Speak Now or Forever Hold You~ ..~~ b~ ~~
After their third date, David Emerson and Brooke Cale are ready
to marry. Such haste does not sit well with David's older brother
Troy, and Brooke's older sister Sydney, who want to stop them.
Their plan to delay the wedding is working perfectly except for
one hitch. Sydney can't seem to keep her mind off Troy. And
Troy is fighting hard to not believe in love at first sight.

Once Upon a Dream by Sally Laity
On the verge of turning the big 4-0, librarian Grace Farrell
grudgingly realizes her dream of a June wedding is collecting
dust like her hope chest. Then Mitchell Haywood strides
through the door of her mundane existence. He's writing about
small Pennsylvania towns and needs to do research at her
library. Mitch turns up something he didn't anticipate. Will
Grace find it too good to turn down?

Something Old, Something New by Yvonne Lehman
When Daniel Gallo moves his grandfather Peppino into a
retirement home, he can't help but notice the home's marketing director, Kay English. She notices Daniel, too, but concerns herself with Peppino's adjustment by arranging for him
to meet her widowed great-aunt Ella, also a resident. The
elderly couple begin matchmaking for their young relatives,
and soon find themselves caught up in the whirl of romance.

Wrong Church, Wrong Wedding by Loree Lough
Piano tuner Breena Pavan has had her share of sweet and sour
notes—on and off the job. Like when she lost the invitation to
a friend's wedding, and attended the wrong church, and the
wrong ceremony! But could that be considered an accident
when she sat beside horticulturist K~~ ~~ ~~~~
beautiful music as this romance b~

Veda Boyd Jones

Sally Laity

Yvonne Lehman

Loree Lough

BARBOUR
PUBLISHING

© 1998 by Barbour Publishing, Inc.

ISBN 1-59789-287-4

Published by Barbour Publishing, Inc., P.O. Box 719, Uhrichsville, Ohio 44683, www.barbourbooks.com

 Member of the
Evangelical Christian
Publishers Association

Printed in the United States of America.
5 4 3 2 1

Speak Now or Forever Hold Your Peace

Veda Boyd Jones

Dedication

For Elaine and Merle Dean, my sister and
my husband's brother, who married nine years
before Jimmie and I.

Chapter 1

"Are you crazy?" Troy Emerson sat up straight in his swivel desk chair and turned the full force of his penetrating gaze on his younger brother. That look from his steel blue eyes had pinned David down countless times in the last few years, but this time his brother didn't flinch.

"I don't care what you say. I love Brooke, and I'm going to marry her." There was a no-nonsense tone to David's voice that Troy had never heard before.

He took a deep breath and pushed away from his desk. He had reacted with his emotions and not his mind. With measured steps he walked to the window and looked down from his Community Bank office on the twenty-fourth floor of The Tower Building. Below him the traffic on the busy Tulsa street looked small— almost like toys that his young brother had played with not that many years ago. And now David was talking about a wedding?

"Marriage is a big step," Troy said in the reasonable voice he used with his employees. He'd been trained to use a calm approach to problems dealing with emotions. If he could weaken David's intensity, he could talk to him and get him to listen to a pragmatic proposal.

"I want to spend my life with Brooke," David said.

"I understand that." Troy turned back and faced his brother. "And I'm not arguing with it. I'm just wondering if now is the time. You met Brooke during spring break. March. This is May. You've known her less than two full months. Don't you think there should be an engagement period?"

"We're not getting married until August. We're working this summer, then we'll get married before the fall semester starts."

"So you're both going back to school?"

"We have scholarships. And we'll work part-time to pay the rent. It will work." The way David said that, as if convincing himself, gave Troy hope that his brother's position could be changed.

"Would it be easier if you both finished college before you married? Brooke will be a sophomore, won't she?" He knew she was nineteen and David was twenty. Way too young to consider marriage. Why, Troy was twenty-eight, and he considered himself too young to settle down. His plan was to wait at least until thirty. He'd have a good-sized savings account by then, enough to afford a down payment on a nice home, and then he'd consider marriage and a family.

"It would probably be easier to wait," David said, "but we don't want to. We've talked about it, and we've decided. Tonight I'm going to talk to her father."

"Have you talked to Mom and Dad?" Troy asked.

"This morning. They said they were the same ages

10

as we are when they got married."

"But that was a different time. A generation ago couples got married younger."

"They understood," David said with a challenge to Troy that he should also understand. "We'd better hurry. I told Brooke we'd meet them at a quarter till twelve to beat the rush."

Troy glanced at his watch. They were going upstairs to the Tower View for lunch. As big brother, he'd thought he'd treat David and his girlfriend to lunch on their first full day back home for the summer. Little had he expected the news that David had given him.

"Them?" The pronoun finally registered.

"Brooke's telling her sister about our engagement, so I thought we'd have a little celebration."

"Isn't this a bit premature? What if her father doesn't give his blessing tonight?"

David lifted his chin. "He will. He wants what's best for Brooke. And that's me," he said with a grin. "Let's go. I want to get there before they do."

Sydney Cale had been delighted when Brooke suggested she meet her for lunch. She had missed her younger sister when she'd gone away to school. The University of Oklahoma wasn't actually that far away—just a two and a half hour drive from Tulsa. The first semester Brooke had come home at least once a month. But since she'd met David Emerson, she'd not made it back at all until now that the semester was over.

Sydney had met Brooke's boyfriend when she visited her sister in Norman one weekend. He seemed nice and was a handsome boy. Certainly Brooke was smitten with him.

Sydney looked up from her computer screen and saw Brooke approach her cubicle at the engineering firm. She saved what she was working on and grabbed her purse.

As they walked into the hall, Brooke said, "David and I are getting married."

"You can't be serious," Sydney said as they waited for the elevator that would take them to the top floor restaurant.

"But I am. We're going to get married in August, right before we go back to school." Brooke's wistful smile stretched across her face. "Imagine me—Mrs. David Emerson. He's going to talk to Dad tonight. And I'd like you to help me with Mom."

"What are you going to do? Tie her up? Gag her so she can't tell you that you're too young to get married?"

Brooke gave her a look that said she knew she'd get this reaction from her older sister, but it didn't matter.

"They'll understand. They only want what's best for me."

"True. And best is for you to finish college before you get married. Why can't you wait a few years?" Sydney asked.

"A few years! I want to spend the rest of my life with David. Right now the months until we say our vows seems like forever, and I want you to be maid of honor."

"I'd be honored to, when the time is right. To everything there is a season, and I'm not convinced this is the right season." Sydney shook her head. How was she going to get through to Brooke? This was not a sensible way to approach life. She needed to make the girl see reason. "You must be able to support yourself. Haven't you listened to anything Aunt Dot has told us?" she said as they entered the elevator which already held a handful of people. A half-dozen more crammed in after them.

"Aunt Dot has been warped by life."

"That's not true," Sydney defended her favorite aunt. "Her heart was broken once, but she adjusted to it. Thank goodness she was able to take care of herself. What if she'd depended on a man? Where would she be?"

Others turned to look at her. She'd broken the elevator code of silence.

"Sorry," she whispered to her sister. "We'll talk about this over lunch." The elevator doors opened again at the top floor and the crowd piled off. "Did you say you had called for a reservation? The Tower View fills up fast—even at a quarter till."

"I said it was taken care of. David actually called."

"David is here?"

"Didn't I mention that we were meeting him and his brother?" Brooke wore that innocent look of hers that didn't fool Sydney. "We wanted to talk to both of you about the wedding. He's going to have Troy be the best man," she explained as they walked to the door of the restaurant.

Sydney started to protest, but it was too late. Before she could give their names to the hostess, David materialized out of nowhere and escorted them to a table, where a man stood beside the ceiling-to-floor windows.

"Hi, Troy," Brooke said gaily. "This is my sister, Sydney."

Sydney extended her hand, and he shook it firmly, then he pulled the chair out for her. She could tell the two males were brothers, but Troy had a much more commanding air about him. She should have expected that. He was quite a bit older, no longer a collegiate, but a man on his own in the world. It wasn't fair to David to compare them.

"Troy, did you know about this before today?" Sydney asked, her hands palms up to show she was overwhelmed by it all—the marriage plans and even lunch at the upscale Tower View.

"I've known about ten minutes," Troy said and handed her a menu.

"What do you think?" Sydney asked.

His razor-sharp glance went to David, but he didn't directly answer her question.

"Brooke's a wonderful girl."

"You're sweet, Troy," Brooke said. "Are you going to be the best man?"

"When the time is right," Troy said.

Sydney studied him. He had used the same words she had used earlier. He must have the same opinion of the nuptials as she did. He was smiling, but his blue eyes said he disapproved. Interesting.

The foursome ordered soup and sandwiches. David and Brooke talked softly about how to handle the evening's tête-à-tête with her father.

"David tells me you're a structural engineer," Troy said.

Sydney nodded. "For Albertson's—fifth floor. You have the advantage on me. I didn't know about you until we were headed up here."

"I work at Community Bank."

"Here?"

"Twenty-fourth floor. I guess with eight-hundred people working in this building, it's not odd that we haven't met. But I'll be watching for you from now on."

She smiled at his remark. "I have a friend who works at the bank. Isn't the twenty-fourth floor for management?"

"I'm a new vice president, a lending officer. But we have a fist-full, so you don't have to be too impressed with the title."

So, he wasn't conceited, but he was very confident. She liked that. She also liked how his wavy brown hair dipped over his left eye, how he looked directly at her when he talked, how he seemed to agree with her about the proposed wedding.

The wedding. She had been so taken with Troy that she was ignoring the reason for this lunch.

"I've only met your brother one other time, but he seems like a very special person."

"Hey, I heard that," David said and grinned. "Thanks. Since you think so, how do you think I should

15

tackle your dad tonight?"

"Tackle may be the right way to do it. I doubt he'll be thrilled. You're both so young for such a major commitment." Sydney chose her words carefully so she wouldn't offend David, but she intended later to lambaste her sister.

She felt Troy's frank gaze and glanced his way. There was a connection here; she felt it. They were in sync. Now if they could figure a way to convince the young couple that they should delay the wedding.

"We thought about getting married in Norman," Brooke said. "There's a darling chapel where we've been going to church, but we decided it would be easier here in Tulsa since we'll both be working here this summer. We're going to talk to Reverend Ritter tomorrow."

"You have this all planned out," Sydney commented.

"We've talked about it for weeks." Brooke held up her hand. "Stop. I know what you're going to say—that we've only known each other a short while. But it's long enough."

"I asked her to marry me on our third date," David said. "I guess it was love at first sight. We know this is right. We know it." He reached for Brooke's hand. "We love each other. There's no reason for us to wait."

"We don't want a giant wedding, just close friends and family," Brooke said. "We're thinking maybe two hundred people."

"Just a small wedding," Sydney said with a touch of sarcasm. "White dress, cake, flowers, pictures?" She'd been in several weddings in the last couple of years as her friends married, and she knew the drill. It seemed like an awfully lot of expense, plus time and energy fussing over details. One friend had sobbed on her wedding day because the groom's cake was supposed to be chocolate, but it was white. Another had broken out in hives a few minutes before the ceremony and walked down the aisle with huge red welts on her arms and neck. "Why not elope?"

"I've never thought of myself as goal oriented, like you are," Brooke said slowly. "But if there is one thing I want in my life, it's a happy family. I want a husband to love, and I want to raise his children. David is the husband I want." The tender way she looked at David made Sydney take a quick breath. "And I want to start our life together in the right way—with the people we love surrounding us in church."

Sydney exhaled. Her baby sister sounded so mature. She exchanged a lightning glance with Troy. He looked as touched as she felt.

"Well," he said. "It appears that you two know what you want. Here's to the happy couple." He lifted his water glass and the foursome clinked and drank a toast. Sydney blinked back tears.

Luckily the waiter appeared at that moment with their food. While Brooke and David traded sandwich halves, Troy leaned toward Sydney. She could smell the muskiness of his cologne, and his closeness made her heart beat faster. Did he feel the same excitement she felt?

"We've got to put a stop to this," he said with his lips close to her ear. "We have to come up with a plan."

Chapter 2

O ne meeting after another took Troy's time when he returned to his office. Lunch had gone better than he'd anticipated, thanks to Sydney Cale. Now there was an attractive woman with good common sense.

In his mind's eye he saw her as she'd been at noon, her shiny brown hair touching her shoulders and turned under in a sophisticated style, her gaze direct, and deep smile lines near the corners of her mouth.

The vibes coming from her were unmistakable. She was as opposed to this wedding as he was. It wasn't in what she said as much as what she didn't say. She didn't gush and talk about roses and white dresses. She didn't lecture the young couple on their lack of experience in life's practical matters, she just didn't say much at all about the subject, as if she were thinking it through before opening her mouth.

If there was one type of woman he admired, it was the level-headed type who considered pros and cons and then made decisions. He would expect nothing less of a structural engineer. She had to be very strong in math and have an analytical mind. *She must be a list maker,* he thought, as he crossed two items off his yellow legal pad.

He added another line. "Call Sydney Cale." He wasn't sure what they could do to stop the wedding, but together maybe they could think of something. He looked up her name in the phone book, but it wasn't listed. He'd have to call her at work. Albertson's Engineering had a half page ad in the yellow pages, and he jotted down the number next to her name. Her firm was one of the best in the business. Albertson's payroll account was here at the bank, and he'd visited with the partners whenever they wanted to buy office cars and finance them. He didn't recall Sydney's name on any of the documents, but then she was young, maybe twenty-four or so, and probably only had a year or two experience with Albertson's, not nearly enough to make partner.

His secretary buzzed him, and he took a call, which led to another call and another. It was nearly four o'clock when he finally punched in Albertson's number and got Sydney on the line. He identified himself and asked how her afternoon was going, then got to the point.

"Correct me if I'm wrong, but don't you feel Brooke and David are rushing into marriage when they should finish school before considering such a big step?"

"Absolutely. They're too young for a major decision like this, and they need that pointed out in a subtle way."

"I skipped the subtle part when I told David he was too young," Troy said with a wry chuckle.

"I'll admit I was caught unaware, too, and blurted out something about their age and the need for a woman to be independent. But I think we can undo that harm and get with a new program if we think about it."

"Do you have something in mind?"

"My first thought was to stand up and yell when the minister says, 'Speak now or forever hold your peace.' "

"That would be most interesting," he said and laughed.

"Actually I have a second idea, but it's not fully fleshed out."

Troy's intercom line buzzed. "Mr. Desser to see you," his secretary said.

"Listen, I've got an appointment now," he said into the receiver. "Why don't we discuss this over dinner. Are you free this evening? I could throw a couple of steaks on the grill and we could work out a plan." He'd thought about taking her out, but his apartment would insure privacy while they schemed and plotted.

"Sounds fine. Can I bring a salad?"

"Sure," Troy said and gave her his address. "Seven o'clock?"

"I'll see you then," she said and hung up.

Troy replaced the receiver and straightened his tie before his secretary ushered in his next appointment. *That went rather well,* he thought. He mentally added a note to stop at the store on his way home.

Sydney didn't normally go to a man's apartment for dinner on the first date. That was why God made public restaurants, she had reasoned. First dates were always so unpredictable. That was the time to get to know a guy, learn his background, discover his values.

She should know; she'd had a ton of first dates, and she'd had lots of second dates, too. But by the third date, she'd usually turned her would-be suitors into brother figures. With no spark apparent, the relationships had become simple friendships.

But she'd made an exception of her first date routine with Troy Emerson. For one thing, this wasn't a first date. It wasn't a date at all. Lunch hadn't been a date either; it had been a family meeting of sorts, and that was just what this was going to be. And the second thing was, and she had no reason for this, but she trusted him. She had instantly liked him. She knew bits and pieces about his brother, gleaned from an infatuated sister, and she knew a little bit about his family.

She'd even done some detective work. She'd called her friend Pam who worked in human resources at Community Bank.

"Troy Emerson is a hunk," Pam had said. "Tall, dark hair, blue eyes. He has a regal air about him, but has the cutest grin."

"I know what he looks like," Sydney said. "I wondered what he's like as a person."

"Kind, considerate. Sharp memory, always remembers people once he's met them. Smart. Why are you asking? He didn't ask you out, did he? Tellers around here line up just to see him walk down the hall."

"His brother has asked my sister to marry him." Okay, that wasn't a direct answer to Pam's question, but she didn't want to be grist for the rumor mill before the building emptied at quitting time. Sydney was glad she wasn't speaking to her friend in person. Pam had a way of looking at her that demanded the whole truth, and nothing but the truth.

"You could be his in-law?" Pam asked.

"That would be stretching it a bit. He'd be my sister's brother-in-law, if they go through with the wedding."

"And why wouldn't they?"

"No reason. Thanks for the information. I've got to get back to work." With a promise of lunch sometime next week, Sydney hung up.

When quitting time came at five o'clock, she didn't stay late to finish what she was working on, as was her custom. Instead, she marked her spot on the drawings she was checking and grabbed her coat. She needed to stop by the grocery store since she had nothing for a proper salad in the refrigerator.

Actually, she had little in her refrigerator. She knew her fast food diet wasn't particularly healthy, but it beat spending time alone in the kitchen, preparing a meal for one. Sydney's idea of a gourmet home-cooked meal included soup out of a can and a TV dinner she could pop in the oven. Those frozen dinners were actually pretty good, and the variety was endless.

Sydney passed the crowd at the elevator and turned to the stairs, her usual way to exit and enter The Tower Building. She was only on the fifth floor, and she considered the staircase her own personal Stairmaster. Once at the basement level, she followed the lighted walkway to the parking garage and to her little Buick. She was one of the first to exit the garage into Tulsa's busy five o'clock traffic. The grocery store was on the way home, and she took a few minutes in the produce area deciding if Troy was the type who liked mushrooms and blue cheese sprinkles in a salad. Then she eased her car into the traffic again.

Her apartment near Riverside Drive and 21st, was actually a remodeled carriage house, in the same Spanish architectural style as the nearby mansion, but in miniature. A prominent lawyer had renovated the big house. Sydney had computed the structures. It was on the job site that she'd seen the carriage house and asked the lawyer if he was remodeling it, too, for a rental. He'd planned on tearing it down, but reconsidered, and Sydney had moved in as soon as it was completed. She was no caretaker, but the lawyer had said her presence would be a crime deterrent. She had full use of the well-kept grounds, which covered two acres of very pricey real estate.

She drove through the large gates toward the back of the property to the carriage house. On the verandah, she sorted through the mail. For a moment, she closed her eyes and took in the sweet scent of roses from the flower garden behind the mansion. Then with purpose, she strode inside, quickly showered, washed her hair, and blow-dried it into soft waves that framed her face. She pulled on jeans and held up blouses and discarded them, all the while lecturing herself for being so silly over meeting Troy Emerson for supper. She'd decided on a plain white shirt with a feminine pink blazer when the phone rang, and Brooke asked if she was coming over for supper.

"No, I already have plans," Sydney said.

"But you said you'd help me with Mom while David talks to Dad."

Sydney thought back over their earlier conversation. "No, I said you'd need me to help you tie her up. I'm sorry, Brooke, but I can't come over. Surely you and Mom can have a civil conversation about this. After all, you'll soon be a married woman."

"But Mom will want to be in on the conversation with Dad. You know how she is."

"Because they're always a team, make joint decisions, that sort of thing?"

"Right."

"Then perhaps you and David should talk to Mom and Dad. Maybe you should talk like adults talk to adults." Sydney hoped she was keeping the sarcasm out of her voice. She didn't want to offend her sister, she just wanted her to see reason. Marriage was a grownup thing, nothing to be gone into lightly.

"Of course. That's what we'll do. We want their blessing on our marriage, but if we don't get it, it's not going to stop us from getting married in August. Did I tell you we've found an apartment? We can get it the first of August and have time to fix it up before we're married on the fifteenth. School doesn't start until the twenty-fifth."

"You have it all planned out, don't you?"

"Almost to what we'll serve at the reception. I'm so

24

excited. This is a dream come true."

"Well," Sydney said, stalling for time because she didn't know what else to say. "Well, I've got to get ready. I'll talk to you later after you've dropped the bomb. What time are you planning this little meeting?"

"David will be here at seven. Where are you going?"

"To dinner with a friend." She sure didn't want Brooke to know it was Troy and that they were planning to delay the wedding.

"Male?"

"Uh, yes." The moment she hesitated, she knew Brooke would blow it out of proportion.

"Someone special? Who is this guy? Why all the mystery?"

"A new friend. I've got to run. I'll talk to you later tonight." Sydney hung up before Brooke could ask any more questions. She finished dressing and hurried to the kitchen where she washed and cut up vegetables. Her salad would feed ten people, but she wanted Troy to have plenty. Should she take dressing to go with it? Why hadn't she thought of that earlier? Her refrigerator yielded a bottle of Thousand Island dressing that held about two tablespoons of congealed dressing. Now she'd have to drop by the store on her way to his apartment.

It was already six-thirty. His apartment was in one of the new complexes in the southern part of the city, past 81st Street. With a last check in the mirror, she grabbed her purse and ran outside. At her car, she remembered her salad and hurried back inside to get it.

After a quick detour to the grocery store, she headed

her car south and pulled into his complex of four big buildings exactly at seven. She cruised the parking lot, trying to make out apartment numbers in the growing dusk. After two tours of the lot, she found the right building and followed a concrete path to the interior court-yard, a park-like space. Apartment doorways opened onto this area of trees, grass, and wooden benches with a few scattered picnic tables beside stone barbecue pits.

Troy stood by one smoking pit, holding a soft drink can in one hand and poking at the fire with a long fork. He grinned at her and held up the fork in greeting. He quickly covered the ten yards between them and led her into his apartment.

"Want something to drink? Coke? Juice?"

"Coke sounds good," Sydney said. She set her salad on the bar which separated the efficiency kitchen from the living room. "Nice place." It was definitely a mascu-line home. The furniture was heavy and all earth tones. Not a pink or purple or green spot of color was in the living room. The closest thing to real color was a muted gold throw pillow on the brown couch.

"I'm glad you could come," Troy said as he rounded the bar and handed her a glass of ice and a can. He smiled at her, and his blue eyes twinkled. They were all the color the room needed to make it sparkle. It merely needed him in it.

Chapter 3

"Shall we throw these steaks on the fire?" Troy asked. Sydney followed him outside where he transferred a couple of filets from a plate to the hot grill. The meat sizzled, emitting a charcoal aroma that set his mouth watering. "How do you want it cooked?"

"Medium," Sydney answered.

Good. Pink inside was how he liked steak, too. He should be able to fix this meal without messing it up. Cooking wasn't his specialty. He'd thrown potatoes in the oven when he got home, so they should be okay. That and her salad and the meat seemed like a balanced meal to him.

He quizzed Sydney about her job and learned that she worked under one of the partners who did all the banking paperwork with him.

"You're not like most engineers," Troy said after they were seated at the table for dinner.

"And what are most engineers like?" Sydney asked.

He'd dug a hole now. Of course, the stereotypical engineer in his mind was a male, not a female.

"Well, you don't carry pens in a pocket protector,

27

and you're not reserved."

She laughed. "Engineers have a bad reputation as antisocial, but we're not all that way. I think most of the men take their jobs very seriously. After all, they make buildings stand up. And they stereotype other professions as well. They call architects the glory boys, but they need structural engineers and not just to stamp the drawings. Most architects are quite creative, but engineers figure they all made C's in college structures classes."

"Are all engineers biased against architects?"

"No. And I'm not. Really." She shook her head. "That's just the standard rebuttal about engineers being humorless and stuffy and architects being the social end of the building industry."

"You certainly don't fit the engineer mold," he said again. And she didn't. There was nothing stuffy about her. For one thing, she was gorgeous. Her shiny hair framed a face of wide-eyed innocence and sophistication at the same time. Her eyes were violet. They had mesmerized him at lunch today, and they had that same effect on him now.

"Thanks. I'm also one of three female engineers out of thirty-four at Albertson's."

"Lucky guys," he said without thinking, then quickly amended it. "Has sexual harassment been a problem for you? You see that everywhere on the news."

"There are always guys who push the limit, but once I let them know they've crossed the line, they back off." She smiled impishly. "Do you have trouble with that at the bank? Do female tellers ogle you?"

He knew his mouth had dropped open. How would she know that?

"Sometimes," he said and chuckled. "You wouldn't think a guy would mind being watched, but there are times I wish I looked different. It's as if all they see is a pretty face and not my mind," he said in a falsetto voice.

Sydney laughed as he knew she would, but he was half-serious. Women did ogle him, and he wasn't sure why. He didn't see himself as handsome. His nose had been broken when he played high school football and had healed a little crooked. He thought his eyes were too wide set, and his chin line maybe too strong, but it didn't stop women from looking, and it made him uncomfortable. He was lucky that his secretary, the one woman he saw most at the bank, was in her fifties, happily married, and looked on him as a son who'd made her proud.

Sydney asked about his job, and he explained his loan capacity. He liked what he did. He saw how providing money for homes and businesses made a difference in people's lives, and he liked being a part of building futures.

As soon as they finished eating, Sydney insisted on helping clear up the dishes. Together they loaded the dishwasher, and she stuck the leftover salad in the refrigerator.

"Dinner was terrific," she said, "the steak cooked to perfection."

"Good. I'm glad you were free tonight," he said. "I've enjoyed talking with you."

29

"Me, too," she said and smiled a brilliant smile. "Wasn't there a reason. . ."

"Oh, David and Brooke. I nearly forgot about them. You mentioned on the phone that you had a plan?" He dried his hands and motioned for her to precede him to the living room. She sat on the couch, and he took his TV watching chair.

"Not exactly a plan, more like a thought. I like David. I really do. And he and Brooke may be perfect for one another, but I question if now is the time for marriage. Is two months long enough to really know a person? Has he seen Brooke's temper when she loses at tennis? I'd say her temper is her biggest fault. I've known her all of her nineteen years, so I think I'm a pretty good judge of her personality."

"This isn't major, but David's a slob. I can't count the times Mom has grounded him until his room was cleaned up. I don't know how he can live in such a mess. If he had his own apartment, he'd be the type to have a pile of pizza boxes in the corner and every dish he owned in the sink. I haven't been in his dorm room this past semester, but I saw it in the fall. I'm surprised David's room hasn't earned a health-code violation."

"That's the type of thing we need to point out to Brooke and David. But how?"

Troy got a legal pad and a pencil from his catchall drawer in the kitchen and sat back down in his chair. "Let's make a list of their negative characteristics, and in all fairness, we'll make a list of their positive ones, too. Then we have to show them the other person's real personality, not the one that surfaces on dates, but the real person, warts and all."

"Sounds like a good plan."

"Okay. So, under Brooke's good points I'll put the obvious, 'cute.' And under bad points, I'll put 'temper.'"

"Under David's good points put 'polite.' And under bad, put 'slob.'"

Troy nodded and continued writing. "We've got the hang of this. Let's look at biggies. What about honesty?"

"That goes in the good column for Brooke."

"Same for David. Greed?"

"No, Brooke's not greedy. Now, jealousy could be one of her vices. I remember a few years ago that she had a boyfriend who talked to another girl, and she was furious. I don't know if she's outgrown that, but we could test it."

"Okay. Vanity goes under David's negative side. For being a slob in his surroundings, he's always carefully groomed. Doesn't figure, does it?"

"Could be something he'll outgrow with time. Were you a slob at his age?"

"Never," Troy said, then admitted, "maybe not as neat as I am now." He glanced around. He'd picked the place up before she got there and had taken out the trash. Had he missed a stray magazine or newspaper? Or soda can?

A knock at the door arrested his attention.

"Troy?"

He recognized his brother's voice and then heard Brooke's voice as she spoke to David.

31

"What should we do?" Sydney whispered.

"Hide in the bedroom," he whispered back and pointed to the door. "I'll get rid of them."

Sydney took two steps for the bedroom, then pivoted and took the legal pad from him. "Evidence," she whispered. "Wouldn't do to be caught with the plan."

She disappeared into his bedroom, and Troy answered the door.

"What brings you two out here?" he asked and stepped back so they could come inside.

"My parents don't understand at all," Brooke said. She dabbed a Kleenex at her red eyes. "They say we should wait a few years."

"I thought her father was going to throw me out of the place," David said.

"He was violent?" Troy asked. He could hardly believe that Sydney's father would behave in that manner. He hadn't met the man, but Sydney had said he was also an engineer, and that certainly didn't fit Troy's stereotype.

"He didn't actually threaten me," David admitted, "but I could tell he wanted to.

"We have to convince them that we know what we're doing, but we're going to get married whether they like it or not," Brooke said. "We're both of legal age."

"Mom and Dad said they understood," David said. "Maybe they can talk to the Cales."

Troy wasn't so sure that his parents' understanding included their blessing on this union. Even though they were young when they got married, they had known each other for years. His parents might think a delay of the August wedding would be a good idea.

"Could I use your phone?" Brooke asked, still sniffling.

Troy nodded and started to point to the portable phone on the bar—right next to Sydney's purse! Instead, he said, "Of course, you can." He backed to the bar, and slid the purse off onto the kitchen counter at the same time that he picked up the phone and handed it to Brooke.

She dialed, then spoke into the receiver. "Sydney, it's me. I'm at Troy Emerson's. Call me when you get in."

Did this mean she was preparing to stay awhile? He had to get rid of them.

"Do you mind if I freshen up?" Brooke asked.

Troy nodded. What could he say?

"The bathroom is. . ." She pointed to the only interior door leading out of the living room—the one to his bedroom.

"It's right through the bedroom," Troy said. "Right through the bedroom, Brooke," he repeated in a loud voice. He didn't know what good his warning would do. There was no place for Sydney to hide in there.

Brooke disappeared through the doorway, and he waited for an exclamation when she saw Sydney. But there was only silence.

"Troy, we've got to do something."

He swung back around to face his brother, still half-listening for sounds from the bedroom. He hoped his bewilderment didn't show on his face. He closed his eyes and thought of his professional training in dealing with people, especially those whose loans were refused.

"You've taken the logical steps here. You've talked to both sets of parents. Now you must evaluate their importance. There may be other avenues open to you."

"What avenues? Oh, you mean someone else to talk to them? But who? Wait a minute, you and Sydney?" David answered his own question and rambled on. "That's a great idea. You two can talk to her parents."

"Wait, I didn't say. . . I don't know Brooke's parents. Why would they listen to me?"

"Are you going to talk to my folks?" Brooke said, coming out of the bedroom.

"No." Troy shook his head and looked behind her, but Sydney didn't follow her into the living room. She'd escaped notice, but how?

"You can use those people skills you're always telling me I should develop," David said.

Troy made a mental note to write "bluntness" under David's list of bad characteristics. "Stubbornness" would also go on the list. With a sigh, he took a seat. How could he get rid of these two without seeming cold-hearted?

"What was your parents' objection? That you were too young or that you hadn't known each other long enough to make this decision?"

"Both," Brooke said and sat with her fiancé on the couch.

"Are you sure you don't know the Cales?" David asked.

"Those are just logical objections. You can't have someone else change their minds. You have to prove that you are mature enough to handle this life-altering change. You also have to have time to get to know one another better and for the Cales to get to know David."

"You're right. They've only met him one other time." Brooke focused on David. "When they get to know you, honey, they'll love you as much as I do. You're a genius, Troy. Thanks." She smiled. No, she beamed, and he could see the similarities between her and her older sister. No wonder David had fallen for her.

Sydney. She was somewhere in his bedroom or bathroom. He pictured her standing behind the shower curtain in the bathroom or behind the door in the bedroom.

"Perhaps you should go back to the Cales and explain that you've considered their opinion and the sanctity of marriage and you're going to take this a little slower," he said in an effort to get them out of his apartment so Sydney could come out of hiding. He hoped that she could hear that he'd convinced the kids to delay the wedding. He was rather proud that it had been so easily accomplished.

"Yes, let's go back," Brooke said. "We'll tell them we feel sure we're doing the right thing, but we agree that they need more time to know you, David. Two and a half months till August. By then they'll know you and give their blessing. I guarantee it!" She leaned over and kissed David on the cheek.

Troy sat in stunned silence. A moment ago he'd been quite sure he'd convinced them to wait. Now it looked as if he'd accomplished nothing.

David pulled Brooke to her feet and put his arm

around her shoulder.

"Thanks, bro. We're going to show them that we're adults and can adjust to change and can sit down and have an adult conversation. Talk to you later." He ushered Brooke to the door.

"Oh, Troy. I left my sister a message to phone here, but it might be late when she gets in and calls. She's out with some mysterious hot date."

"I'll tell her what's happened. Good night," Troy said and closed the door behind them. He turned and strode purposefully to his bedroom to find his mysterious hot date.

Chapter 4

"Sydney?" Troy called as he marched into his bedroom.

"I'm here," she answered as she crawled out from the cramped chair space under the desk. Sudden light nearly blinded her, since she was looking at the underside of the lamp when he flicked it on. He helped her to her feet.

"Good hiding place. I thought Brooke would find you when she came in here."

"I know. I panicked, but dove under here before she came through the door." She bent down and retrieved the legal pad and pen from under the desk.

Troy filled her in on the parts of the conversation she'd missed as they settled back into the living room.

"So, if they're going to spend more time at my parents' house, then that's where we can show David a side of Brooke he's never seen. It's perfect."

"And we can have them go to my folks' home and show her how David really is. He seemed older when I visited him at school, but he regresses to younger when he's living at home."

"I know what you mean. My parents treat me like a

kid when I'm there. It's as if they can't let their little girl grow up."

"This time their habit will work to our benefit."

They plotted on how to tackle their siblings, and agreed that a starting place would be with Brooke's temper.

"Can you set up Saturday morning for a tennis match?"

Sydney nodded and pointed at the portable phone. He handed it to her, and she punched in her parents' number.

Brooke came to the phone. "Did you get my message?" she asked in a soft voice. "Did you call Troy?"

"I spoke with him, and he filled me in on your conversation with Mom and Dad," Sydney said truthfully. She just didn't add that she hadn't had to phone him. "So you're going to let them get to know David."

"Yes. In two and a half months, they'll grow to love him like I do. Well, not quite like I do," she said with a giggle. "Meanwhile we're going to plan the wedding."

Sydney rolled her eyes at Troy, who had moved to the couch beside her and was leaning close to hear the other side of the phone conversation.

"So I understand. Listen, Brooke, can you play tennis on Saturday morning? With you getting married in August, I hope we can make the most of the time we have together this summer."

"That sounds like fun. Then I'll meet David afterwards for lunch."

Troy shook his head, and Sydney took a deep breath.

"Oh, if you want to include David, that's okay," she said in what she hoped was an indifferent tone. "We could play doubles."

"With your mysterious date tonight? How did it go?"

"Very well. But he may have to work Saturday." Was that stretching the truth? She had no idea if Troy worked Saturdays. "Do you know anyone we could get for a fourth?"

"Hey, what about Troy? You ought to get to know him. After all, he's going to be my brother-in-law."

"I don't know. He seemed nice enough at lunch, but does he play tennis?" She smiled at Troy. This was like taking candy from a baby.

"He's got the build for it. Did you notice his physique? The guy's a hunk." Sydney turned her head straight ahead. She hadn't counted on Brooke commenting on his appearance.

"Yes, he's nice looking." This time she looked at him and saw his wide grin. She wrinkled her nose at him. "So, can you arrange doubles?"

"I'll let you know. Call you back in a couple of minutes."

"Oh, no. Uh. . .I mean, leave a message on the machine if I don't answer. I'm going to hop in the shower."

"Okay. What time Saturday?"

"Ten?"

"Perfect. Talk to you later."

Sydney punched the phone off and laid it down

on the coffee table.

"If I don't want to be a liar, I'd better go take a shower."

Troy chuckled. "Well, we've got a plan. A starting point for Project Postponement."

When the phone rang, Sydney held up her hand in farewell and walked to the door before he could answer it. "Thanks for supper. I'll see you Saturday."

By the time Sydney got back to the carriage house, Brooke had already left a message. The doubles match was on.

Sydney climbed in the shower for the third time that day. She'd started the day with a morning shower, she'd showered again before going to Troy's for dinner, and here she was getting wet one more time because she didn't want to be a liar. Project Postponement was going to give her dry skin.

She wasn't doing the wrong thing, was she? Meddling didn't come natural to her. She wanted to make her own choices, and she felt others had the right to theirs. But this was her little sister, and marriage was a major life choice.

As she sunk into bed, she turned to God for direction.

"Dear God, thank You for today." She always started her prayers that way, then she talked to God about the day's blessings or troubles. "Please lead me into doing what's right for Brooke. I love her, and I want her happy. I don't want to lie to her, and I don't want to misguide her. I want what's best for her. And I want

Your will to be done. Am I interfering or are You using me to help her? Please show me the way. Amen."

Usually after her goodnight prayer, Sydney felt a peace settle over her. This time the peace didn't come. She felt edgy and uncertain and slept fitfully until morning.

She didn't see Troy at work on Friday, and she wondered why she had expected to. Their paths had never crossed before, but now she was aware that he worked in this building. He was as familiar with the lobby as she was, and that knowledge changed how she looked at The Tower Building and the other people there. She scrutinized the men by the elevator; some of them might know Troy. She perused the women in the eighth floor cafeteria at noon. Were some of these the tellers who gave Troy the eye?

As Troy drove toward his date's apartment that night, his thoughts flew back to the previous evening he had spent with Sydney. He was glad she had left before he'd talked to David on the phone. His brother had gone on and on about how smart Sydney was, and wasn't she quite the looker, too? Finally, Troy had been blunt and said he'd thank his brother to quit pushing Sydney at him. He'd agreed reluctantly to play tennis, and his reluctance wasn't just a clever way to manipulate David without his knowing it.

He was having second thoughts about this plan with Sydney. It wasn't just the disloyal feeling he had; it

41

was the manipulative way he was acting. Although his job required him to control the people who worked in his department and his training had prepared him to deal with irate people and calm them down and lead them to his way of thinking, he had hoped those skills didn't transfer to his personal life in a negative way.

But wasn't he his brother's keeper? The moment David had told him about the wedding, he'd given his opinion and tried to talk sense into him. But what Troy was doing now verged on dishonesty, and he didn't like it.

It wasn't Sydney's fault. She was a breath of spring air, a delight to be around. He liked her sense of humor and the fun that shone in her eyes.

But that was last night, and tonight he was seeing Vicki. She was a wonderful person, assistant choir director at his church, and a good friend. She didn't look at him with that direct look that was so much a part of Sydney. She looked at him in a pleasant way, a thoughtful way, but not a see-to-his-heart type of look that he felt from that structural engineer. There was a connection there, and he wasn't sure what it meant.

The evening went fine. He and Vicki went to a movie and afterwards discussed it over a cup of coffee at her apartment. Then he went home and dreamed about Sydney.

He thought they'd be playing tennis Saturday morning at a public park, but he didn't know of one in the vicinity where David was directing him.

"Turn left on 21st," David said.

Troy had decided to pick up his brother so they could have some time alone, but David wanted to talk about his summer job at a billboard company and not about the proposed wedding, so Troy followed his lead. The subject would come up when they joined the women. Of that, he was sure.

"Take that drive and park by the carriage house."

"Who lives here?" Troy asked. The main house was a mansion with a red slate tiled roof and stuccoed walls. The carriage house had the same Spanish look about it, but on a much less grand scale.

"Sydney rents the little house. Didn't I tell you we were playing on her court?"

"Does she play a lot? Is she good?" Troy asked.

David laughed. "You'll have to judge that for yourself. Let's just say that she's won a few trophies. So has Brooke."

They got their rackets and balls out of the back seat, then walked to the tennis court behind the big house. Sydney and Brooke were already hitting the ball back and forth, warming up. They looked like pros. Both were dressed in tennis skirts, Sydney in traditional white, and Brooke in pale blue with little flowers along the edge of the skirt and the neck of the matching shirt.

Their volleys were impressive, hit hard and barely skimming the net, and landing within inches of the boundary lines. Sydney hadn't mentioned that she was good at the game. He'd thought it would be a friendly way to get exercise. The way they were hitting the ball, it looked like they were out for blood. He was definitely out of his depth. Oh, he liked tennis well enough, and had played some every summer for fun, but he'd never entered even a local tournament. What had he gotten himself into?

"Hi, honey," Brooke called. "You're on my team."

David joined her and Troy walked to the far side of the court. It was a perfect day for tennis. Not a cloud in the sky, a slight breeze, and the temperature was closing in on seventy.

"Good morning, Sydney. It's good to see you again." He didn't want to act too friendly. After all, David and Brooke thought they had only met at that lunch. He would have to act as if he and Sydney were nodding acquaintances instead of a duo who had plotted and schemed to change their siblings' lives.

"Why don't you play up and I'll get the base line shots?" Sydney said.

Troy nodded and took his place at the net. This was going to be a challenge, for he was a dinker. If the ball came to him, he'd stick his racket out and dink it back. He didn't think David was any better, so he was surprised at his little brother's ability to slam the ball back at him while they were practicing.

"You're a lot better than I remember," Troy said when David was also up at the net.

"Brooke and I've been playing. She's taught me the finer points of the game—like get it back across the net."

"Are you ready to begin?" Sydney asked. They tossed a coin to see who served first, then Brooke took the balls and began the match.

At first Sydney was polite. "Good try, Troy." Next she offered advice. "If you move once you see the ball leave her racket, then you should be able to return it. Just judge where it will land. It's okay. That comes with practice."

She ran back and forth across the court, taking the shots he swung at and missed altogether. They lost his serve in four straight serves. Brooke played with the same concentration as her sister, but her demeanor seemed gentler.

As they changed sides, he put his arm across Sydney's heaving shoulders. "It's just a game, Sydney. Simmer down."

She didn't respond, but she didn't tell him how to hit the ball anymore, either. If anything, she became more determined to win the match, even if she had to play doubles by herself.

At the end of the first set, Troy had had enough. She was wiping her forehead with the sweat band around her wrist. He wasn't perspiring. Maybe she did have a point, and he wasn't giving it his all, but she was turning a fun sport into work.

He mimicked her, shifting his weight from one foot to the other while waiting for the ball to be served. It gave him momentum to go after the ball, and he returned one of Brooke's serves for a point.

Sydney didn't say anything out loud, but she tilted her head, as if to say, not bad. It was all the impetus he needed. He wanted to be on the receiving side of her smile, not her grimace.

45

He watched the ball as it left David's racket, as it skimmed the net, as it bounced. He focused on the ball, not on the pretty spring day, not on the easy bantering between Brooke and David, not on the competitive woman on his side of the court.

At the end of the second set, they were tied. The lead see-sawed back and forth in the third set, and finally David and Brooke won it, 6-4.

Sydney shook hands with their opponents. "Good game, David. Brooke, you're getting better and better. Your serves are stronger, and you mix those cross-courts with the straight shots. I predict next year you'll be in the number one spot."

"You play for OU?" Troy asked.

"She's terrific," David said, with pride in his voice. "Didn't I tell you she was on scholarship?"

"I didn't know it was from the athletic department."

Brooke smiled. "I have some way to go to beat Syd. She was number one her freshman year."

"Well, age and not much practice have taken their toll," Sydney said, "but I like the game."

As the foursome walked toward Sydney's carriage house, Troy pulled her to the side and faced her, putting his forearms on her shoulders, his racket resting against her back. She looked up at him with a question in her eyes.

"You're very competitive," Troy said.

"In tennis, I am. It's required if you want to win."

"Do you think we taught David anything about Brooke? Showed him a bit of her dark side?" he asked

46

with a grin.

Sydney's eyes opened wider and she bit her lip. "Did we just show him that his future sister-in-law is a cutthroat player who wants to win?"

Chapter 5

Sydney stared at the phone on her desk. Troy had said he'd call her, but he hadn't. After the tennis match on Saturday, David and Brooke had left for his folks' house for lunch. Troy had stayed a few minutes longer.

He'd told her that he'd been having second thoughts about Project Postponement, that he felt disloyal. She told him that she'd had the same feeling and had prayed about it. Whether to continue with it or not hadn't been decided, but Troy had left with the promise of a call.

She didn't know why he'd want to talk to her again after the way their tennis match had gone. Didn't men like sweet, feminine women? She knew she was aggressive, competitive and one-minded when she was on the court. She could never have been on the tennis teams in high school and college without those characteristics, but she didn't think she carried them over to other parts of her life.

On Sunday, Brooke had gone to the late service at church with David and brought him back for Sunday dinner at the Cales. Sydney had discovered that the Emersons had transferred last year to the same large church that her family attended. She'd never seen Troy there, but she always went to early service. David mentioned that his family went to the eleven o'clock.

Troy didn't call Sunday night. And he didn't call at work on Monday. Now that she thought about it, he couldn't call her at home. Her number was unlisted, and she hadn't given it to him. He could hardly ask Brooke for it or she would wonder why and start with the questions.

And why would he call anyway? The only reason would be to plan their next session of showing Brooke's true side to David, and only if they decided to continue with Project Postponement. Sydney certainly couldn't misinterpret a call as interest in her, no matter that she felt a certain spark when he was around. After their match when they'd faced each other and he had rested his arms on her shoulders, she'd felt that they were in a world of their own. Just the two of them.

"Ready for lunch?" Pam, her friend from Troy's bank, appeared at her desk at the same time that her phone rang.

She held up one finger to indicate just a minute and answered the phone. "Sydney Cale."

It was him.

"I only have a moment, Sydney. Brooke has asked our family to go to your folks' home for dinner tonight. Know anything about this?"

"Dinner tonight? Not a clue."

"Think you could get invited? I'd hate to face your parents alone."

"I'll see what I can do."

"Okay, great. I've got a lunch meeting, so I have to run. See you tonight."

Sydney hung up and immediately punched in her parents' number. "I'll be just another minute, Pam. I've got to. . . Hi, Mom. I hear you're having a dinner tonight. Am I invited?"

"Of course you're invited. Brooke was supposed to call you yesterday. We're counting on you to be here."

"What time?"

"The Emersons are coming at seven, but come before then and you can give me a helping hand in the kitchen. This means a lot to your sister."

"All right. I'll be there," Sydney promised and hung up. "Sorry," she said to Pam. "Where shall we go for lunch?"

"Did I eavesdrop correctly? Are you meeting Brooke's fiancé's family tonight? Including Troy Emerson?"

"It's so important to my sister, she forgot to ask me," Sydney said. "She's a little ditsy these days. Uh, is The Boulevard okay with you? We'd better hurry if we want a table." She hustled Pam out of the office and across the street to the restaurant that catered to downtown business people. They grabbed a table and were quickly served.

"So, was that Troy on the phone earlier?" Pam was not one to let go once she was on the scent of something important.

Sydney glanced away from Pam's all-seeing eyes.

"It was, wasn't it? What's going on? I want to know every detail."

"Nothing's going on. He wants me there tonight, so he has someone to talk to." Sydney wasn't about to confide that she'd developed a huge crush on Troy, just like the single tellers at the bank. "Well, if you must know, he and I are hoping to convince David and Brooke that they should delay the wedding until they know each other better. It's that simple."

"Nothing is simple where Troy Emerson's involved. He doesn't date anyone at the bank, his cardinal rule, but I've heard talk that he's big on playing the field." Pam waved her fork in an all encompassing wave. "A different date each weekend, except for one whose name keeps cropping up. Vicki."

Sydney took a quick breath. She didn't want to hear this, but at the same time she wanted to know more.

"How do you know all this?"

"He talks with his secretary, who dotes on him and is always asking what he's done over the weekend. Since she knows we're all interested, she shares bits and pieces in the break room."

"But you haven't heard about his brother and my sister?"

"No. That hasn't hit the grapevine yet. I'll let you know when it does."

Sydney wanted to ask about Vicki, but she couldn't bring herself to. Then Pam would know she was more interested in Troy than just as a potential brother-in-law for her sister.

The afternoon dragged by until Sydney could escape work. She flew home and changed into white slacks and a short-sleeved blue sweater, then headed for her parents' home.

The smell of baking chicken and the sound of Brooke's frantic voice met her when she opened the front door.

"I'm so glad you're here. Please tell Mom she needs to change clothes now. The Emersons are always early, no matter where they go, and I don't want her caught in those old clothes."

"Calm down. This isn't a summit meeting," Sydney said.

"I know. I know. I just want everything to go perfect. I want his family to like mine. Reverend Ritter says that if you think you aren't marrying the family, then you're mistaken."

"So, you've already started the marriage counseling," Sydney said as they walked toward the kitchen. "Can I take over here, Mom, so you can go change?"

"Thanks, honey. Finish peeling these potatoes. I think this will be plenty. Here wear this." She slipped off her cobbler-style apron and handed it to Sydney.

"Care to give me a hand?" Sydney asked her sister.

Brooke fumbled with a knife and cut her finger instead of the potato. She scurried off to bandage it while Sydney finished the potatoes and put them on to boil.

The way Brooke is acting, this might as well be a summit, Sydney thought and wondered what Troy's parents would be like. She fixed herself a glass of iced tea and wandered into the dining room. The table was set with the good china, and her mother had arranged flowers from her luscious garden as a centerpiece. Nine places. There were nine people. Surely he wasn't bringing a date. No, that was preposterous. Why did the unknown woman Vicki pop into her mind? Maybe David and Troy had another sibling. But wouldn't that have come up in conversation? She went back into the kitchen and stirred the potatoes.

"There are five Emersons coming?" Sydney asked when Brooke returned with her finger bandaged.

"Four Emersons and a last-minute guest," Brooke said.

Sydney gasped and dropped her tea glass, which shattered when it hit the hard tile floor. "Oh!" Brooke picked up the biggest pieces of glass, and Sydney grabbed paper towels and started mopping up the mess, slicing her finger on a shard in the process. Blood oozed and dripped on the knee of her white slacks.

"I can't believe this," Sydney exclaimed, and ran for the sink. She held her bleeding finger under running water and sponged the blood on her slacks with the dish rag.

"Girls, what's going on?" her mom asked from the doorway.

"Just dropped a glass," Brooke said. "We're klutzes tonight."

"Well, relax. We're going to have a pleasant evening. I talked to Jan Emerson this afternoon, and she seems like a down-to-earth type person. I like her already."

The Cale girls arranged hors d'oeuvres and were sitting in the living room talking with their father when the Emersons arrived.

Sydney would have recognized Ralph Emerson anywhere. Seeing him was like glimpsing Troy twenty-five years down the road. Jan Emerson was petite beside him. Her hair was cut stylishly short, and her smile reminded Sydney of Troy's grin. To Sydney's amazement, the woman hugged her.

"I feel like I know you from what Troy and David have said about you. Brooke's certainly proud of her older sister."

"Thanks," Sydney said. "I'm delighted to meet you." She glanced past the vivacious woman to the others coming inside. David was next with Troy and another man bringing up the rear. Brooke took care of the family introductions, but then Troy took over.

"This is our old neighbor, Edmund," Troy said. "It's been what, five years since we've seen each other?" Edmund appeared to be around Troy's age, late twenties.

"Once we finished college, I took a job in Chicago," Edmund said. "I haven't been back since my folks moved. Since I was in Tulsa, I thought I'd drop in. Nice of you to let me come to dinner with the family."

Sydney's relief at the guest being a man made her greet him with extra enthusiasm. "Any friend of Troy's is a friend of ours."

Conversation took off with several discussions going at one time. It was as if the two families had known each other for years instead of just meeting.

Sydney heard her father and Ralph discussing the Drillers, the local minor league baseball team. Jan and her mother discussed the library fund-raiser. David and Brooke looked at their parents with obvious relief that the meeting was going so well. That left Edmund and Troy for Sydney to visit with, and the conversation centered around Edmund's job as a stockbroker in Chicago. He even gave a lecture on last year's mini-crash that forced an early closing of the stock market.

It was with relief that Sydney excused herself to help her mother in the kitchen with last-minute food preparation.

With Sydney gone from the living room, Troy and Edmund discussed old times, but Edmund quickly steered the conversation back to his job and the excitement of the stock exchange. He made banking seem tame by comparison, but Troy was not going to defend his choice of career to Edmund. The two of them had been competitors as long as he could remember. Whether it was who could ride a bike further with no hands to who had the highest batting average in Little League, the two had always been at each other.

"I think I'll see if Syd needs some help," he said. He'd never called her that, but he wanted Edmund to think that she was his special friend. Her warm welcome to his old neighbor had not set well. Troy shouldn't have been surprised when Edmund followed him to the kitchen, but it annoyed him just the same.

The women were bustling around. His mom was pouring iced tea; Sydney's mother was slicing chicken; Sydney was mashing potatoes with an electric mixer.

"Need a hand?" he said over the whine of the motor. "I've mashed a few potatoes in my time."

Sydney's eyes widened with surprise. "I had no idea you were so domesticated."

Troy glanced at his mother. She raised her eyebrows, but didn't comment.

"I can help," Edmund said. "I have more experience at ordering from a menu than cooking, but that's what I get for being so busy. No time for the fine art of cooking."

Troy could barely suppress a groan, and he hoped Sydney was seeing through this clown. She didn't seem fazed by his conceited remarks, but smiled up at him. She handed Troy the mixer she was using, and led Edmund to another counter.

"As Jan fills these glasses, would you carry them into the dining room? Right through there." She motioned toward an arched doorway, then she walked back to Troy and plopped several pats of butter in his potatoes. He stopped the mixer while she poured in milk.

He leaned toward her. "Stay away from him," he said in a low voice and was shocked that he had said it.

"No problem," Sydney replied.

"I'm sorry. I mean—"

"I know what you mean," she said and smiled at him. "Need more milk?"

Chapter 6

S ydney hadn't been home five minutes from the family dinner when the doorbell rang. She peeked out the hole, then opened the door.

"I don't know your phone number, but I know where you live," Troy said. "And I wanted to talk."

"Come on in." She waved her hand toward the living room, and he took a seat on the couch. She sat in a chair across from him.

"I wanted to explain about Edmund. We've known each other a long time."

"But not as friends." That was obvious from the way Troy had acted. Oh, he'd been polite and listened to Edmund talk, but there'd been a frown line across his forehead most of the evening.

"For fifteen years we lived side by side. I couldn't make a move that he didn't know about. If a friend came over, he was right there, too. If I made something in Dad's workshop, he'd make something even better."

"Sounds like he had an inferiority complex and was out to prove he was just as good as you."

"Or better," Troy said.

"And still does. After all, he's in the stock exchange,"

she said it with the high-and-mighty emphasis that Edmund had placed on it.

Troy chuckled. "You've pegged him right, but I felt I should apologize for my attitude this evening. I really try to live my life by the Golden Rule, and I didn't succeed tonight."

"I doubt that Edmund noticed that you were less than interested in what he said. You weren't impolite. I imagine that only your mother and I noticed."

"Why did you notice? My mom is a given. She knows what I'm thinking before I think it, but I knew that you knew, too. Okay, I shouldn't have told you to stay away from him, but it was more than that, wasn't it?"

She didn't know what to say, so she remained quiet. How could she explain the connection she felt for him? He reached out his hand to her and she took it. Without hesitation, she sat beside him on the couch and looked at him. She knew he was going to kiss her from the look in his eye, and it was what she wanted, too.

It was a gentle kiss, a meeting of souls and a pledge of something more. Then he kissed her again and again.

The phone rang, and Sydney reluctantly pulled away from his arms and answered it.

"Syd, how did you think it went? Everyone seemed to like each other," Brooke said.

"The evening went very well. Our parents got along great."

"Dad and Ralph are going to the ball game tomorrow night. Isn't that something?"

"Sounds like progress to me," Sydney said into the

receiver, but she gazed at Troy while Brooke gushed on about the good relationships developing between the Cales and the Emersons. Troy picked up a pencil and notepad from the end table.

"Phone number?" he wrote on the pad and handed her the pen.

Sydney smiled and wrote her number for him.

"It was a good evening," she said again to Brooke. "Good night."

"It's time I was saying good night, too," Troy said as she hung up the phone. "I'll call you."

"Does that mean you want to continue with our plan?" She hoped it meant more than that—that he wanted to call her solely because he was interested in her.

"Continuing to point out character traits they're not aware of can only help them in the long run." He stood, and she walked him to the door. Before he left, he tilted her chin up and kissed her once more.

Sydney got ready for bed in a daze. She knew there was something special between her and Troy, and his wonderful kiss deepened what she already felt for him. That spark between them was quickly becoming a flame. Their three times together might not be classified as dates, but she had a much stronger emotional reaction to him than she'd ever had to a man before. She climbed in bed and held her nightly talk with God.

"I know You've sent him to me for a reason. He's a strong Christian who works at living the life You'd want him to. Is he the special one You've sent for me?"

For a full week, Troy fought the urge to call Sydney Cale. Something was in the air between them, and he wasn't sure what it was, but it didn't fit into his life plan. Over the weekend he'd had a first date with a woman he'd met at a friend's house. As first dates went, it was most pleasant, but when he'd taken her home and given her a brief kiss goodnight, he was dissatisfied. Sydney's image flashed in his mind, and he wanted to be holding her, kissing her.

What he needed, he decided after he'd reflected on it the next few days, was to get to know Sydney Cale better, then he could get her out of his mind. He could use the cover of Project Postponement to ask her out, so he wouldn't be misleading her into thinking he was personally interested, and he'd make a list of her negative points, just like they were doing for David and Brooke.

With a sense of fair play, he made a column for her good points, too. Under the negative side he wrote "competitive," but he felt compelled to add "necessary for sports." Under good points he wrote:

1. *Christian woman.*
2. *Can communicate with me without words.*
3. *Kisses like an angel.*
4. *Cares about her family.*
5. *Smart, good at math.*
6. *Straightforward.*

At work, he pulled the list from his briefcase, read it again, and reached for the phone.

"We need to start spending every spare minute we can with David and Brooke," Troy told Sydney on her work extension.

"I agree," Sydney said, thrilled that she'd be able to spend more time with him, too. "If you're free tonight, I'll check and see if they can go with us to my great aunt's. Reverend Ritter has told them that they are also marrying the family, and they should meet as many members as they can."

"I thought Friday night we could all take in a movie. Getting them to agree on a choice will show David's willful side. He always wants his way."

"Perfect. I'll get back to you," Sydney said, then made a few calls to set up the evening's entertainment, for any evening spent with Aunt Dot was entertaining.

Troy picked her up that evening, and they met David and Brooke at Aunt Dot's home in the southern part of Tulsa. When Aunt Dot had moved there, it had been a farmhouse, set back from the road. Now it was surrounded by Oral Roberts University on the north and giant apartment complexes on the south. She'd turned down countless offers to sell, called it her home, and said she wasn't going to leave it.

"Aunt Dot is my dad's aunt," Sydney explained to Troy as they sauntered up the long walk to the front porch where the others sat on wicker furniture. "She never married and is quite independent. If anyone can show Brooke that it would be better to wait to get married until she's had some time on her own, it will be Aunt Dot."

"I told Aunt Dot our plans," Brooke announced as soon as Troy was introduced.

"And I gave them a piece of my mind," Aunt Dot said. "Now you folks ready for some homemade ice cream? I mixed it up after you called, Syd."

"Peach?" Since Sydney had been a youngster, Aunt Dot had made her favorite ice cream whenever she came for a visit.

"Would I make you any other kind? Peaches are from the deep freeze, but they'll be nearly as good as they were last summer."

They sat on the porch in the twilight of the warm June evening, eating ice cream and talking about the future. Aunt Dot was always big on discussing goals, and she had a knack of drawing the most intimate dream from a person. Through the years, Sydney had confided her successes and failures. Tonight David and Brooke talked about the family they wanted after they finished school.

"What about you?" Aunt Dot looked at Troy with a penetrating gaze. "What do you want out of life?"

Troy laughed uneasily. "My long range goal is to marry in a few years when I'm financially secure, buy a house, have a family. Live the American dream. Have a wife who loves me, a cheerful home to go to after a day's work, and kids who respect me."

"You make a good living now?" Aunt Dot asked.

He seemed taken aback. Sydney gave Aunt Dot a look asking her not to put him on the spot. After all, they were here for Brooke's and David's benefit.

"Yes. I draw a good salary, and I like my work. I hope I help people make positive changes in their lives."

Aunt Dot nodded and looked thoughtful. Later when Sydney helped her take the empty bowls to the kitchen, she said. "Don't let him make the same mistake I did. There's no need to wait until there's plenty of money. A little sacrifice can bond a couple together."

"Then you think David and Brooke should go ahead and marry?"

Aunt Dot shot her a sly look. "I'm not talking about David and Brooke. I'm talking about you and Troy."

So Aunt Dot could see the invisible connection that stretched between them, too. That shouldn't have surprised Sydney, but it did.

On Friday night Troy picked up David first, then Brooke, then Sydney for their movie date.

"What movie should we see?" he asked and winked at Sydney. He expected an all-out war, with David fighting to win the battle.

"I read the reviews in the paper this morning," Sydney said. "There was some spy thriller and a comedy."

"That spy movie sounds good," David said from the back seat, just as Troy figured he would.

"It doesn't matter to me," Brooke said. "I'm easy."

"What do you like, Troy?" Sydney asked.

"Nothing too silly," he said. "I like a good mystery."

"What do you mean by silly?" Sydney asked. "Slapstick humor?"

"No, romantic comedy. I don't like unrealistic situations, and those verge on fantasy land. What's your favorite kind?" Troy glanced over at his front seat passenger.

"Romantic comedy," Sydney said. "I like to come out of a movie theater smiling, not thinking about some deep meaning and heavy plot. And not scared half to death, either."

"Why don't we compromise?" David suggested. "There's a foreign film festival downtown. That might be fun."

"You mean with subtitles?" Troy asked. He'd been to a foreign film in college, but it wasn't an experience he wanted to repeat. He'd come out of the film feeling like an idiot, not knowing what he'd just seen. Some of the subtitles flicked on and off the screen so fast, he hadn't been able to read them.

"Of course, with subtitles. How else could we understand it?" David asked.

"That sounds like fun. Something different," Brooke said. "You're full of good ideas, David."

"Sydney?" Troy asked and glanced her way again.

"Okay by me. It'll be an experience," she said.

Troy turned the car toward downtown. It'd be an experience all right, but probably not a good one. He parked on a city lot, and they walked back the three blocks to the theater and waited a good ten minutes in line. Who would have thought a foreign film would have been so popular? Certainly not Troy. He restlessly shifted his weight from one foot to the other, then slightly begrudgingly paid for the tickets for a movie he didn't want to see.

"I'll buy the popcorn and sodas," David said and walked toward the refreshment counter with Brooke.

Troy looked at the one-dollar bills he was folding and saw that the cashier had mistakenly given him a ten for one of them.

"I've got to get back in line," Troy said and explained the situation to Sydney, who stood with him until he had exchanged his ten for a one, then they joined the others.

At least the theater was a wonderful change from the small strip-like theaters that were now in clusters of ten or more around Tulsa. This old theater with its high domed ceiling had been renovated and could seat hundreds in a luxurious setting.

"Isn't this cozy? Boy, girl, boy, girl?" Brooke said once they were seated with each couple sharing a tub of buttery popcorn.

It got cozier once the lights went down. Troy rested his arm on the back of Sydney's chair and let it settle down around her shoulders. She leaned toward him. He concentrated more on the clean smell of her hair than on the movie, although it was much easier to follow than the one he'd seen in college. This one had a plot, and that plot was a mystery.

After the movie, Troy suggested they do something on Saturday night, too.

"Brooke's coming over to watch a video," David said. "We're saving as much money as we can this summer to carry us through the school year, but you can come over if you want to." In the rearview mirror, Troy saw David exchange a puzzled glance with Brooke.

Troy dropped Brooke and David off at his folks' house, then he drove Sydney home.

"You were a good sport," Sydney said as he walked her to her door. "And so was David. I don't think he was particularly keen on seeing that film, although it was his suggestion, wasn't it? Did he get his way? If he controlled the choice, it was in a subtle way."

"Well, maybe he's outgrown that willful attitude. Anyway, why do we watch movies but foreigners watch films?" Troy asked.

Sydney laughed. "I think it has something to do with sounding cosmopolitan or sophisticated. I'm not sure, but it was a good film. I enjoyed the evening."

"Me, too. Up for watching a video with them tomorrow night? I'll figure out a way to get us all into David's bedroom so Brooke can see what a slob he is."

"Oh. . .right. The plan."

She sounded as if she had forgotten about Project Postponement, and for the moment, as he pulled her in his arms to kiss her good night, he forgot about it, too.

Chapter 7

Project Postponement was way down on Sydney's list of things to think about. What took up most of her thinking time was Troy Emerson. She cleaned her house on Saturday morning, humming as she dusted and swept and vacuumed. She wanted the place clean and homey when Troy picked her up for their rendezvous with David and Brooke.

She'd met Troy a little over two weeks ago, and she'd spent a few hours plotting and scheming with him, but mostly she'd spent time getting to know him. She knew it was too fast, but she'd fallen in love with him. Just when it had happened, she didn't know, but the feeling enveloped her. She felt brand new, as if every moment was glistening, every moment held joy.

She got ready for their Saturday night date with care, choosing comfortable jeans and a white shirt with a mauve vest. She wanted to look casual; after all it was a watch-TV date. But she also wanted to look stylish.

Her choice of clothes was the uniform of the night, although Brooke wore white jeans and David's jeans had holes in the knees. Troy's jeans were creased, which didn't surprise her at all. She couldn't see him ironing, but sending his clothes to a laundry fit her conception of his lifestyle.

"Do you still have those old baseball cards?" Troy asked David when they were all sitting in the family room. "Some men at the bank were talking about what kind of investment they were and if they had a good return these days."

"Hey, I'd forgotten all about those," David said. He glanced at Brooke. "This might be another item to add to our financial portfolio."

"Financial portfolio?" Sydney knew they were saving for their life together, but this sounded a bit much.

"Where are they?" Troy asked. "In your room?"

"Yeah, somewhere."

"Could I see them?" Sydney asked. "Do you have anyone I might recognize?"

Brooke laughed. "You'd know Mickey Mantle and Babe Ruth and that's only if you read the names. Can we look for them?" she asked.

Good, Brooke was falling right into their trap. David shrugged and walked down the hall. Troy was on his heels, so Sydney followed, and Brooke trailed after her.

"I thought you said this would be messy," Sydney whispered to Troy. The bed was lumpy, but made up, and the room was tidy by what she considered male standards.

"What happened to you?" Troy asked. "You're neat."

David grunted from inside the closet.

"I think he's neat, too," Brooke said and laughed at

her little joke. "He used to be such a slob, but I told him there was a place for everything and everything should be in its place."

"You sound like Mom. Since when are you Miss Shipshape?" Sydney asked.

"Since I met David. You wouldn't believe him, Syd. He'd throw clothes on the floor right beside a laundry hamper. His roommate wasn't much better. We agreed that we'd both be neater, so I've had to work at it, too."

"Here are the baseball cards," David said, his head still in the closet. "Do you think we could get much for them? Do you have one of those guides that tell their value?"

Troy took the box that David held out and flipped through the cards.

"You can't really change a person, you know," Sydney told her sister.

"Reverend Ritter says that, too, but I disagree. If you have a bad habit, and if you know it's not a good one, then you can work on it. I read somewhere that three weeks of practicing a good habit can change a bad habit. David and I have listed qualities in each other that we are concerned about, and then we discuss them."

"But you can't change a person's values like that," Sydney said.

"No, but I don't want to change David's values. He's perfect the way he is. I just want him to look at habits that might get in the way of our marriage."

Sydney followed the others down the hall and sat

next to Troy on the couch while they watched a movie. She'd seen it already, but didn't say so. Troy must have seen it, too, for he glanced at the screen now and then, but organized the cards by years and teams.

"You ought to take these to a dealer for an appraisal," Troy suggested. "Some of these rookie cards could be valuable."

"Great," David said. "On my lunch hour Monday, I'll do it. Ready for another movie. This one's an oldie that Brooke wanted to see."

Troy glanced at Sydney then toward the door. It was all the signal she needed.

"Actually, I need to have an early night," Sydney said. "I'm taking on the second grade classes alone tomorrow, and I have to go over my lesson."

"We've got to talk," Troy said on the way to Sydney's house. "Plan Postponement isn't working. I heard what Brooke said about changing habits, and I'm beginning to think these kids know what they're doing."

"They seem well-suited to each other," Sydney said. "Do you have the list with you?"

He nodded and patted his shirt pocket.

"Then let's reassess what we've learned so far."

As soon as they arrived at the carriage house and Sydney had fixed them some coffee, they sat at her kitchen table with the paper in front of them.

"This isn't much of a list," Sydney said.

"I know. We never finished it once they interrupted us that first night at my apartment, but it's a start. For Brooke we have temper, which we didn't actually see on

70

the tennis court." He grinned across at her. "But I saw yours."

"Yes, you did see my worst side. We ought to play again, and I'll do better."

"Why not give me lessons? Isn't that what Brooke did for David? Believe me, he used to match me terrible stroke for terrible stroke. Now he's a stronger player."

"A good idea. Then we can play them again and beat them."

"There's that competitive edge coming out again," he said and laughed. He looked back at the list. "The only other negative trait we have for Brooke is jealousy, and that was iffy. You mentioned in high school she was jealous once."

"Yes. Let me think about how to pull that one off. And David?"

"We covered slob, but he's trying to break that habit. Can you believe those two? Who would have thought they'd be this mature about bad habits?"

Sydney nodded in agreement. "Vanity," she read from the list. "I haven't seen an example of that. His jeans tonight had holes in the knees."

"True, but he probably thinks that's stylish."

"What about pressed and creased jeans?" Sydney asked and pointed at him.

Troy was silent a moment. "Point taken, but I like them that way. One of the few luxuries I allow myself is to send out my laundry. I'm basically a frugal person."

"I'm not criticizing, just pointing out a character trait. Now, can we think of anything else? I don't think they're guilty of the ten deadly sins. Let's face it, David and Brooke are pretty good people."

"True, but are they made for each other?" he asked.

"I don't know, but that's not our choice. That's for them to decide. We just want them to be informed decision makers." She looked down at the short list again. "I'll work on the jealousy angle, but it may not pan out."

"They aren't at the same job, so there's no opportunity for her to see him talking with anyone else. Where else—"

"Tomorrow at church," Sydney interrupted. "They're going to the same service now. Is there some girl there who could talk to him?"

"I'll come up with someone. Brooke told me you go to early church."

"Yes, I need the worship time before I teach my second graders. I could probably use it afterward, too."

They formed yet another plan. After her Sunday school class, Sydney would meet Troy in the fellowship hall where his adult singles class hung out before the second service. There were always single women there, and Troy would get David in a conversation with one of them and see where it led.

With the plan made, Troy stood up to leave. As was now their custom each time they parted, he kissed her goodnight. But each night the kisses grew longer and more tender and more meaningful. And each night, Sydney wanted more.

The next morning, armed with her teacher's

72

quarterly and materials for a flower craft to reinforce appreciation for God's world, Sydney marched into her Sunday school room. Early church had given her the comfort and the strength to face her charges, thirty-two second graders. Normally there were two classrooms for this age, but today Sydney was doing double duty because the other teacher was out of town. By the time the bell rang for the end of Sunday school, she was ready for a break. She had glue on her fingers, a bit of the sticky goo in her hair where she'd brushed it away from her face, and a mark from a permanent black marker on her cheek from a boy who accidentally stuck his hand up at the wrong moment.

She put away the extra supplies, washed her hands and scrubbed at the mark, but it was going to stay a while. With hurried steps, she made her way to the fellowship hall where she was to meet Troy. There must have been a hundred people there, but she spotted him immediately. He was holding a cup of coffee in one hand and a cookie in the other and talking to an attractive blond. She turned her head, and Sydney recognized Vicki Higgins, the assistant choir director. Surely that wasn't the Vicki that the bank grapevine had paired with Troy, but all evidence pointed to the contrary.

A sharp pain stabbed at Sydney's heart and turned it green as she watched Vicki put her hand on Troy's arm. She didn't know Vicki well, but of course, she had seen her with the choir and at Sunday school committee meetings.

Sydney took a few quick breaths, then turned to

leave. Troy hadn't seen her, so she could slip away and he might think she'd been delayed.

"Good morning, Syd," Brooke called in a cheery voice. Her sister was followed into the fellowship hall by David and his parents.

With no escape available now, Sydney smiled and exchanged pleasantries with the Emersons. She really liked them, but right now she longed to be swallowed up by a large hole. She risked a glance toward Troy and saw he was walking straight for their little group with Vicki in tow.

Troy had spotted his family and Sydney and was ready for another installment of Project Postponement. It had been easy to convince Vicki to flirt with David. She would be an older woman for him, but what male wouldn't be flattered to have a pretty blond like Vicki make over him.

He greeted Sydney, who said, "hello," but then looked at his mother instead of at him. His mother wasn't even talking. Vicki was doing her part and gushing over how good it was to see David.

"Are you working here this summer?" Vicki asked.

"Yeah, at the billboard company," he said. "Same one I worked for last summer."

"That looks dangerous. Do you like working that high in the air? Some of those billboards must be three stories up."

Troy tuned her out and focused his attention on

Brooke, who was talking to his mother. Sydney wasn't contributing to the conversation, but stood as if entranced with Brooke's views on how nice it was to have cookies between Sunday school and church. Why wasn't she nudging Brooke to pay attention to David and Vicki?

She glanced at him, and he saw hurt and disappointment in her eyes. He'd been amazed at how well he and Sydney communicated with looks, but this time he wasn't understanding her. What had upset her? Had something happened in her Sunday school class? She had a line on her cheek, and he took a step closer and traced it with his finger. Her gaze locked with his while his finger slid over her smooth skin.

"A boy accidentally marked on me," she explained without him asking. So, their unspoken communication line was back. But the hurt was still in her eyes, and she turned them away from him and looked at David and Vicki.

They were still carrying on a fairly animated conversation, but Brooke had joined in. Instead of showing signs of jealousy, Brooke was smiling and asking Vicki questions about the choir. She must have outgrown the jealous streak that her sister had seen years earlier. Or maybe she was so secure in David's love, that it couldn't be threatened.

Troy looked at Sydney, and the truth hit him. She was acting the way he'd expected Brooke to act. That hurt look about her—was that a result of him talking to Vicki? But they were friends. Oh, they'd gone out a few times because it had been convenient, but the last time he'd seen Vicki, they'd talked about how they were better friends than dates. They valued their friendship too much to call it a relationship. But Sydney couldn't know that. Actually, she couldn't even know that he'd dated Vicki. So, he was on the wrong trail here. Wasn't he?

All he knew was that he wanted to wipe that hurt out of her eyes. He wanted her to look at him with the same trust that Brooke had for David. He wanted Sydney to be as secure in his love as. . . What was he thinking?

He felt as if the floor had moved underneath his feet, and he reached for Sydney's shoulder to steady himself. In an instant his carefully made plans, of being at least thirty with a fat savings account and a new home before he married, were gone. What he needed in his carefully ordered life was this woman. And he wanted her now.

"Sydney," he said and led her off to the side of the group. "Would you have Sunday dinner with me? We need to talk."

Chapter 8

S ydney sat beside Troy in the pew during the second service. She was glad she'd already heard the sermon, because she didn't hear a word of it. Her thoughts were on the man beside her.

He'd had the most incredulous look on his face when he asked her to Sunday dinner, and she knew what it meant. He loved her. She was certain of it.

When the minister paused for silent prayer, she poured her heart out in thanks to God and asked that He guide her future.

"Where are we going?" Sydney asked when church was over. "Your parents' house?"

"No, some place where it's just you and me. I'll be over in a few minutes to pick you up, but first I need to talk to my folks."

Once Sydney arrived home, she immediately hit the bathroom and used every cleaner she had to get the mark off her cheek. It came off, leaving a red place where she had scrubbed so hard. She freshened her makeup and sat out on the verandah to wait for Troy.

When he arrived, he had taken off his suit coat and carried a large sack with him. "Got a blanket? Could we eat a picnic here on the grounds?"

Sydney went inside and got a large blue gingham tablecloth out of the linen closet. "I know a wonderful spot for a picnic," she said when she returned.

He took her hand as they walked to a bushy area on the edge of the property. Fragrant blooms gave off a sweet smell as she led him through the bushes on a narrow path, which led to an interior clearing about ten feet in diameter.

"I don't know who cleaned off this spot, but I consider it my secret think place," she said as she spread out the tablecloth.

Troy sat down and patted the area beside him. Once Sydney was seated, folding her skirt underneath her, he unpacked sub sandwiches and sodas from the bag.

"Hungry?" she asked.

"No, I'm too excited to be hungry," he said.

"Excited about. . ." She waited for him to finish her sentence.

"Us. About us." He took a deep breath, let it out slowly, and held out his hand to her. "I love you, Sydney."

Sydney put her hand in his, closed her eyes and said, "Thank You, God." She opened her eyes. "I love you, too."

He pulled her into his arms and kissed her, once, twice, three times.

"I know this is sudden," he said when they finally pulled apart. "I can't explain it, but I know it's love that I feel for you, and I know it's right. Normally I let my mind rule my emotions, but this time my heart is ruling my head. I feel like I've known you forever." Mentally he went through the list of her characteristics that he'd written. "I've seen you when you were angry, competitive, romantic, kind, jealous—"

"Jealous?"

"I think you were as jealous of Vicki as I was when Edmund came with me to your parents' home for dinner."

"You're right." She told him what the office grapevine had whispered, and he explained his relationship with Vicki.

It was her turn to describe his qualities. "I know you are smart, honest, good-looking, conniving—"

"Honest and conniving?"

"Honest in that you returned ten dollars to the theater cashier when you hated standing in line. Oh, I'll add 'impatient,' too, and 'good sport,' since you really didn't want to see that film. And you are conniving, because it was your idea to show Brooke and David that they hadn't known each other long enough to make a major commitment like marriage."

"I've reconsidered my stand on that."

"Then I'll add 'able to change his mind' to your list of good qualities," she said.

"And for the record, you were the one to come up with Project Postponement. I just thought we had to stop them from making a mistake."

"You're right," Sydney said. "We agreed about that. We're in sync about a lot of things, all the things that matter. We both believe in God and want to serve Him by living up to His standards. We both believe in family and all that means." She shifted away from him so she could hold his hands and look him in the eyes. "You told Aunt Dot that you wanted children. How many?"

"How does four sound?"

"Sounds like a happy family," she said and smiled.

He took her hands in his. "Will you marry me?"

"Yes, oh, yes." Again she found herself in his arms.

"When?" he asked and kissed her. "Soon," he answered his own question and kissed her again.

"If it was practical, I'd marry you tomorrow," she said, "but I think we'd better do this right. Talk to our parents and all."

"Actually, we should start by telling David and Brooke," Troy said. He picked up his sub sandwich. "Suddenly I'm ravenous."

They ate their subs and interrupted each other with questions and answers about each other.

"I want to know everything about you," Sydney said. "What was your most embarrassing moment?" She laughed when Troy described part of his costume falling off when he was in a school play.

"Did you have pets as a kid?" Troy asked.

"A dog. Strictly an outside dog. My mom wouldn't let him in the house."

"Sydney," Troy said when they had packed up the sandwich wrappers and folded the tablecloth and were walking back to the carriage house. "I want to spend the rest of my life getting to know you better."

"I can't think of anything I'd like more," she said.

They stopped walking and she looked up at him, and he kissed her once again.

They talked until late and then they talked some more. It was as if their admission of loving each other had freed them to talk about anything that entered their minds.

"We have work tomorrow," Sydney said.

"I know. I'm leaving, but I don't want to. Did you say you'd marry me tomorrow if it were possible?"

She laughed. "Of course, but I think there are a few matters to take care of first. Like a blood test and marriage license."

"Oh, yes. But you will marry me soon?"

"I can hardly wait. Goodnight, Troy."

His goodnight kiss was long and thorough. "I'll see you tomorrow," he said and finally let her go.

Sydney had to hold the phone away from her ear. Pam's excited voice must have reached the next office cubicle.

"You won't believe this, but Troy Emerson was asking about marriage licenses," Pam said.

"How do you know this?" Sydney might have to alert Troy that his secretary didn't keep secrets.

"He asked some people in the elevator. In the elevator, can you imagine?"

Sydney wasn't ready to announce to the world that she was getting married, so she hedged around the truth. "Do you think he could be asking for his brother? Remember he's planning to marry Brooke in August."

"Oh, I guess you're right." Pam's voice sunk an octave. "Got time for lunch?"

"Not today, but soon," Sydney said and hung up. Today she met her fiancé for lunch and they talked over plans for the evening. They each made afternoon calls, and that evening, Sydney sat with Troy in the Tower View restaurant, nervously awaiting her sister and her fiancé. After they arrived and they had all ordered, Troy made the announcement.

"Sydney and I are getting married."

Brooke and David exchanged a look, and Brooke burst out laughing. "I told you," she said. "You owe me a million dollars."

"You knew?" Sydney was amazed.

"Of course. It's in the way you look at each other. It's in the way you say each other's names. Same with us," Brooke said and pointed at David then herself. "Love shows. When are you telling Mom and Dad?"

"Tonight. And we're getting married as soon as we can," Sydney said.

"Are you going to elope?" Brook asked.

"Do you two feel you've known each other long enough to make such a major commitment?" David asked.

Sydney looked at Troy, and he held out his hand and took hers in it.

"I've been waiting all my life for him," Sydney said. "Now that I've found him, I don't want to delay the life I've dreamed of."

"Why not wait a few years?" Brooke asked. "Isn't

that what you wanted us to do?"

"We've changed our minds about that," Troy said. "We think you're mature adults who can make your own decisions."

"And we think you know what love is," Sydney added, "and so do we."

Brooke whispered something to David and he flashed her a quick smile.

"Why not set the date for August fifteenth?" David suggested. "We've already booked the church."

Epilogue

Sydney looked across the mirrored room at her sister, who stood a vision in white lace and tulle. Brooke's traditional gown was full-skirted and made her small waist look even smaller.

Her own wedding dress featured a straight skirt and was made of white satin. Aunt Dot adjusted Sydney's short veil and sniffed.

"You girls are beautiful today," she said. She wiped her eyes and stepped into the hallway.

"No tears for me," Sydney's mom said. "This is a glorious evening. My daughters are marrying fine men tonight. Our family's growing, and I'll find out what it's like to have sons."

"And I'll find out what it's like to have daughters," Jan Emerson said.

Sydney couldn't remember two months flying as fast as the two months since that June day when she and Troy had confessed their love to each other. She and Troy and Brooke and David had spent countless hours together, planning their weddings and reception. They had painted the apartment in Norman last week and moved most of the younger couple's belongings into it. In the last two days, they had moved Troy's furniture into the carriage house where Sydney and Troy would live.

Yet in some ways, the two months had seemed to drag by. Sydney could hardly stand the wait until she and Troy would be a married couple.

Aunt Dot poked her head back in the changing room. "Okay, it's time. The ushers are ready to seat the mothers."

Sydney drew a deep breath. The moment had finally come. With quick hugs to the brides, the older women were ushered out of the room, leaving Sydney and Brooke alone.

"Are we ready for this?" Sydney asked, feeling a sudden nervous flutter in her stomach.

"I am," Brooke said. "I'm more than ready. Let's go."

Sydney opened the door, and the sisters walked quietly to the vestibule of the church where their father waited.

When the music signaled time for the bride's walk, Brooke took her father's arm and disappeared into the sanctuary.

"Dear God, thank You for this special day," Sydney whispered while she waited for her father to return. He came and offered his arm to her, and she stepped into the doorway. A long way off in the dim candlelit sanctuary, she saw Troy, handsome in a black tuxedo. His gaze never left hers as she floated down the aisle.

His look said, "I'm scared, too. This is a big step, but it's the right one for us." She nodded and beamed, and he smiled.

The minister began the ritual. When he came to the part where he said, "Speak now or forever hold your peace," Troy squeezed her hand.

They exchanged conspiratorial looks while Brooke

and David looked momentarily puzzled, then the minister, having waited the customary moment and having no response, continued the service.

Veda Boyd Jones
Veda writes romances "that confirm my own values," including the award-winning *Callie's Mountain* (**Heartsong Presents**). She has also written several books in the American Adventure Series for boys and girls ages 8-12 (Barbour Publishing). Besides her fiction writing, Veda has authored numerous articles for popular periodicals. A sought-after speaker at writers' conferences, Veda lives with her husband, an architect, and three sons in the Ozarks of Missouri.

Once Upon A Dream

Sally Laity

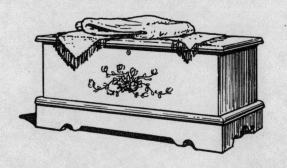

Dedication

To Dianne. . .treasured sister,
lifelong friend, with love.

Chapter 1

*H*is eyes glittered with evil as he fingered the edge of Lenore's velvet cloak, a devilish sneer twisting one side of his thin mustache. "At long last. . .you are mine."

Lenore shuddered, her terrified gaze raking the dank confines of the cave. How would Guilford ever find her here? Surely the heavy rains had washed away all evidence of their passage through the wooded hills. She swallowed, gathering her courage. He would find her. He had to. Straightening her back, she lifted her chin and met the malevolent count's smug countenance. "Never. I shall never belong to you."

He laughed then, a sinister sound that clawed its way up Lenore's spine. "Dream on, my pet. This night will be ours alone. No one on earth, save I, knows where you are."

"You, sir, misjudge me!" The triumphant masculine voice echoed from the drafty entrance.

Lenore's heart leapt. Guilford! He had come!

Her joy quickly evaporated at the sound of two swords released from their scabbards. As the sharp blades clanked relentlessly against each other, she struggled to break free of the rope cutting into her wrists. *Please, Lord God in heaven, let my Guilford be the victor. Let our love know the joy of sweet fulfillment. . . .*

The library door squeaked on its hinges.

Startled, Grace Farrell all but slammed *Guilford's Rose* into the drawer of her large walnut desk. She rarely read for pleasure during working hours, preferring to save that pastime for her solitary evening hours. Mustering her composure, she reached up to smooth her french twist and assumed a matter-of-fact air as one of her most regular patrons entered.

"Hi, Grace. Nice weather for ducks," quipped short and round Hattie Birch who then disposed of her dripping umbrella in the stand beside the door. After brushing lingering raindrops from the sleeve of her raincoat, the older woman crossed the carpeted room to an assortment of mismatched shelves that fairly sagged from the increasing collection of published works. "Has the gardening book I requested on loan come in yet?"

"Yes, it has." Rising, Grace made her way around the desk to the bookshelf where she kept the special-order volumes. "I was just about to call you and let you know it arrived earlier this afternoon."

"Oh, good. Good." Hattie accepted the book from Grace's hand with a huge sigh of relief. "Lawrence and I, we've been looking to do something different this year in the garden. Maybe try some newer varieties of vegetables and flowers."

"That should be challenging." With an inward smile at the little woman's compulsion to possess the most accomplished green thumb in all of Luzerne County, Grace held out a second volume. "I took the liberty of selecting this one on English tea roses for you as well, in case you might be interested."

"Why, that's downright sweet of you," Hattie said, beaming. "I'm always telling my husband how helpful you are."

"Will there be anything else?" Grace asked, moving to the counter to stamp the due dates on the cards and tuck them inside.

"Well—" She tossed a furtive glance over her shoulder. "Think I'll browse through the fiction. My Lawrence says love stories are sappy," she added on a sigh, "but I don't let his opinion get to me. I kind of enjoy the reminder of how it was when the two of us first fell in love."

"I understand."

Hattie regarded her with a pointedly questioning stare, one Grace recognized all too well. "Of course, everybody knows a refined lady like yourself probably prefers the type of books my husband considers beneficial. No offense, mind you—"

"None taken," Grace assured her. "Many new titles have arrived since your last visit. Take your time."

She heard Hattie's footsteps meander the length of the romance section, pausing now and again.

Grace cleared her throat, weighing the pros and cons of making a suggestion. "I've. . .heard good comments about the new Violet Birchfield release, *Wishful Thinking*. Some of the other ladies at church seemed to enjoy it." *And I, too, thought it was ever so charming,* she wanted to add.

"Really?" came Hattie's voice. "I'm quite picky. I don't care much for anything too racy."

"I don't believe that one would offend anyone. It's an Inspirational."

"You don't say. Hmmm, yes, here it is." She paused, as if scanning the blurb on the back cover. "Well, it does sound enticing. Guess I'll try it."

Grace smiled politely as Hattie came and handed her the paperback to stamp and add to her other selections. "Well, happy reading. I'm sure you'll enjoy these."

As Hattie nodded, her gray-streaked hair reflected the overhead lights but the effect was brief as she turned to retrieve her umbrella.

When the door closed behind her, Grace exhaled in relief. Better not be so careless in the future. The last thing she needed was for the whole town to know that "Old Maid Farrell"—a nickname that rankled her more with each passing year—was in the habit of devouring every single romance novel that found its way into the library. At thirty-nine, Grace was more than aware of her reputation as a dull, passionless spinster—after all, she herself had worked very hard to give that impression. But what else could she do, when so many of the blind dates arranged by her well-meaning friends had ended in disaster?

Grimacing at the memory of those painful encounters, she took comfort from her decision to refuse all future efforts at matchmaking. And those well-meaning friends had finally given up, apparently believing her desperate yet feigned attempt to act as though she were beyond such concerns.

As if anyone were ever truly beyond the need to love and be loved! Exhaling wistfully, Grace schooled her disappointments into line and looked at the wall clock. Nearly time to close for the night.

She opened the desk drawer and took a quick glance around before removing *Guilford's Rose* from its hiding place. The cover art revealed the typical flaxen-haired beauty, long unbound hair streaming halfway down her back as she cowered from a dark-caped villain. And looming over the cad was handsome and dashing Magnificence Personified, his sword at the ready.

Grace had to admit the plot struck her as rather trite but at least the novel would help occupy some of a too-quiet evening. So far the story seemed to be moving along at a fast pace, and she had yet to come across anything objectionable. However, if she encountered a scene that made her blush, she would quickly reroute the book to another library in the district rather than add it to her shelves. Grace considered it her mission in life to look out for her mostly conservative readers, many of whom were personal acquaintances and members of the local Bible church she attended. Of course, should someone wish to read one of the more explicit novels, she'd be happy to order in the specified title.

She added the novel to two other new releases already in her tote, then put on her half-glasses and took out the ledger to see if all currently due books had been returned.

Another squeak of protest from the door cut through

the silence. She peered over her spectacles as a tall muscular stranger strode purposely toward her, the clumping of his shoes muffled by the blue tweed carpet. "Yes? May I help you?"

"Actually, I hope you can, Mrs."—he leaned back to read the brass nameplate on the desk—"Miss Farrell. I'm Mitchell Haywood. A woman at the Wyoming Valley Historical Society pointed me in this direction a little while ago."

Puzzled, Graze focused on the man's hooded green eyes, noting that their dusky hue complemented the plaid shirt visible beneath his unzipped leather jacket. "And how may I be of service?" she prompted, suddenly remembering to remove her reading glasses.

An amiable grin added considerable appeal to his long, angular face and creased the skin around his eyes. "Actually, I'm a writer. I'm working on a series of books about America's small towns, places that might have been eclipsed by larger and more commonly known locales yet have unique histories people might find interesting."

"I take it you're not from around here."

"Right." As if from habit, he raked his fingers through a silvering temple of light brown hair. "I'm on assignment, you might say. I recently finished similar collections on New York and Connecticut, and now have been prevailed upon by my publisher to put together one on Pennsylvania."

"I see." Detecting a subtle blandness in the man's tone and rather lackluster expression, Grace sensed that he found this particular assignment less than appealing. She calculated mentally the raft of information such a project could entail. Then she checked her watch.

"Oh! Sorry," he offered with a wry wince. "Kind of late in the day for me to be coming by, I know, but I really didn't expect to start in immediately. I just wanted to make sure I'm in the right place so I can begin tomorrow."

With a thin smile, Grace nodded. "Rest assured, Mr. Haywood, our library contains a treasure trove of records and information that should be of benefit. I'd be delighted to steer you to what you're looking for, first thing in the morning. We open at nine."

"Fine. See you at nine, Miss Farrell." He flashed a toothy grin and waved as he took his leave.

Having automatically returned the gesture, Grace lowered her arm and watched after him, taking in his long, sweeping stride and somewhat noble bearing. Very few new faces came through her door. And to think he was a writer, no less. This was a first for her small library. These days most books of merit were researched at university library complexes or even on the Internet. Nice to know some people did things the old way. And getting to assist in the project in some small fashion might be a refreshing change—certainly a far cry from her seldom varied routine.

The cheerful thought lifted her spirits. The steady rain that had put a damper on the day's traffic had begun tapering off, taking with it much of the heavy gloom of the storm. She collected her belongings, then crossed to the coat closet for her raincoat and boots before locking up for the night.

Moments later, as she inserted the key into the door of her cream-colored Buick, Grace glanced up to see a burgundy Jeep Cherokee roll through a shallow puddle in the unpaved parking lot. Her eyes met another parting wave from Mitchell Haywood. She gave a polite nod as he passed by.

Tomorrow could prove to be a very interesting day.

Mitchell Haywood assessed the strawberry blond librarian in the rear-view mirror as he waited to pull out onto the wet pavement. The refined, symmetrical features of her patrician face were complemented by eyes of a gentle azure blue, he recalled, eyes with a demure quality to them. Though she appeared quite tall for a woman, she carried herself with a casual grace that made her quite approachable. Strange that someone so attractive was unattached—but then, she could be divorced, not that it was any of his business.

All he wanted was for her to display the same competence tomorrow that she showed today. He planned to make quick work of this task so he could continue on his way.

To Mitch Haywood, spring was one season that could best be appreciated in milder, sunnier climes. A person didn't have to see many TV weather maps to deduce that much of the Northeast was often plagued by cloudbanks that stretched all the way to Kansas.

As Mitch watched the librarian tip her head and get into her sedan, he realized the road had cleared. He directed his attention forward again, applying pressure to the accelerator as he headed toward the highway to Harvey's Lake.

The Back Mountain seemed to contain the same esthetic blend of old-fashioned and modern homes he had noted all along the drive from Wyoming Valley, a route that had taken him through an assortment of both sparsely and liberally populated towns and rural areas. Now as the storm drew to a close, the subdued light of day added another kind of quiet charm, making the bright April greens in the meadows echo the deepening hue of the thickly treed hills so in abundance. Mitch found the meandering country roads a welcome change from the boring, sterile freeways he'd been navigating the last few years. Something about this more placid pace soothed a person's spirit, and he wondered if he might even enjoy the couple of days he'd calculated spending here. Nearing the outskirts of the lake and the campground where he'd parked his travel trailer, he mused over some of the questions he'd ask Miss Farrell in the morning.

Then, unaccountably, the vision of the librarian's silly half-glasses perched slightly off-kilter on her nose came to his mind and he chuckled. And for some reason he couldn't fathom, he wondered if she always wore her hair pulled back that way.

Chapter 2

"**Y**ou shall have no need to fear anything or anyone again, my love," Guilford declared, drawing Lenore into his strong embrace. "That diabolical count will rot in the dungeon of Markham Prison, my men and I will see to that!" Gesturing to a duo of muscled companions waiting near the cave entrance, he indicated for them to lead the defeated villain away.

Her head resting in the comforting hollow of Guilford's shoulder, Lenore felt her heart throb almost painfully within her ribs. She had prayed to be rescued before the evil count carried out his sinister intentions—and yet, she had been plagued by serious doubts. For a short span of time she had felt devoid of all hope. Nevertheless, she gazed up at her champion through the thick fringe of her lashes and smiled sweetly. "I shall forever be in your debt. Pray, how am I to repay you?"

A slightly mischievous glint appeared in her knight's hazel gaze. "I'm sure we shall think of a way, dear heart. We'll have all of a lifetime together."

Lenore blushed prettily.

"I shall ask your father for your hand this very night."

"Surely a love such as ours could not possibly be denied," she whispered. "Father will doubtless give us his blessing, *and I shall wed you on the most magical night of all, Midsummer's Eve, but a fortnight away."*

He drew her closer. "Then 'twill be ours alone, for all time, to blossom and grow. . .our love a flower, and you my beautiful rose." Bending his dark head, he touched his lips to hers.

The words wrapped themselves around Lenore as the kiss deepened, stealing her very breath and filling her with ecstasy. She could ask no more of life than to be cherished by the most handsome and daring knight in all of Breckenshire.

When at last they drew apart, Guilford took her small hand in his. "Come, then, my beauty. 'Tis time I take you home." Striding out into the moonlit night, he lifted her effortlessly onto the back of his noble steed, then swung up behind her.

And together they rode toward love's destiny.

Grace stared incredulously at that final sentence for a full minute before closing the book.

Love's destiny.

Could it be possible that such a thing actually existed? Could one truly experience the bittersweet agonies described in fictional stories like this? She had dreamed so, in her much younger years, imagining a handsome young man proclaiming his undying passion, pleading for her hand in marriage. They would wed in June, of course, for the added romance and promise, and then would live happily ever after.

But those grand dreams had never come true. Not for her.

She sighed, rocking slowly in her calico-cushioned rocker. At least the story had served its purpose and helped to fill the quiet evening. And even a plot as romantically predictable as this one was better than the typical fare offered by network television.

Grace removed her reading glasses and laid them under the hobnail lamp on the end table, then rose and headed for the bathroom. As she turned on the taps of the claw-footed bathtub, carefully adjusting the temperature, she poured a handful of scented crystals into the swirling water.

Moments later, having gathered her nightgown and turned down her handmade quilt, Grace eased herself into the luxurious warm water. The bubbles tickled her skin and crackled just below her ears as she leaned back against the smooth white porcelain. She relaxed and closed her eyes, letting her mind drift over the day's events. . .to Mitchell Haywood.

She couldn't help wondering what sort of person the writer was, where he was from. He seemed decent enough, if she were any judge of character. The short time he'd been at the library had shown him to be mannerly, if not thrilled at the thought of being in the area. Best to stay on her guard, though. First impressions could be deceiving.

Still, she surmised with a small smile, his face was quite arresting. Elongated and strong, with just enough lines to lend character, and with adventure-seeking green eyes. If nothing else, having a stranger around would liven up her humdrum existence. She yawned and reached for her nylon pouf, pouring on a dab of moisturizing body soap before washing her arms.

The next morning on her way to work Grace grimaced with chagrin as she reflected on the ridiculous dream she'd had during the night. Funny how it had seemed to make such perfect sense in the foggy netherworld of half-sleep! In her dream she herself had taken Lenore's place in *Guilford's Rose,* dressed as a medieval maiden, her hair unbound and billowing dramatically around her like a golden cloud while two virile males, vying for her hand, engaged in a clashing sword fight.

A warm flush came to her face. Thankfully, no one would ever believe the town librarian had such utterly nonsensical fantasies. Greatly relieved, she determined to forget the ludicrous dream.

That was easy to do when she pulled into the library lot and spied the Jeep Cherokee already occupying a space just beyond where she normally parked. Obviously Mitchell Haywood kept to a rigorous research schedule when he had a project underway. She plucked her purse from the seat before exiting her sedan.

Tall maple and oak trees flanked either side of the squat wooden building, shading the whole front, and their filtered light added a touch of briskness to the clear spring morning as Grace neared the entrance.

She heard the door of the Cherokee open and close, and on the edge of her vision she caught the writer's brawny form.

"Morning, Miss Farrell," came his hearty voice as he joined her and mounted the front steps.

Grace dipped her head politely. "Mr. Haywood. You must be quite anxious to begin."

He gave a nod of agreement and grinned, the skin beside his eyes crinkling.

For a fleeting second Grace stared. There was something odd about his friendly smile. Something. . .familiar. And as she directed her attention to unlocking the door, a tiny flicker of deja vu came to her mind. She had seen him in her dream! *Could he actually have been—?* Mortified at such a notion, she deliberately dismissed it along with an accompanying twinge of humiliation and did her best to assume a very businesslike air. "Come in, won't you? It won't take a moment to point you toward what you'll need to get started."

"I shouldn't be underfoot for long," he proclaimed confidently, following her inside.

Grace fought the impulse to arch her brows. Obviously he didn't expect unassuming Cragle Memorial Library to hold much data he would consider of use. She flicked on the light switches, trying to ignore the impression that he observed her movements as she made a quick circuit to raise the window shades. After stowing her purse in the desk, she led the way to a small side enclosure just off the main room. "This is our Local and Area History room," she announced, opening the door and stepping inside. She turned on the light as he came in behind her.

With no little satisfaction, she saw surprise register

in his expression as he took in the array of files and books, the detailed maps along the length of one wall, and the multitude of aged photographs displayed art-fully on the neutral wallcovering.

Discomfited, he looked her way. "I am impressed. I have to admit, I had a few doubts when that woman from the historical society down in the valley sent me out here."

"To the sticks?" Grace offered with a straight face, knowing that for all it lacked in size, Cragle Corners more than compensated in setting and neighborly in-habitants. Tucked in a narrow valley between the higher hills of Dallas and Lehman townships, the hamlet with its scattering of charming homes and small businesses had easy access to all the larger towns nearby.

"More or less." A humble-pie grin spread across his broad features as he set his briefcase down on the work table and opened it.

"You must have spoken to my old school friend, Pam Rogers," Grace affirmed, watching him take out a laptop computer and notepad. Unable to stop herself, she babbled on. "Pam knows I share the same fascina-tion for local history as did the founder of our little library—who, by the way, managed to acquire a collec-tion of diaries and artifacts equal to those in any of the larger libraries in the county. We also have an impres-sive offering of memoirs from the original settlers and some of their descendants, along with copies of the numerous books written about this area over the years."

"So it would appear."

"Yes. Well, I'll leave you to your work." Pivoting on her heel, Grace halted and turned back. "I suggest you pick any small town on the map and delve into its history in the files. Mountain Springs, for example, ran quite the ice harvesting enterprise in its day. And Harvey's Lake was the 'in' spot for high society years ago. At one time it was fashionable to take an excursion train from Wilkes-Barre for a day of picnics and a cruise on the steamboats. Even little Noxen was once a major railroad center for three prominent local industries. Many seemingly insignificant villages had their own uniqueness in years past. Of course, my friend Pam no doubt mentioned some of this already. If you have any questions, I'll be at the desk."

"Thanks, Miss Farrell. That's very generous of you."

Closing the door after herself, Grace leaned against the jamb momentarily. *I cannot believe I jabbered on so much!* She collected herself and went to her desk to check her calendar. Then her watch. In mere minutes second graders from Faith Academy, the Christian school a stone's throw away, would traipse through the doorway two by two for Miss Grace's Story Hour. She hurriedly arranged some small chairs in a semicircle.

The door opened right on time.

"Morning, Miss Grace," the dozen bright voices sing-songed as they streamed inside, their cheeks pink from the crisp spring air. As usual, half took seats, and the others sat cross-legged on the floor in front of them. Their willowy blond teacher, Abigail Hughes, appeared more like an older sister to the brood than their teacher as she perched on a chair off to one side and looked on.

Grace smiled at the lot and lowered herself to the seat facing them. "Good morning, boys and girls." She picked up the juvenile fiction book she'd chosen and turned the front cover illustration forward for the children to see. "This morning we'll be reading *A Promise Is a Promise,* by Jennifer Bacon. I think you'll enjoy this story."

Mitch looked up from his laptop as a chorus of oohs and aahs rang out in the next room. Absorbed in his work, he'd been completely unaware that anyone had come into the library. But when a collective giggle broke forth, he got up to see what was happening.

As he opened the door a crack and peered out to the main room, he saw a small group of children paying rapt attention as Miss Farrell read to them from a storybook. He chuckled and began to turn away. Then his gaze fell upon the librarian's face. . .and stayed there.

For someone who appeared at first glance to be so staid and proper, she looked immensely appealing surrounded by children, her features soft, slight, and animated. With her hair fashioned into another french twist, the stylish lines of her coordinating blazer, and her soft jersey dress, she made a very feminine picture. But lest she catch him staring, Mitch quietly closed the door and returned to the chore at hand.

Concentrating on the village of Mountain Springs, as she had suggested, Mitch immersed himself in the file records, sorting out and jotting down the various details he found of interest. The place certainly must have been a bustling enterprise at one time, providing lumber during the milder months and then switching to harvesting the lake ice during the cold winter. Once he finished gathering the pertinent data, he'd drive there to take photographs for his book. Then he'd come back and research another town. He was particularly curious to know the original history of this part of Pennsylvania in regard to Indian activity, and what part, if any, these towns played during the Revolutionary or Civil Wars— but that interest was purely personal and not necessarily pertinent for this project. He continued scanning through the wealth of information before him.

"Excuse me?"

Engrossed in his notes, Mitch hadn't even heard the door open. He looked up and met the librarian's polite smile.

"Sorry to disturb you, Mr. Haywood," she began, "but it's past lunch time. I thought I'd tell you there's quite a nice lunch menu available just down the road at Millie's Diner."

"Is that where you eat?" he asked with a glance at his watch.

"Oh, no. I'd have to lock up to do that. I bring a sack lunch and eat at my desk. I just thought you might be hungry."

Mitch nodded and grinned. "Yes, in fact, I am. I wasn't even watching the time. Guess I'll go grab a bite."

"You can just close this door," she added. "No one will bother your work while you're out."

"Thanks." As the librarian returned to her desk, Mitch saved his work on the disc and shut the lid on the laptop, then got up. "Can I bring something back for you, Miss Farrell?" he asked on his way to the exit. "Pie? Coffee? Milk shake?"

"Thank you just the same, but I must watch my waistline." She put on her small spectacles and bent her head to resume whatever she was doing.

Once outside, Mitch found the freshness invigorating as a pine-scented breeze stirred the leaves on the trees. No need to drive, he decided, since having passed the eating establishment a few times already, he knew it was fairly close, just beyond the brick church. He set out at a brisk pace, admiring the few small homes on either side of the road.

As he walked, he replayed in his mind the sight of the librarian surrounded by all those happy little faces. What would possess a woman as slim as she to think she must watch her weight? Seemed to him she looked fine. Just fine.

Chapter 3

Surveying yet another display of God's handiwork, Mitch breathed a prayer of thankfulness. He never tired of seeing new places and reveling in nature's glory. While his previous visits to Pennsylvania had been limited to Philadelphia and the historic battlefields of Gettysburg, the lush rolling vistas he had encountered while driving the width of the state awed him. He hadn't expected to discover such an abundance of quaint little towns nestled in the irregular contours of the hilly terrain.

Positioning his camera on the portable tripod, he felt his jacket growing warmer in the sunshine as he peered through the lens at Mountain Springs Lake. Beneath fragile mare's tail clouds, the glistening surface of the water mirrored a sky of clearest blue.

The area surrounding the lake gave evidence that a vital community had been in existence at one time. Second-growth trees and underbrush now covered hills that once had been stripped clean of their virgin hemlocks and hardwoods. Now primarily a hunting area, the remains of a dilapidated chimney and a scattering of crumbled building foundations were duly noted by Mitch.

After reading about the village's heyday, it was not hard to imagine the workmen's shouts and banter ricocheting off the hills, the chopping of axes felling the lush timber, and the roar of logs careening down chutes into the splash dams below.

Mitch could also envision the dazzling white of winter, when the grating of gas-powered saws filled the frosty air and acres of lake ice were being scored by horse-drawn plows and cut into floats thirteen feet square. Once the floats were cut into smaller chunks and planed to uniform thickness in the mill, the ice found a ready market in the iceboxes of houses, hotels, and restaurants. Railroads also used immense quantities in both passenger cars and the refrigerated ones carrying meats and perishables to faraway markets. But the arrival of electricity had brought an end to the harvesting of lake ice.

Selecting another picturesque angle, Mitch snapped several more frames, then rotated the camera to photograph other views. He always enjoyed this facet of his work, furnishing a liberal assortment of both current and historic photos of every town he wrote about, knowing they added appeal to the finished product. His one regret was that it seemed a shame to keep such wondrous sights all to himself. The best camera—and the most descriptive adjectives—fell short in capturing the essence of a truly breathtaking setting like this one.

Perhaps the time he spent here wouldn't be so bad after all.

Grace finished dusting her cozy two-bedroom house and returned to her parlor to change the music coming from the stereo speakers. The plaintive melodies of the alto sax were too subdued for her mood just now. She scanned through her CD collection and chose some Irish folk tunes instead, for their cheery lilt.

Mr. Haywood hadn't seemed to mind the mere half-day the library remained open on Saturdays. He had come in early this morning, as usual, and closeted himself in the history room until lunchtime. Then with a jaunty wave he took his leave until first thing Monday.

Afterward Grace wished she had broached the subject of Sunday services. Something about him seemed compelling—perhaps even lonely. Being a traveling man, he might appreciate an opportunity to mingle with some friendly locals. If he were still around next weekend, she'd make an effort to work in an invitation to worship. After all, he was under no obligation to come, and it was her Christian duty, she assured herself.

Grace went to her homey kitchen, gratified by the sheen of the freshly scrubbed tile floor as she turned the burner on under the tea kettle. Alternate weekends she gave the place only a lick and a promise; with no one else living here the house stayed tidy. But today she had whipped through with the mop and polish, plumping pillows and restoring the rich glow to the bright country furnishings. Now that her work was done, a cup of tea would be welcome.

As the tea steeped, she picked up two of the novels she'd brought home and scanned the back cover copy. *Spring of Enchantment*, with its romantic cover art, won out as she returned to the parlor to curl up with the book and the steaming mug. Something to keep her company until Monday.

A shaft of sunlight sliced through an out-of-position slat in the miniblinds and warmed Grace's forehead. She stretched and yawned. What a pity to have to part with such a wonderful dream. She smiled to herself as she slowly returned to consciousness.

Funny, it was awfully bright for seven o'clock, Grace thought as she glanced at her bedside clock, then bolted upright. It wasn't seven after all—but half past eight! She had never in her life slept so long—and on a workday morning, yet.

Flinging covers aside, she dashed to the bathroom for a minute-long shower and then returned to throw on an outfit picked at random. She fastened her chin-length hair back in a bow clip to save time, and then without further ado she was out the door.

When Grace pulled into the library parking lot, she saw Mitch Haywood in a somewhat relaxed stance by the entrance, leaning against the handrail, his arms crossed. Her gaze met his, followed by another rather uncomfortable flicker of deja vu.

Having read late into the night, her mind had been unwilling to relinquish the story of the petite heroine and her towering lover. Now in a vague snatch of memory, Grace recalled that the raven-haired beauty in her dream had managed in some bizarre way to grow in stature as the plot progressed, ending up almost nose to nose with the handsome hero—himself tall, long-faced, and extremely charming. . .not to mention *familiar*.

Grace rolled her eyes in consternation and exited her car. Was she so desperate that her subconscious found it necessary to latch onto any handsome stranger who happened across her path? This insanity had to stop. She blew some wayward hairs out of her face and charged up the steps.

"I do apologize, Mr. Haywood," she began, rummaging through the keys on her ring. "I assure you, I am rarely tardy. I don't know what to say."

When she glanced up, she found him actually grinning, his jade-green eyes twinkling. "No worries, Miss Farrell. A fine-feathered choir has been entertaining me while I waited."

"All the same," she babbled on as they entered the building and she hurried to turn on lights and raise the shades, "I'm sorry. I know you've a schedule to keep and do not need any delays. There won't be any school children coming in this morning, so I'd appreciate it if you'd let me make up for the inconvenience by lending you a hand."

"That's not necessary, really."

"I insist. It's the least I can do."

A comical half-smile played at the corner of his mouth. "Well, then, sure. If it would make you happy."

As he occupied his usual spot at the long table and opened his portable computer, Grace did her best to recapture her image of efficiency. It wouldn't do for the writer to leave the area with a poor impression of

Cragle Corners. *Or of me,* her conscience intimated, though she refused to dwell on why that seemed so important.

More than aware of his every move as she worked, Grace quickly delved into file records on a few of her own favorite places, beginning with Stull, another present-day ghost town, once famous for its tannery. She extracted material on Harvey's Lake as well, no longer only a get-away for people of means but popular among locals and out-of-towners. Then she flipped through data on other nearby locations, pulling out some written memoirs of the open-air big band concerts once so popular in Fern-brook, plus various other items of interest. She knew from instinct what information a writer would consider of merit and for her the morning passed in a blur.

Mitchell, on the other hand, had problems maintaining a serious expression. True, he had been antsy at first, when he'd arrived at the library only to find it locked up with no one around to open it for the day. But when Miss Farrell hustled across the lot in a tizzy, her face flushed, her hair less than perfect, no one in his right mind could fail to see humor in the situation. Up until that moment everything about her seemed to fit together in a tidy package. Somehow he sensed the librarian expended considerable effort to maintain that unflappable reserve she presented to the world. He couldn't help admiring her spirit.

A sidelong glance revealed her still somewhat flustered but determined, extracting data from the various file drawers. Mitch surmised without even looking at

115

the material she stacked in precise piles by his elbow that the woman had undoubtedly saved him tons of work. He would probably accomplish more in this one day than he had all together since his arrival, and that knowledge touched him deeply.

A strange rumbling sound cut into his thoughts.

Since it had drifted from the librarian's direction, Mitch pretended not to notice. But when he heard it a second time, he easily recognized the grumbling of an empty stomach. He checked his watch. Then cleared his throat. "Bring a lunch today?" he asked casually.

A hint of pink crept over her fine cheekbones. She looked like a kid caught with her hand in the cookie jar, debating whether or not to come clean. Then, as if with great reluctance, she shook her head. "I-I'm afraid there wasn't time."

"Hey, no problem," he said with an understanding smile. "With all that we're getting done this morning, we can sure afford a breather. I'll run over to Millie's and grab something for us to eat. Back in a jiffy." Without another word, he was out the door.

Grace watched after him until the sound of his footfalls faded. Then she relaxed. How embarrassing to have a demanding stomach, but after all, she was only human. No point in ruing her shortcomings.

True to his word, Mitch returned bearing a veritable feast—which, with obvious delight, he spread out on the smaller spare table in the workroom. He motioned for her to be seated.

Grace didn't need an engraved invitation—not for

turkey breast sandwiches on rye bread, steaming bowls of vegetable soup, Millie's warm apple pie, and coffee.

"I asked her what you usually order when you eat there," Mitch explained. "Sounded so good, I got two of everything."

"How thoughtful," she said. "It looks delicious. I. . . I hope you don't mind if I pray before I eat. It's my custom."

"Not at all. It's mine as well."

Caught unawares by his easy confirmation, Grace forgot after her closing "Amen" exactly what she had prayed. But she couldn't forget how hungry she was and the food tasted every bit as delicious as it looked. As she ate, her eyes instinctively roamed to Mitchell Haywood. The man had already witnessed her at her worst yet he hadn't rubbed it in. Besides, he had no designs on her, nor was he the product of some well-intentioned matchmaker's scheme. Grace could think of no reason why she shouldn't be herself around him. With that assurance, she felt little pieces of her well-constructed armor begin to melt away.

Across the table from her, Mitch also seemed to be relishing his meal. "How long have you been a librarian, Miss Farrell?"

She looked up. "Seems like all my life," she admitted quite candidly. "And. . .I don't suppose you could possibly call me Grace." She came within inches of adding that calling her Miss Farrell made her feel as old as Methuselah.

"As you wish. My friends call me Mitch." He took a

drink of his coffee and then put the cup down. "You were born around here?"

"In Wilkes-Barre, actually, but I've lived here in Cragle Corners for most of my life. I've never been more than a hundred miles from home—in any direction." She paused. "And where might you hail from, Mr., I mean, Mitch?"

He grinned disarmingly. "You name it, I've been there. But originally I was born in the Midwest. Peoria, Illinois. Served a stint in the navy, went to college in Indiana—that's where I studied photography. Of course," he continued on a quieter note, "until my wife passed away a few years ago, I pretty much stayed in one spot. We had a home in Terre Haute. I kind of became a roving journalist after she died, took assignments anywhere they'd send me."

"I'm sorry," Grace offered softly, not knowing what else to say. So that was the reason she had discerned a lonely quality about him. One he tried to bury in work. She wondered if he had other family, anyone who cared about his welfare or remembered to pray for him. "Have you any children?"

He shook his head. "Nope."

"Do you enjoy what you do?" she asked after a slight pause. "The traveling and all?" She hoped he didn't think she was prying but the very concept of an adventurous and independent life such as his seemed utterly fascinating to a homebody like herself.

His expression remained open and friendly. "Yeah, I like it a lot. Not much to grumble about when somebody's paying you to go places like Paris, the Holy Land, or the Far East." He grinned again, as if caught up in some remembered scene.

Noticing that they had both finished eating, Grace rose. "Well, that was absolutely delightful. Thanks, Mitch, for the nice lunch. Next time will be my treat. . . I-I mean—" Never in her life had she taken the initiative that way. Surely he'd think she was forward. Aware of a wave of warmth cresting her cheeks, she clamped her lips together and quickly began clearing the table of styrofoam dishes and plastic silverware, restoring its former orderliness, and her former dignity.

She did not bother to look his way as she disposed of the remains in the wastebasket. "No sense letting the afternoon get away from us. I've dug out some records on a few more nearby towns for you to look over. If you run out of work before tomorrow, just let me know and I'll gather another batch. Meanwhile, I'd better check my desk and see what needs attention."

The high-pitched ring of the cellular phone sounded. Reclining on the bed in his trailer, Mitch closed his Bible and answered the summons.

"Hi, Mitch. Grady here. How's everything going?"

"Fine," he told his editor. "Turns out I've been able to unearth a ton of of stuff you're gonna like. First on the anthracite mining industry in Wyoming Valley, and now all kinds of other neat details on some of the smaller burgs in the area. I figure enough's been done on the

Pennsylvania Dutch culture. Time to showcase a few other facets of the state."

"Sounds good. Think you'll be much longer?"

"I wouldn't imagine so. A couple days, a week at most."

"Great. Well, I'll check back with you in a couple days."

"Sure, Grady. Talk to you then."

It wasn't until he'd hung up that Mitch remembered the little dig he had planned to insert when his editor called, about how much more he'd have preferred to be covering spring in the Rockies or some other more exotic locale. Now the intended remark didn't seem quite so applicable. Especially since he was actually starting to enjoy this assignment, working in that unexpected treasure house of a rural library—with Grace Farrell.

For Mitch to have someone with whom to share a meal was a welcome change. And he had nothing against basking in her pleasantly resonating voice, either . . .or treating his nose to the subtle fragrance she wore.

No, he really wasn't in too much of a hurry to finish, he thought with a smile.

Not just yet anyway.

Chapter 4

G race was finishing her morning devotions over a second cup of coffee when the phone rang. She frowned and reached for the receiver, unable to imagine who would be calling at this hour. "Hello?"

"Hi, Gracie. It's me, Pam."

"Good thing you identified yourself," she teased. "I wouldn't have recognized your voice." Smiling, she relaxed back against the kitchen chair, visualizing the lissome brunette who had been her closest friend forever, or so it seemed.

"Oh, come on," Pam said facetiously. "Didn't I call you a mere month or two ago?"

"Wait, and I'll check my calendar," Grace quipped. "There's probably a red circle around the day. I sure wouldn't have let such a *big occasion* go by unnoticed."

"Oh, sure. Like the phone doesn't work from your direction, girl."

"I know, I know." Grace giggled. "I'm just as bad as you. What's up?"

"Oh, nothing much. I know you'll be leaving for the library shortly so I won't keep you. I was just wondering if the hunk I steered in your direction last week ever showed up. . .a writer, working on some book on Pennsylvania. He looked up a bunch of stuff down here at the historical society on coal mine disasters, then asked if I knew of any other areas of interest. And you know how partial I've always been to the Back Mountain—not to mention jealous of you for landing that neat position in our old stomping grounds, while I had to settle for this job down here in the valley."

"Yes, I do, and yes, he's been by. In fact, he's still here. I think he was kind of floored at how much actually went on in these parts in the old days. I personally dumped a ton of research files in his lap yesterday."

"Ah. Trying to keep him around, huh?" Pam cajoled in her typical, suggestive way.

"Don't be silly. I'm just making sure he does our proud commonwealth justice."

A laugh skipped over the wire. "So. . .what do you think of the guy?"

Grace knew Pam was fishing. She rolled her eyes. "What's to think?" she answered evenly, aware that except for a few unbelievable dreams, she had managed quite successfully to keep herself from thinking much of anything about Mitchell Haywood. "He is, after all, just passing through, remember," she couldn't help adding —an inward reminder she admitted was as much for herself as for her girlhood friend.

"Yeah. Right. Still—"

"Paamm!" Grace exhaled in exasperation. "He seems decent enough, okay? But the minute he finishes his research, he's out of here. End of story." She glanced at the clock. "Listen, I'll catch you later, okay? I've got to run."

"Sure. You know I can't resist baiting you. He is

122

handsome, though, don't you think?"

It was easy to picture the knowing smirk behind the question. "You never give up, do you?" Grace remarked with a shake of the head.

"Are you kidding? My very best friend in the entire world is going to waste and it's just not fair!"

Unable to stay annoyed after a comment like that, Grace felt her mood soften. "You're too much. But yes, he is handsome. . .not that it matters a hill of beans. Anyway, have a good day."

"You, too. Let me know if anything exciting tran- spires."

"Right. I'll do that. My love to Steve and the kids. 'Bye for now." Chuckling to herself, Grace replaced the receiver and got up to collect her purse and coat.

"Thank you, Miss Grace," the youngsters chorused, as if they'd been coached by a choir director. Hand in hand they paraded past her on their way outside.

"You're most welcome. See you next Tuesday."

"I think they really got into that story," Abby Hughes commented airily from the end of her line of charges. "It should make for some pretty cute pictures this afternoon."

"I can imagine. Why not have them bring their drawings to show me next week?"

"What a great idea! I'm sure they'd be thrilled."

Grace returned the teacher's parting smile and closed the door after her. Then remembering she still had today's storybook tucked under her arm, she returned it to the juvenile section and straightened the chairs before heading for her desk.

Mitch exited the history room just then.

"Out of work already?" Grace asked him lightly.

"You can't be serious," he replied. "Just hungry is all. Shall I—"

She shook her head. "I had plenty of time to prepare a lunch this morning. Thanks for asking, though. Enjoy your meal."

He threw her a peculiar look as he left—but she was positive the disappointment she read on his face was a product of her own active imagination. Surely he couldn't expect her to impose on him on a regular basis. Yet the profound stillness of being alone seemed suddenly unbearable. She was getting far too used to having Mitch around. And that was not good. Not good at all.

Mitch didn't broach the subject of having lunch together again until later in the week.

"But I fail to see much virtue in letting the perfectly good food I brought from home go to waste," Grace hedged.

"I don't have a problem with that, if a sack lunch is what you prefer," he assured her. "What I do have a problem with is eating by myself over at the diner, while you eat alone in an empty library. Isn't it far more practical for two responsible adults like us to dine together?"

She contemplated his reasoning but did not reply.

"Besides, I'd like to hear what it was like to grow up around here. I've been a city boy most of my life. When I went hiking in the woods or fishing, it was on vacation, not a daily activity I took for granted like a lot of the country kids."

"Okay, okay!" Raising a hand in defeat, Grace relented. "Go get yourself some food, for pity's sake. I'll wait for you."

"You sure take a bushel of persuading," he shot in return, quite appreciating this more relaxed side of her he'd begun to glimpse a few short days ago.

In less than twenty minutes he was back, devouring a charbroiled steak sandwich while she nibbled on her tuna salad and carrot sticks in a far more civilized fashion. In between bites she talked candidly about her girlhood experiences in this rural setting.

". . . but nobody ever did 'fess up to dying the cat green!" She smothered a giggle. "Turned out it was only food coloring."

Mitch found himself reveling in the soft intonations of her voice and the enchanting word pictures he credited to an obvious love of books. "So, you pretty much enjoyed living out here in the sticks, then," he grinned, tossing back at her the phrase she had used to great advantage.

"I couldn't imagine being anywhere else. I've read about many exotic places but the Back Mountain is all I've ever known."

The opposite of his own life, Mitch conceded. Ever since Laura's death had brought an end to their eighteen-year marriage, he'd been ricocheting around the world like a marble in a pinball machine. At the time it seemed the only way to handle his loss. He sloughed off this sudden pensive turn of thought and returned to the present—noticing that Grace had swallowed her last bite and was folding her napkin.

Mitch had been waiting for such an opportune moment. "Aha!" he bellowed. "You can't refuse this, now, can you?" With a flourish he produced two slices of Millie's cherry pie from the styrofoam container he'd brought. He waved one piece under her nose.

She elevated an eyebrow in chilly regard. "Oh, I see precisely what you're doing, Mitch Haywood. Fatten the lady up, then be on your way. Less than chivalrous, I must say."

But Mitch could tell from the sparkle in those azure eyes of hers that she was anything but serious.

The following day, as Mitch navigated the irregular circumference of Harvey's Lake in search of likely spots to photograph, he thought about his lunch with Grace.

To his regret, the librarian had reverted back to the more severe hairstyle she'd worn when they first met. He had preferred the slightly softer style from the morning she'd overslept, and couldn't help wishing she'd leave it free altogether once in a while. She seemed completely oblivious to its glorious color, its incredible sheen. Did she even have a clue how the sunshine turned her glorious mane into spun gold, or that under the fluorescent library bulbs it shone like a new copper penny? His fingers all but ached to run through the soft silkiness he could only imagine.

What are you thinking, blockhead? he railed as a surge of guilt rushed through him. *Get a grip!* But it wasn't the easiest thing in the world to eradicate Grace Farrell from his mind, to forget the musical laugh that emanated from her more and more often lately. Miss Staid Librarian was far more witty and captivating than she let on. How on earth could someone like her still be running loose? There must be a real shortage of males in this backwoods Eden, at least males with any kind of brains. *And if you had any brainpower yourself, you'd wind up this assignment of yours and get out of here while it's still possible.*

"Maybe it's already too late," he rasped in the silence of the Cherokee's interior. And his own words stopped him cold.

Belinda sloshed the rag around inside the bucket, then squeezed out the excess water. She must have written twice as many sums and vocabulary words on the blackboard today as usual, what with that visiting dignitary from the school board making his annual rounds and reporting on the progress of the district students. Well, at least the dreaded ordeal was over. Relieved, she washed

the grainy slate surface thoroughly to remove every last streak of chalk dust.

She had barely finished the chore when the sound of approaching hoofbeats drifted through the open window. Having dismissed the children half an hour early, she frowned, wondering if an uninformed parent were coming by to pick up one of the youngsters. She dried her hands, then walked to the door and stepped outside.

Only a dozen yards away, she noticed something disturbingly familiar about the tall rider's silhouette against the blowing field grasses on either side of the narrow dirt road. And the way he sat his mount was even more familiar. Belinda placed a hand to her throat. "Travis?" she gasped.

Coming up on the small country school building, the slim, wiry cowboy swept his Stetson from his sandy hair and grinned in the way that once wielded power enough to melt Belinda's untried heart. "Hello, little lady. I've come back, to take you away from here, just like I said I would." Without so much as waiting for her reply, he swung down from his sorrel gelding and started toward the wooden steps.

Belinda felt her knees go wobbly. This was what she'd always wanted, always hoped for, wasn't it? She'd waited so long. Watching down the road for him until her eyes burned, listening for the faintest hint of his voice, dreaming through the long lonely nights, trying to convince herself he'd keep his promises.

Only he hadn't.

She remembered the very moment her hopes had died

within her. Remembered weeping her heart out as she finally relinquished all those tender dreams she'd held onto for so long.

And now there was Brad Sawyer to consider. Brad, her betrothed. . .steady, reliable Brad, who even at this moment was on his way back from Cedar Springs with the ring he'd saved up to buy her. Tonight they would announce their engagement to their friends and family. She clutched the handrail.

"Aren't you glad to see me?" Travis asked confidently, coming closer with each sure movement of his lithe body.

He was near enough to touch now.

He reached for her.

Belinda took a step back. Hardening her resolve against his bewildered expression, she hiked her chin. "No, Travis. I am not glad to see you. You're too late."

The tea kettle whistled, its shrill whine not to be ignored. Sighing, Grace tucked a bookmark into the novel, but she couldn't resist giving an encouraging pat to the closed paperback as she set it down. "Good for you, Belinda. I was wondering if you'd work up spunk enough to dump that cad."

Then, amused that she was actually talking to a book, Grace shook her head. "You know, old girl, you could use a few hobbies besides reading."

"Oh?" she asked herself in a slightly higher pitch, feigning shock. For effect, she pressed her fingertips to her throat, just as she had pictured the heroine doing. "And what makes you say that, pray tell?"

"Well, look at you," came her own more dignified

reply as she poured the steaming water into her bone china teapot. "You're actually starting to believe this stuff."

Grace laughed. The sound echoed in the quiet confines of her house and, for a few fleeting moments, she almost felt like crying.

Chapter 5

As the library's limited Saturday hours drew to a close, three giggly teenagers finally checked out their selections, after a frantic half-hour of indecision. Grace breathed a sigh of relief with their exit. The weekend rush had been more hectic than usual, with a steady stream of patrons coming and going throughout the morning. The girls were the last to leave.

Except for Mitch.

He had taken to leaving the door to the history room open, and she had been mindful of his presence despite the confusion of people coming and going.

After placing the last few returned books atop the already loaded cart, Grace made her rounds around the room, tucking each volume into its proper place on the shelves. Nearing the doorway to the history room, she paused, her fingers still resting on the cart's handle.

Mitch glanced up at her, then at his watch. "Sorry. Am I keeping you overtime?"

"Oh, no. Not at all. I still have a few things to do before I can lock up."

He nodded, but started gathering his papers together anyway.

Grace nibbled her lower lip for a few seconds, watching him. "I was wondering if you might be interested in coming to church tomorrow. . .if you're not otherwise occupied. I might be able to introduce you to an old-timer or two who'll talk your ears off."

His movements halted.

"Of course," she added hastily, "I've never inquired about your personal beliefs, so don't feel you're obligated in any way to accept."

A slow smile spread across his lips. "Well, let me put your mind at ease, my friend. I accepted the Lord as my Savior when I was just a kid, and it's a rare Sunday that I'm not worshiping with other believers, no matter where I happen to be."

The news didn't come as a complete surprise but Grace was gratified to hear it, nonetheless.

His grin gained in exuberance. "In fact, I really appreciate the invitation. The red brick church across from Millie's Diner?"

She shook her head. "No, I go to Heritage Bible, about two miles from here, just this side of the lake highway. It's not quite as grand but the people are friendly and the preaching is excellent. I think you'll like it."

"Just name the time," he said, snapping the latches closed on his briefcase, "and I'll be there."

A handful of puffy clouds floated across the bright May sky and a mild breeze rustled through the trees bracketing the clearing occupied by Heritage Bible Church.

Grace arrived at the attractive fieldstone building just as the bell in the tower announced the dismissal of Sunday school classes, and the semiorganized scramble began between the fellowship hall and the sanctuary. So far Mitch had made a practice of being punctual, if not early, but as she scanned the parking lot, the burgundy Cherokee was nowhere in sight. It took some effort to squash the pang of disappointment trying to creep in.

"Hi, Grace!" Jovial Hattie Birch tugged her short, bespectacled husband in Grace's direction and started up the steps with her. "Larry and I, we just want you to know how helpful those gardening books have been, isn't that right, honey pie?" She cut a glance to her mate but didn't wait for him to respond. "I'll be in on Monday to renew them."

"I'm glad they were of use," Grace replied. "I'll look forward to seeing you tomorrow."

As they crossed the foyer and entered the spacious ivory and oak interior of the sanctuary, they went their separate ways, the Birches to the last pew on the right, while Grace took her usual spot in the fourth pew on the left, nodding and waving to church friends along the way.

Grace had barely sat down before Mitch slid in beside her with his customary cheerful grin. "Morning," he said quietly, giving the church the once-over. "Nice place."

He had come after all! With a surge of pure elation, Grace smiled in return, only to observe the tickled glances and knowing smirks pass between those around her. How quickly everyone jumped to the conclusion that the two of them had a personal relationship! Bristling inwardly, she decided to rectify the matter with a few introductions.

Just then, narrow-faced Pastor Thomas stepped up to the pulpit. "Good to see so many folks out to worship on this Lord's Day. Let's ask God's blessing on our service."

The other worshipers would just have to contain their curiosity until after the benediction, Grace decided. She wondered if they'd be able to concentrate on the sermon.

Or, for that matter, if *she* would. Directing her train of thought to a safer route, she mused that perhaps those well-meaning friends deserved to wonder a little. It wouldn't hurt them to discover that she was actually capable of keeping company with an attractive man without any assistance from them. She stifled a smile and made an effort to center her attention on the prayer, even though she was acutely conscious of Mitch's shirt sleeve feathering her bare arm.

". . . We ask these things in the name of Your Son, Jesus Christ," the pastor finished. He raised his balding head and smiled at the congregation. "Now let's stand and turn to hymn number forty-seven, 'What a Friend We Have In Jesus.'" He motioned for the pianist to begin the introduction.

As Grace and Mitch shared the single hymnal from the rack directly in front of them, she was pleasantly surprised by the timbre of his rich tenor. A refreshing sound, his voice did not slice through her ears the way many tenors in the higher range often did. Blending with him on the soprano part, she endeavored to stave off the warmth that threatened to creep up her cheeks when he shot an approving glance at her. And a considerable portion of Pastor Thomas's ensuing sermon on the sixth chapter of Romans sailed right over her head.

After the service Grace drew Mitch to a gray-headed gentleman in herringbone tweed. "I'd like you to meet Luther Beck, only one of the most knowledgeable residents of Cragle Corners! Mr. Beck, meet Mitchell Haywood, a visiting writer."

Mitch took the elderly man's gnarled hand and shook it warmly, noting the surprising strength of the bony grip. "Glad to meet you, sir."

"Same here. A writer, is it?" Luther Beck rasped, peering up at Mitch, who towered head and shoulders above his slightly stooped frame. "Well, well. What kind of books do you write?"

"Actually," Grace supplied, "he's working on a project about this area's history. Isn't that interesting?"

"Why, it surely is, it surely is." The shrewd, faded blue eyes twinkled as they fastened on Mitch. He tilted his head toward Grace. "Tell you about the Colonel, did she?"

"Colonel?" Mitch echoed in puzzlement. From the corner of his eye he saw Grace smile and step away to mingle with a few stragglers who still remained inside the church. He figured she had made certain he'd met everyone else by now, but something told him she had saved the best for last.

"Yep. Colonel Robert Bruce Ricketts, our own Civil War hero. Also happened to be a distant relation on my mother's side. One of them cousins twice removed or somethin' akin to that. Anyway, we're kinda proud to claim him on the family tree."

"A Civil War hero, you say."

The silver head nodded. "Battle of Gettysburg, it was."

Mitch could have kicked himself for not having the foresight to bring his pocket tape recorder from the trailer. All he could do now was pay close attention and make mental notes. "I'd sure like to hear more about him—if you have a few minutes, of course."

"I can do better'n that, son. If you're not tied up for dinner, my Lilly's got a roast goin'. She didn't come to service 'cause her rheumatiz is actin' up. But she loves company. We'd be right glad to share a meal with a visiting writer. And Gracie, of course," he added with a sly grin. "My wife always cooks a ton of food. We live just over the next hill."

Mitch hiked an eyebrow as he caught Grace's eye and she gravitated back to him. "We've been invited to Sunday dinner. Are you free?"

Seated next to Mitch at this veritable Sunday feast,

Grace sampled the carrot and raisin salad and smiled appreciatively at the frail but very able wife of their host. No doubt Lilly Beck's nimble fingers had also fashioned the colorful needlepoint accents and crocheted doilies which complemented the traditional mahogany furnishings of their modest home. What a shame that such artistry was losing place to today's hectic pursuits.

Grace switched her attention to Mitch, who by all appearances was in seventh heaven at this opportunity to enjoy real home cooking. She had discerned a fleeting look resembling homesickness when he first entered the dwelling, and it made her sad for him, always being on the road, when it was so evident he enjoyed people. He seemed genuinely interested in Mr. Beck's reminiscences about his boyhood in this rural setting.

"What was it you were telling me at church," Mitch finally prompted during a pause in the conversation, "about your family's hero?"

"Oh yes. Colonel Robert Bruce Ricketts," the old man began.

"Help yourself to more mashed potatoes, you two," Lilly Beck urged, her hazel eyes sparkling behind rimless eyeglasses. "I got so used to cooking for those strapping sons of ours, I invariably make too much. 'Course, the two of us can eat the leftovers for days so I don't suppose it matters any."

Smiling at the birdlike woman, Grace picked up the partially empty bowl and passed it to Mitch.

". . .'course, the colonel was just a captain at the

time," Luther Beck was saying. "And the consolidated battery he commanded—comprised of three officers and a hundred and forty-one men—was handed the chore of facing seventeen hundred Louisiana Tigers on Cemetery Hill. The order was to hold the position until the last extremity."

Mitch dished himself more of the potatoes and then forked another slice of roast beef from the platter while he listened.

"When them rebels let out with some fiendish yells and rushed the battery and all its infantry supports, Captain Ricketts charged his pieces with canister and poured in a stream of deadly volleys. Now the infantry, lyin' behind the stone wall in front, turned tail and ran, leaving the captain to face the brunt of the attack."

"Less than a hundred and fifty men, against a force of seventeen hundred?" Mitch asked incredulously.

"Yep." Mr. Beck gave a satisfied nod. "He knew just how much the enemy coveted that particular prize, and that the heart of the entire Union army was throbbin' for him in that desperate hour. So he kept every man at his post, guns blazin'. By the time it was over, dead bodies littered the field in front of them. Barely six hundred of them terrible Tigers were able to slink away in defeat."

"That's some story," Mitch affirmed, chewing slowly.

"Only one of many," the older man stated. "He was soon promoted to major, then commissioned colonel of the First Pennsylvania Light Artillery. When he was discharged he came back home, and him and his brothers bought up a passel of land on North Mountain. About eighty thousand acres, all told. A good chunk of it's a state park now, just down Route 118 a piece. A right pretty place, too. Gracie should show it to you before you move on."

Grace held her breath as Mitch swung a playful glance toward her. "How about it, *Gracie?*" he asked lightly. "Any plans for the afternoon?"

"Well, I really should help with the dishes," she hedged. "It's so kind of Mr. and Mrs. Beck to be sharing this delicious meal with us." But inside Grace knew the true reason she was hesitant to extend this outing. Mitch's efficiency as he gleaned information at the library every day was one thing, but this relaxed side of him was even more fascinating.

A little too fascinating.

"Oh, just let me serve up some of my apple pie and then you young folks can just run along," the older woman said. "Luther and I have all day to do dishes."

Well, Grace's reckless side reasoned, Mitch would soon be leaving Pennsylvania for good, and she'd never ever see him again. What would be the harm in enjoying a few extra hours in the company of this charming man the Lord had brought across her path? Perhaps it would serve as a consolation prize for the solitary life she had known for so long.

"Sure," she blurted out, not quite meeting Mitch's gaze. "I love Ricketts Glen."

Chapter 6

Rickett's Glen State Park basked in spring's glory, all green and woodsy as the majestic giant pines, hemlocks, and oaks of North Mountain came into full crown. The thick overhead canopy created by towering trees more than five hundred years old blocked out all view of the sky above. And on the ground, a light breeze rifled across fallen trees and young ferns, carrying with it the moist odor left over from the recent rains.

Grace savored her companion's unconcealed enjoyment as they crossed hand-hewn wooden foot bridges and hiked leisurely up the Falls Trail along Kitchen Creek. Reaching "The Glens," where two branches of the creek unite at "Water's Meet," they stopped to catch their breath.

"This place is awesome," Mitch said, reading the plaque that had been set into the rocky cliff commemorating the park as a national landmark. He gaped at the wild Y-shaped gorge the descending creek had carved into the rocks and popped the lens cover off his camera. "I never cease to be awed by the beauty of God's creation."

"It is lovely, isn't it?" Grace commented as he went to work snapping pictures from a variety of angles. "No matter how often I come to the park, I'm always captivated by its beauty. But to see Rickett's Glen at its absolute best, you should come in autumn when it's wildly painted in broad strokes in the colors of nature's palette. It's truly a sight to behold."

Suddenly conscious of a growing intensity in Mitch's gaze, Grace averted her eyes. Once again she was aware of how utterly masculine he looked in his band-necked teal shirt and gray slacks. She intended to keep the mood light. "There are more falls ahead," she informed him casually. "One of them, Ganoga Falls, has several tiers, and drops almost a hundred feet."

"Really."

She nodded. "Of course, if you're too tired. . ."

"Me?" he teased. "I'm not the one wearing fancy Sunday shoes. I should have taken you home to change before I made you tramp through the woods."

Grace almost laughed aloud, remembering how she had tried on almost everything in her closet this morning before finally settling on a denim skirt with matching vest, silk blouse, and leather flats. "I'm fine."

"Well, I'm game if you are. How many falls are on this trail, anyway?"

"At least twenty-two that have names, I believe, and a few more without. Adams Falls, which we admired below the parking lot, is the most beautiful of all as it plunges over those three cascades. Of course, that's my opinion."

"Then," he made a wide arc with one arm, "lead on, Miss Grace."

"As you wish." Peering dubiously up at her amiable

companion, she stepped past him. "I should warn you, though, the trail ahead has some steep grades."

"Tsk, tsk. And you with slick-soled shoes, too," Mitch responded, easily catching up to her. "Well, not to worry." He offered her his hand, eyes twinkling.

A tiny voice inside warned Grace against letting herself rely on him. But when she caught a heel in an exposed root and almost stumbled, the mere thought of how utterly humiliating it would be to trip and fall right in front of him made her swallow her nervousness and slip her fingers into his.

Somehow, she had known his touch would be warm. And strong. As his grip tightened securely around hers, the most delicious sensation she had ever experienced tingled through her being, spiralling all the way from her head to her toes.

She surmised that if she had married years ago, the way her best friend Pam and most of her other schoolmates had done, she might have known many wonderful outings similar to this one, with the man of her dreams.

The man of her dreams. . .

Grace almost couldn't breathe.

Of its own volition, her gaze shifted to the handsome writer beside her. And she knew that all too soon she would pay a high price for allowing her heart to progress beyond a few fanciful dreams. . .for falling in love with Mitchell Haywood.

Mitch filled his lungs with the fresh mountain air. It felt good to be stretching his legs like this, and with such pleasant company. He'd been working at such a pace for the last several years, he could hardly remember what it used to be like to have someone to share thoughts with on the spur of a moment, or someone to talk to at night.

Not that he ever intended to put down roots again and start over. He'd already been blessed with one rare and lasting love in his life, and he figured that was as much as anyone deserved. But there was no harm in enjoying this special day, and he was doing that to the fullest. It would be nice to look back on every now and then.

He'd been delighted when he'd arrived at church to discover Grace attired a little more casually, and better yet, wearing her hair down. Shining like new copper in the sunlight, the red-gold ends curled softly over the collar of her blouse, making her appear youthful and innocent. And enticing.

He released her hand to photograph Ganoga Falls, which she had announced as the highest one in Rickett's Glen, and then the magnificent scenery on all sides. The photos wouldn't necessarily have a place in this book on Pennsylvania, but if he ever did a series on waterfalls, they might come in handy. Satisfied with the views he'd captured, Mitch turned to take Grace's hand again.

She had strolled a few yards away and now sat lost

in thought at the creek's edge, legs curled under her, her fingers trailing in the cold rippling water. Gazing at the glorious sight she made in this rustic setting, Mitch realized that in the time he'd known Grace, he had been watching her come to life before his eyes, like a butterfly emerging from a cocoon.

The rushing current overpowered the sound of his footsteps, and as he approached she retained the same dreamy, faraway expression. From his vantage point, he saw a ray of sunlight highlight her perfect profile in finest gold.

He stopped and focused the camera, then clicked the shutter. This photo wouldn't go in any book. It was strictly for him. For the memory of this day. He feasted his eyes another second or two longer, then nonchalantly tramped over to her.

"Oh, am I holding you up?" she asked, coloring slightly as she sprang to her feet.

"Not at all." *And even if you were, it wouldn't matter.* Mitch's gaze centered on her lips, soft and rosy and slightly parted, and alarm bells went off in his head. He cleared his throat. "Say, since we've made it all the way up here to the highest falls, maybe we should call it a day."

A faint hint of disappointment on her face vanished so quickly he wondered if he had imagined it. "As you wish. I've hiked the park trails a hundred times." Brushing off the back of her skirt, she started heading in the direction from which they'd come.

Mitch watched her stroll away, head high, shoulders

straight, her skirt and silky hair swaying with each step. And a conviction he'd been trying to ignore reared up in his consciousness. *Mitch, old boy, I think it's time you were on your way.*

Grace couldn't help noticing Mitch wasn't his normally chatty self on the drive back to the church parking lot to pick up her car. But she wasn't about to ask any questions. She had more than enough of her own jumbled thoughts to sort through.

When he drew up beside her Buick, she looked at him and smiled in an effort to restore their earlier camaraderie. "Well, thanks. I had a wonderful time, Mitch. Hope you enjoyed the park."

"What's not to enjoy?" he answered matter-of-factly. "It's certainly one of God's masterpieces. No Niagara or Angel Falls, of course, but with a distinct beauty of its own. The up close and personal kind." He grimaced, then released a deep breath, visibly relaxing as he did. "You, uh, usually go to the evening service?" he asked on a gentler note.

Grace shook her head. "I never used to miss, but my night vision isn't what it used to be." She kept her tone cool and easygoing, hoping to forestall yet another invitation. If she didn't leave now, she'd really make a fool of herself.

She opened the Jeep's door and stepped down. "Guess I'll see you tomorrow, huh?" she finally said.

He only nodded.

Yet something lingered in his expression, unspoken words that hovered between them, and Grace sensed that Mitch was as aware of the moment as she.

The moonlight tinted the landscape an ethereal silvery blue. Running, panting, she made it to the seclusion of the birch grove where the slender tree trunks swayed on whispers of the night wind.

"Over here," came the low murmur.

She turned, her woolen cape a swirl of lavender that settled around her ankles. "Is it really you?"

"None other, my darling. I could not stay away." Each word brought him closer, until he enfolded her in his arms.

"I was afraid you wouldn't come," she breathed. In unspeakable wonder, she melded her soft form against his warm, muscled strength and closed her eyes. A bittersweet ache enveloped her heart as he rocked her in his embrace, stroking her hair with one hand. "Everyone said I'd be alone forever. 'Old Maid Grace,' they called me. But they were wrong. All along, they've been wrong." She tipped her head back and searched his face. "You do love me, don't you, Mitch?"

He merely smiled, and the backs of his fingers lightly grazed the curve of her cheekbone, tracing a path through the joyous tears she could not hold back.

The moisture on her cheeks rendered Grace awake. She sat up in the darkness of her solitary bed, clutching the sheet to herself in growing awareness.

"A dream!" she gasped. "It was only a dream."

The indescribable happiness she had scarcely grasped a fragile second ago withered into the sinking reality, then shrank to nothing. And the remaining traces of her tears were washed away by a flood of new ones. . .the kind that knew only sadness and profound loneliness.

Chapter 7

G race kneaded her throbbing temples, wishing the pain reliever she had swallowed before leaving home would cure her headache. Hopefully the concealer she'd applied to the dark circles under her eyes would do its job. After only a few hours' sleep she feared she was in for a very long day.

There was no sign of the Cherokee when she arrived at work.

Ten o'clock passed. Eleven. Then, a little before eleven-thirty, the distinct sound of a vehicle pulling into the parking lot wafted through a partially raised window. Grace resisted the temptation to rush over and peer outside.

As the door opened she held her breath, her flagging spirit rising, only to fall flat.

"Hi, Grace!" Hattie Birch exclaimed cheerily as she scurried across the room, books clutched in the crook of one arm. She set them on the counter, separating a paperback novel from two gardening books. "I need to renew this pair, but I'd like a different romance."

Unable to muster more than a semblance of a smile, Grace stamped the new due date inside the hardcovers while Hattie went to peruse the fiction section.

"Where's our author this morning?" the older woman

queried from a few aisles away.

"He hasn't been in yet today," Grace replied smoothly. "Some of the time he spends doing field work, taking pictures for his book." But the explanation didn't hold water. Mitch hadn't mentioned any such possibility when they'd been together yesterday.

"Well, it's good to see he's a church-going man," Hattie declared, stepping into view on her way back. "How's the book coming?"

"Mr. Haywood seems pleased with it." *At least, I assumed he was,* she almost said. A smarting behind her eyes curbed the impulse. She reached for the novel the woman had selected and dated the card. "These will be due in two weeks."

"See you later, Grace," Mrs. Birch said with a genial nod. Gathering her selections, she departed.

In the oppressive stillness of the empty library, Grace's every move seemed to echo. She sagged against the back of her chair and folded her arms. *Where are you, Mitch?* But the only answer that came to her was one she refused to accept: He hadn't come today because he hadn't wanted to.

She rose and crossed to the window overlooking the parking lot. *Dear Lord, Mitch should be here, working on his project, like every other day. I don't understand.* But that was untrue. She did understand—all too well. He must have discerned her innermost feelings in her eyes or her actions, and now he wanted out of here. The knowledge only added to her misery.

In desperation she discarded her untouched lunch

and threw herself into a frenzy of work, dusting, tidying, tapping uneven index cards in the file cabinet into place, lining up book spines a precise half-inch in from shelf edges. . .anything to keep from thinking. Anything to make the day go by.

Endless hours later, as quitting time approached, a vehicle pulled into the parking lot.

The fine hairs on Grace's neck pricked up.

The door opened, this time admitting Mitch.

Without his laptop. . .without his briefcase.

Without his smile.

At the sight of his ominous demeanor, Grace felt her heart thud to a stop. Her insides went quivery. She could almost perceive the axe that was about to fall. "Hello," she forced past the clog in her throat. "We missed you around here today."

He gave a cursory nod. "Grace. . ." He started toward the desk. "I finished up the last of the pictures. There's nothing more left to do."

Nothing? her heart demanded. *Nothing at all?* Her pulse gathered speed, throbbing with such intensity it was hard to hear over the rushing in her ears. *Don't let me fall apart, Lord. Please, don't let me fall apart.*

"I didn't want to leave without saying good-bye. I. . .don't know how to thank you for all your help."

"Oh, please." Grace rolled her eyes, gathering every ounce of dignity she possessed, hoping it would be enough to get her through this dreaded farewell. . . through the ever-so-gallant little speech he apparently thought would suffice. . .after the wonderful day they

150

had shared together *only yesterday.*

But she'd known from the start that this moment would come, she reminded herself sternly. She straightened her spine. Long years of practice wrenched forth her old business-as-usual air, and with a toss of her head, she manufactured a smile. "It is my job, you know. 'Be nice to the tourists.' I hope the finished product does us justice." Her use of *us* made her cringe.

Mitch's piercing gaze roamed her face. "I. . .I'll never—"

"Oh, would you look at the time," Grace cut in, aware she was down to her last shred of composure. "I need to close up." Snatching her shoulder bag from the bottom desk drawer, she fished for the keys and willed her legs to stand, her knees to keep from buckling, as she rounded the desk. Methodically she moved about, pulling down the shades, straightening an out-of-place chair at one of the tables, turning off all but the main light switch.

So far, so good. Now only one thing remained. She could do this. After all, hadn't she been the star of the senior play? Fixing her expression to one she hoped appeared calm and serene, Grace stepped to the desk again and extended her right hand to Mitch, steeling herself against the touch of his fingers closing around it. "Much success with your series, Mitch Haywood," she said, a little too brightly. "It's been. . .interesting, collaborating with you." The next word almost stuck in her throat. "G—good-bye."

For a heartbeat he didn't release her hand, and she saw his attention slide lower, focusing on her lips.

Terrified, knowing that if he dared to kiss her it would be the absolute end of her, Grace withdrew her fingers while she still could. "God keep you in your travels." Crossing to the door, she pushed against it and stepped out into the growing dusk, leaning against the door more for support than courtesy. Holding herself together for all she was worth. Waiting.

Her silent plea did not go unheeded. After only a slight hesitation, Mitch walked to the exit, his gaze meeting Grace's faltering one as he paused briefly on the threshold. Then, with a half-smile, he raised a hand and gave her shoulder a light squeeze. "So long, Grace Farrell," he said softly.

She swallowed hard, somehow managing a nod until he passed and went down the steps to the Cherokee parked next to the landing.

Stifling the sob gathering deep inside her, she kept her back turned, struggling to make her fingers stop shaking long enough to lock up for the night. . .while the sound of his familiar strides rang in her ears, while she heard the Jeep's door open and close, the ignition start.

It took the last speck of her tattered strength to look up and give a final wave when Mitch drove past. Out of her life.

And then the floodgates collapsed.

How she ever made it to her car, she would never know.

Completely drained, both physically and emotionally,

Grace splashed cold water over her tear-swollen eyes and nose, avoiding a look in the bathroom mirror at the morbid damage wrought by hours of weeping. After last night she'd thought there couldn't possibly be another tear inside of her. . .but she'd been proven wrong.

Well, enough was enough. Unless she intended to spend the rest of her life in a dark house feeling sorry for herself, it was time to pull herself together. Someone *her* age, she reasoned bitterly, should have acquired brains enough along the way not to have put herself in such a wretched position in the first place. But just like a silly schoolgirl, she had convinced herself she could play with fire without being scorched. Well, she would live through this, more's the pity. If there were one thing she was accomplished at, it was being alone. Being *unloved*.

She sniffed determinedly. When it came right down to it, she wasn't any the worse off for having had a pleasant little diversion in her otherwise predictable life. Mitch Haywood, with all his charm and appeal, had befriended her in a way no other man had done. And, she reminded herself, they'd both known from day one that he was only there temporarily. She'd been the fool for letting down her guard. But that was water under the bridge. Just like in a romance, the hero had ridden off into the sunset, gone on to his *destiny*, leaving her to hers. Eventually she would find the strength to look back on the good times and at least smile, if not laugh.

Small comfort, but it would have to do.

"Morning, Miss Grace," the second graders chorused, huge smiles lighting their sweet faces.

Closing the door after the last pair to enter, Grace took her place in the semicircle.

"The children have something to show you this morning," Abby Hughes announced airily, her own youthful countenance aglow. She nodded to her charges and, almost as one, they proudly unfurled the rolled pictures each of them had brought along.

As Grace scanned the simple crayon drawings depicting last week's story, her heart went out to the children. "Why, they're beautiful! May I put them up on the bulletin board so that everyone who comes to the library can see your wonderful work?"

The dozen smiley faces nodded.

"Good. That makes me very, very happy. Well," Grace went on, "I have a new book to read you this morning, boys and girls. This one is called *A Surprise for Mr. Greenwood* by Randall Phillips. How many of you have a pet?"

"I have a kitten," one girl announced, her pigtails bouncing.

"I only have goldfish," a freckle-faced boy said, wrinkling his nose. "We live in a 'partment."

Grace smiled. "Well, this story is about a very special pet. Let's see who can guess what it is. . . ."

At the close of storytime the little pairs marched dutifully out the door again.

Their teacher waited to bring up the end, concern apparent on her fair face as she turned to Grace. "Is everything okay?" Abby asked kindly. "You look a little pale today. Are you catching a cold?"

"I'm fine. Just a bit tired."

Abby appeared satisfied. "Well, see you next Tuesday, then."

"Right." Grace smiled after her and closed the door. *Next Tuesday, and the next Tuesday, and every Tuesday after that. . .for the rest of my life.* Pressing her lips together, she drew a deep breath and returned to her desk.

"So, how's tricks?" Pam asked over the phone. "Our hero writer still around?"

Grace switched the receiver to her other ear and poured tea into her mug. "Mitch? No, he finally finished what he was doing and moved on to the next assignment. Two weeks ago." Blessedly, the pronouncement was already losing a portion of its sting. "What's new down in the valley?"

"Nothing much. I wanted to check to see if you're planning to be home next weekend. Jamie wants to celebrate his birthday with a picnic at the lake and we'd sure like you to come along. I called early so you'd have time to arrange for it."

"What's to arrange? I'm free anytime after noon every Saturday. It sounds like fun."

"Great. We'll see you then, at our usual spot. And I want to hear all about Mr. Dreamboat. Catch you later."

As the line went dead, Grace's smile followed suit. The last thing her mending heart needed was to dredge up memories she was expending considerable effort to erase. But perhaps this would be just another step on the way to healing. Besides, she realized, she was getting awfully good at directing pointed conversations to other—safer—topics.

She took a sip of tea and reached for her Bible. . .the only love story her heart had been able to handle lately.

Chapter 8

G radually, after increasing the time she normally spent in her daily prayers and Bible
reading, Grace reached a peaceful acceptance
of her fate. When home alone, she no longer hated herself for having discovered her very human nature. And
at work, where the memory of Mitch's presence still lingered in some intangible way, she no longer hated him
for demonstrating that love didn't always have a happy
ending—as it did in romance novels.

Now whenever she thought of Mitch, she found
herself holding him up before the Lord, asking God to
watch over him as he dashed about the world on assignments. She speculated that perhaps the Lord had
brought him into her life for that very purpose: Once
again he would have someone who cared enough to
pray for him.

Well, whatever the reason, Grace affirmed inwardly,
she shouldn't have too much difficulty relating the bittersweet interlude to her best friend, come Saturday.
And in the meantime, she had rows and rows of fanciful love stories to get her through the lonely times.

The weekend brought mild temperatures and clear

157

skies. Anticipating the outing with Pam and her kids, Grace donned ivory linen slacks and a soft knit top of delphinium blue. She collected from her pantry a few snack items for the picnic, then left for the library.

The morning proved to be a slow one as the sporadic traffic on the street outside passed right on by. It was a perfect opportunity for dusting the upper shelves and tops of the bookcases, a chore she tended to put off as long as possible. Tucking the feather duster under one arm, Grace lugged the wheeled ladder from the storage closet and set to work.

The menial task did have a good side, she concluded as the hours ticked by. On the ladder's fold-out shelf rested a goodly stack of tempting novels and nonfiction works she was acquiring during the process. Finished with the last section of shelves, she climbed down and gathered her cache of books together. She then tucked all but one of the books into a spare desk drawer to be checked out at a later date. But *So Still the Night*, a historical romance whose back-cover blurb sounded the most inviting, she slipped into her purse to take home. Then she wheeled the ladder to the closet at the back of the room.

On her return she stopped dead. Her heart lurched.

"Hello, Grace." Standing just inside the door, a very real Mitch Haywood straightened to his full height.

Grace had not heard a vehicle drive up, much less anyone come in. She felt the blood drain from her face as a curious blend of elation and anger melded into confusion. "W-what are you doing here?"

A lopsided smile curved his lips, a perfect complement to the enigmatic expression he wore. "Well—" He slowly started toward her. "Thought I might do another series—about Pennsylvania's military heroes. With Colonel Ricketts such a great opener, I figured you'd probably be able to put your hands on records of other local men and women of renown."

Lost in the voice she'd tried so hard to forget, Grace could only stare him. But the relentless pounding of her pulse would not abate—not with her stubborn heart refusing to face the possibility of surviving yet another parting. . .not with it trying to memorize the unexpected sight of him even now. And he was coming closer by the second.

A few feet from her he stopped, and his expression became softer. "Actually, that's not quite true. I. . .came back because I wanted—*needed*—to see you again." He took another step.

Grace took a small step herself, backward, her gaze mesmerized by a determined glint in his. "Y-you seem to be taking a lot for granted."

He gave an off-handed shrug and flicked a glance around the room, then smiled. "Well, no books came flying at me when I came in. I hoped that meant I had a fighting chance."

Grace was too mixed up to return the smile. And too busy trying to stay the warmth she felt rising from her collar to her hairline. "I-I think you—"

"—should never have left here," he finished for her. "I never even kissed you good-bye."

A tiny gasp escaped. She hiked her chin and retreated a few more inches. "Don't be silly. W-we aren't . . .we never—"

"Yeah, I know. Strange, isn't it?" A corner of his mouth curved upward. "Every now and then I need to have my head examined. Like a few weeks ago, when I drove out of here. I had convinced myself I could forget you, Grace Farrell. . .but there was this picture I'd taken—" His words trailed off.

Those dusky green eyes had never left her face, and Grace felt Mitch had the advantage over her. For all her lifetime of reading about love, she'd never learned how to play the game—if that's what this was. Surely he could see into her very soul, could detect feelings she hadn't been able to suppress. She inched her foot backward again but her heel touched the wall. She swallowed.

As if he sensed her panic, he didn't come any closer. But from a mere arm's length away he reached up, lightly brushing his fingertips over the curve of her cheekbone. Watching, waiting, studying her.

It was all Grace could do to keep her knees from buckling. She thought she had seen his hand tremble a little, and her own entire being was far from steady. She couldn't remember what fictional heroines did in situations such as this. But a peculiar ache crimping her insides grew stronger as she gathered courage enough to look into his eyes.

After the briefest hesitation Mitch exhaled audibly and reached out to her. She did not resist as he drew her into his arms.

Closing her lashes against an exquisite contraction of her heart, Grace felt her breath catch in her throat. Perhaps a taste of such infinite joy would give her strength to endure another parting, if she had to. She smiled and returned the embrace. "Oh, Mitch. . ." The steady throbbing of his own heart against hers gave her precious confidence.

For a timeless moment he held her close. Then, easing away a little, he searched her face, and slowly brought his lips to within a fraction of hers, as if giving her the chance to turn away. To flee.

It was the furthest thing from Grace's mind. All on their own, her lips parted slightly and she pressed closer.

Nothing had prepared her for the wondrous reactions that would stir within her with Mitch's kiss—the most reverent one she had ever known—or for the undisguised passion she glimpsed in his eyes when it ended. But she desperately needed to know the truth. "You came all the way back here just to kiss me goodbye?" She held her breath, almost dreading his answer.

A rakish grin appeared. "You think I'm the 'kiss and run' type?"

"I can't really say, now, can I?" Grace countered.

"No, I suppose you can't." He ran his fingers through his hair and moved aside. "Look, I realize your work day is not over yet. Are there any immediate matters you need to take care of?"

She glanced at the clock on the wall and shook her head. "It's almost noon. Everyone knows the library closes early on Saturday."

"Good," he said, nodding. "We need to talk." He took her hand and escorted her to her desk. As she sat down he drew up a chair for himself. "First, and foremost," he began earnestly, "thanks for not throwing me out. I. . .had to go for broke."

Relaxing somewhat, Grace smiled. "You mean, you really weren't as confident as you appeared?"

"Far from it, I assure you. And I want to be completely honest with you," Mitch went on. "When I first came to Cragle Corners, it was under protest. To keep my job."

"Yes, I sensed that." She picked up a pencil near her fingers and idly toyed with it.

He nodded again. "Granted, I liked the slower pace of life I found once I got here. I liked the mountains, the trees, the curving country roads—you name it. Even so, I planned to wind up all my research in a day or two. But for some reason I dragged it out, made it last a whole lot longer than necessary. Of course, I convinced myself I was just taking my time so I could do a thorough job. Now, looking back, I see that was just a smoke screen."

He paused, but she made no comment.

"When I drove out of here," he said, taking up where he'd left off, "I tried to go as fast and as far away from here as I could. Only I kept thinking about you. Seeing your face—even when I *wasn't* staring at the picture I'd taken of you at the park. Your voice kept me awake nights. I relived all the talks we'd had, remembering your telling me you'd never been more than a hundred miles from home in your life. And I—" Mitch's eyes turned heavenward and he filled his lungs, releasing the breath in a rush. "I knew I could change all that . . .if you'd come away with me."

"What?" As Mitch's last phrase made it through to her consciousness, Grace felt herself becoming light-headed. "Y-you want me to. . .to—"

"Oh, man!" he muttered, rubbing a hand across his face. "I knew I'd muddle this up. No, that's not what I mean at all." He reached for her hand, enclosing it in both of his as he looked directly into her eyes. "What I'm trying to tell you, Grace Farrell, is that it wasn't my editor who brought me here, and it wasn't my job that made me stay. It was the Lord's doing. All of it. He meant for me to come here so I would meet you. So I would grow to love you. . .and want to marry you. We were destined to be together. I truly believe that."

Destined to be together! The very thought sang to Grace's heart to the accompaniment of a thousand violins. "You—you love me?"

That endearing grin of his lit up Mitch's whole face. Jumping to his feet, he came around her desk, gently drawing her up into his arms. "Yes," he murmured against her hair. "I love you. And I'm asking you to marry me. I'm not a total gypsy, by the way. . .I do have a pretty nice log house on Lake Michigan where we can live between assignments. But the rest of the time I'd like you to come along with me wherever I go. I want to show you those places you've only read about."

All her dreams, *all* of her deepest longings—and

Mitch too? "I-I can't believe it!" Grace heard herself say.

"The only thing is," Mitch said hesitantly, "we'd have to get married in a couple days. There's a festival I'm supposed to cover in Japan in two weeks. . .unless you'd prefer to wait until I'm finished and can come back. I'm willing to wait."

Grace's stomach chose that moment to let out a rather embarrassing growl.

"Don't you ever eat?" Mitch teased.

She could only giggle. "Yes, I eat, and yes, I love you. And yes. . .I will marry you."

A brilliant grin lit up his face. "You mean, before I go to Japan? It wouldn't give you time for a big elaborate wedding, or anything. . . ."

Grace let her eyes freely roam Mitch's face. "Oh, who needs an elaborate wedding? June is right around the corner. My whole life I have dreamed of being a June bride. I would marry you now, Mitch Haywood. This instant. Only. . . ."

He blanched. "Oh, yeah. I know it'll be hard to find someone to fill your position here at the library right away."

Another rumble made its voice heard and Grace blushed. "Could I interest you in a picnic? There's someone who'd like the chance to get to know you a little. And by odd coincidence, she'd kill to have my job."

"You're kidding."

"No."

Mitch chuckled and hugged her hard. "Then, we're out of here, Grace, my love."

Grace leaned down to retrieve her purse from the desk drawer, then, hand in hand, she walked with him to the door to lock up. Within minutes Mitch was assisting her into his Cherokee.

Suddenly she halted. "Oh, I forgot something! Would you wait just one second?"

"Sure." He grinned and climbed in his side while she dashed back into the library.

Unzipping her purse, Grace removed *So Still the Night* and set it on her desk with a light pat. "Sorry, old friend. I won't be keeping company with you just now. I have my own date with destiny."

Heart singing, she all but ran back to Mitch. . .her destined love. The two of them had some plans to make.

Sally Laity

An accomplished writer of contemporary and historical romances, Sally's novel, *Dream Spinner*, contained in the *Inspirational Romance Reader–Historical Collection No. 2* (Barbour Publishing), is a bestseller. She recently coauthored an inspirational romance series set during the Revolutionary War entitled "Freedom's Holy Light" (Tyndale House Publishers). Sally makes her home in Bakersfield, California and is married with four children and ten grandchildren. She enjoys writing inspirational romance because it is an avenue for her to openly share her faith.

Something Old, Something New

Yvonne Lehman

Dedication

To Ella Groves, whose lifelong Christian service and beautiful inner spirit is the inspiration for this story; Pat Winebrenner, Marketing Director at Highland Farms Retirement Community for her invaluable cooperation; Marilyn Stevens, Activities Director, HFRC; Albamae, Frances, Maxine, and Peg, HFRC residents; Howard for his "Abraham suggestion"; Lori Marett for her critique; and to Susan Johnson for her encouragement.

Lay not up for yourselves treasures upon earth, where moth and rust doth corrupt, and where thieves break through and steal: But lay up for yourselves treasures in heaven. . . For where your treasure is, there will your heart be also.
MATTHEW 6:19-21 (KJV)

Chapter 1

Peppino Gallo couldn't swat a fly or smack a mosquito without thinking about how that truck smashed the life out of his Marybelle when she pulled out in front of it. He couldn't lift his eyes toward heaven without questioning, "Why?" He figured God wasn't going to answer. He'd been asking for over two years now.

All the well-meaning advice hadn't help a bit—neither had counting blessings nor the passage of time. He and Marybelle had over fifty years of married life together—now that had ended. He couldn't live in the past, his present was meaningless, and he could see nothing bright about his future.

Golden years?

Humph! They looked dull gray to him!

After an unpleasant afternoon of grumbling about wanting to be independent, not wanting to be a burden to his family, and maybe he shouldn't have sold his house, his grandson, Daniel suggested, "Let's go check out another place."

"We've looked at every available place in town," Peppino replied. "Why waste our time?"

"Humor me, Pops," Daniel implored.

Peppino lifted a bushy white eyebrow, the color of

his thick wavy hair. Beneath a handlebar mustache, his lips twisted into a wry grin. "That's my line, Danny-boy. I'm the old one. You're supposed to humor me."

"Just this once," Daniel pled, and the next thing Peppino knew they sped along Highway 70."

That was fine, until Daniel turned off at a big green sign with huge white letters. Peppino's eyes widened. "You took a wrong turn, didn't you, boy?"

Daniel got a strong feeling this might not be a good idea. "I've heard it's a great place. The Hensons said their parents moved out here. You know them. They—"

Peppino interrupted. "Well, I know a few who are spending their lives behind bars, but that doesn't mean I want to be locked up in prison."

"Pops," Daniel pleaded. "This is not a prison—"

"Same as!" Peppino growled. "It's an old folks' home."

"It's not that," Daniel protested.

But the old man's face was red, like he was about to explode. "You think I'm ready to be put out to pasture!"

Daniel pulled off onto the side of the road and switched off the engine, concerned about his grand-father who could do anything he wanted, live wher-ever he wished. He had the money. He had the time. He still had his health. He just didn't have the will. "You know we can turn around and go back to Dad's house right now."

"I've given that a try, Daniel. A whole year. But Drake's got his real estate business. Oh, I commend him for being a hard worker, but I rarely see him. And Marta, bless her heart, means well, but she treats me like I'm in my second childhood." He sighed. "And the teenagers—they're good kids but they drive me insane with their noise and energy."

Daniel could see Peppino's point. As much as he loved his family, he couldn't live with them either. "You know you could share my apartment."

"Your apartment?" Peppy snorted. "At your age, the last thing you need is an old codger like me cramping your style."

At thirty-two, Daniel had had his style cramped a time or two already. "You know I don't feel that way," Daniel said with both affection and dismay.

"Well, you should. I've lived my life. You haven't even started yours yet."

Haven't started? Daniel marveled. But it wasn't his own life that concerned him right now, but Peppino's saying, "I've lived my life."

He started the engine. "You want to go home with me? Or to Dad's?"

Peppino threw up his hands. "To the old folks' home—where I belong!"

Daniel stepped on the gas. "It won't hurt to get a little information about the place." They rounded a curve and immaculate green lawns appeared: a lovely community of houses, condos, main building, apartments, lush foliage against a background of majestic western North Carolina mountains, sidewalks bordered by low hedges and flower beds with a profusion of red, purple, orange, yellow, and white flowers. He gave a low whistle. "This

171

place is like a resort."

"Yep," Peppino agreed, "the last resort!"

Ella Hayes noticed the red convertible parked outside the Administration Office, but it made no immediate impression upon her. She was hurrying along the corridor of Skyland Retirement Center, after having visited her friend June in the Health Care Unit. It was a little past five, but she'd just pop in and see if her great niece was still in her office.

Her mind really was on June's sprained ankle when she found herself at Kay English's doorway before she realized it. She heard a male voice at the same time the receptionist said, "Kay's busy right now."

"Oh, I'm so sorry," Ella apologized, when two men and Kay looked at her. "I didn't realize you had another appointment tonight."

Kay smiled. "This is my aunt, Ella Hayes," she said, and both men stood. The older one nodded briefly, but the young, good-looking man smiled warmly. My, he was handsome with that smooth olive skin, dark eyes, and dark wavy hair.

The older one said, "No need to apologize. We didn't have an appointment—" His words stopped abruptly. He looked suspiciously at the younger man. "Did we?"

"No, sir," the younger man declared. "We could come back another time."

"No, there's no need. Aunt Ella is a resident here.

She could tell you a lot about the place." Kay gestured toward the men. "Meet Daniel and Peppino Gallo."

Ella felt like apologizing for Kay's appearance. Oh, she was definitely the picture of a conservative, career woman in that navy blue suit, with her auburn hair pulled back in a twist. She wished this good-looking Gallo man could see her with her hair down and her gray-green eyes sparkling. But Ella knew Kay would disown her forever if she made any such remarks. She controlled herself and said what was right. "I'm really sorry to barge in, Kay. I just wanted to remind you about the Philharmonic concert at seven in the Assembly Room." She smiled at the pleasant young man and the frowning older man. "You two are welcome to join us. The public is invited to these events."

Kay dared not look at Daniel, but kept her eyes on Peppino as he muttered a half-hearted, "Thank you," then declined the invitation. Kay hoped neither would suspect that the white-haired, seventy-five-year-old woman with the sweet voice, clear blue eyes, and innocent expression was an incurable match-maker.

Kay also hoped they didn't notice the color she felt creeping into her face. For something to hide behind, she picked up her reading glasses and perched them on her nose. "Oh, Aunt Ella. Would you have the cooks fix me a plate? I'll eat in your apartment, then we can go to the concert together."

"Glad to," Ella said, her eyes reflecting the mischief running around in her head. "Nice meeting you gentlemen."

173

"What kind of living arrangements are you interested in, Mr. Gallo?" Kay asked, as they returned to their chairs.

Peppino sighed, sitting stiffly, looking like a defeated man. Apparently he wasn't eager to get down to the business of a retirement center.

"My wife and I had discussed a condo," he answered.

"Oh, your wife will be—?"

"No!" he replied shortly. "That was years ago. She's no longer with me."

Is he bitter—or hurt? Kay wondered. *Does that mean she left him—or died?* She reached for two packets. "You can look these over and ask any questions," she advised, peering over the top of her glasses and handing brochures to both Peppino and Daniel.

She understood Peppino's reluctance. It wasn't easy contemplating making a major lifestyle change—at any age. She'd done it several times—when her parents died, when she moved in with Aunt Ella, then when she moved again to an apartment when Aunt Ella moved here.

She looked into the concerned eyes of Daniel Gallo. He cared. Kay cared. But, if Peppino Gallo didn't want to be here, then he might be better off elsewhere. And yet, something about him tugged at her heart. And Daniel's expression seemed to plead, "Do something!"

But she was only the Marketing Director—not a miracle worker.

Then she smiled. Her face relaxed. She was well-acquainted with the Master Miracle Worker—God Himself. And she'd witnessed many of His miracles here in this place. She doubted that any words would make a dent in the hard shell of Peppino Gallo. He reminded her of a Doubting Thomas. What she needed to do was whet his interest in the Center.

She picked up a ring of keys from her desk and stood. "Let's take a little tour," she suggested.

Chapter 2

Kay led along several hallways and through lounge areas, until she stopped and unlocked a door. "Come on in," she said, "the couple who live here gave permission for me to show their apartment while they're away. At the moment, they're cycling through Holland."

Peppino was skeptical. "How old are they?"

"Seventies," she said. "Most people come here when they're still young enough to join in the activities."

"Activities," he repeated blandly, as if he hadn't expected there would be any.

Kay quickly mentioned just a few things that included intellectual activities, the arts, opportunity for knowledge and development of talent, woodworking shops and outdoor trails, shuffle board, golf. . .and before she could even mention all of them, one glance at Daniel revealed he too was pleasantly surprised at the quality and variety of services offered at the Center.

"I've heard this is a fabulous place, but I suppose I thought more in terms of a nursing home," Daniel admitted.

"You've visited nursing homes in the area?" Kay questioned. Peppino didn't appear to be a candidate for that.

"With our church," Daniel said. "We've had services at several homes." He glanced at his grandfather, who was looking over the kitchen. "Pops is a terrific singer."

"Not any more," Peppino replied adamantly, without turning toward them. "What's to sing about?"

Kay watched a somber expression fall on Daniel's face. He obviously cared deeply for his Pops, and apparently was active in church. Good qualities, there! Not bad-looking, either.

Peppino joined them in the living room. "This is not a nursing home, although we have the Health Care Center for residents who are ill, or get hurt," Kay pointed out. "It's a retirement center. Most of our residents claim to lead fuller lives than before they came here."

After showing them the living room, bedroom, closet behind folding doors along one entire wall, and the compact, fully-equipped kitchen, Kay took them out to the balcony where they looked out upon spectacular mountain vistas in all directions. "The lower apartments each have a patio and a garden spot."

"Do the residents keep the gardens, or is there a gardener?" Peppino asked, interested.

Kay smiled. "That's up to the resident. You can do as much or as little as you like here. We also have a garden plot where anyone who wants to can grow vegetables. Also, you may eat all your meals in the apartment or in the dining room."

Peppino and Daniel exchanged warm glances. When Peppino walked closer to the railing and peered down upon the flowering gardens, Daniel looked at Kay

177

and nodded, an approving smile on his lips as if he were pleased. She smiled back and suddenly felt the warmth of the fading sun on her face. Mercy, she hoped the freckles across her nose weren't standing out like copper pennies against a blush. She was too old to blush. But it wasn't often—frankly, not in the three years she'd been here—that such a handsome young man toured the Center. Usually, middle-aged couples accompanied parents or older couples came alone.

After leaving the apartment, Kay took them through the Garden Room, explaining, "Most guests and residents agree this is our most beautiful and intriguing indoor setting."

"Sounds like a real mountain stream," Peppino said, walking toward the center of the spacious room that featured an indoor court within a twenty-foot square stone wall, two feet high. "Rather looks like the outdoors too," he commented with an approving nod, taking in the lovely ornamental pool, surrounded by the rich foliage of colorful flowers, shrubs, and trees.

"Complete with goldfish," Peppino added approvingly, almost smiling at the creatures swimming around in the pool. On the right was a curved bridge against the stone wall. Water flowed down the rocks, under the bridge, and into the pool.

"I like this," Daniel said, as Kay watched him lift his gaze to the space above the inner court that reached all the way to the skylight where natural lighting enhanced the scene. Surrounding the space on the floor above was a high wooden railing, where one might stand and look down upon the enchanting court below. The cathedral ceiling slanted to the height of another floor and from a center beam hung a great wooden chandelier with globes inside square boxes.

Kay was sure Peppino's interest was whetted, and her suspicions were confirmed when, as soon as they returned to her office, he said, "Maybe I should see a condo. If everyone's as active as you say . . ."

His voice trailed off as Kay shook her head. "We have a three- to five-year waiting list for everything but the apartments," she said. "But, if you do take an apartment, it gets you into the system and you're more likely to get a condo later if you decide on that."

Neither Daniel nor Kay spoke, but their eyes silently communicated the same sentiment: hope that Peppino might realize the opportunities here.

Peppino contemplated the possibilities, many of them aloud. "I want to be independent."

Daniel nodded. "But you've said you don't want the upkeep of a house and yard anymore."

"True," Peppino nodded and Daniel realized he and his grandfather were actually having a conversation, instead of a heated stand-off, for a change. "And if I decided to take off and climb the Alps, I could."

They all laughed, but Daniel said pointedly to Kay, "He really could!"

Seeing the sudden light in Peppino Gallo's eyes for the first time, Kay suspected there was a lot of life in that man yet. Already, she found him charming, even in his obvious doldrums. He just needed to steer that self-pity into something more productive. And considering who had the apartment next to the available one, she just might have the answer to his problems!

"You indicated there is an available apartment?" Peppino questioned.

"Like the one I showed you, except it's on the lower floor," Kay said. "It's available now for contracting, but the furniture can't be moved out until next weekend."

Peppino turned to his grandson. "Do you want to go ahead with this, or wait? You know you have the biggest wedding of the season coming up the end of July."

Wedding? Kay thought with a sense of chagrin. *So, Daniel's getting married. Well, isn't everyone—except me?*

"Getting you settled is my first priority, Pops," Daniel said. "But don't worry about the wedding. I've got that under control." He nodded at Kay then, as if she should proceed with the plans. His gaze was warm and searching.

Her gray-green eyes fell to the papers in front of her like an unattached leaf falling from a tree. *Jealousy and envy get behind me,* she admonished herself silently and searched her calendar. She cleared her throat and addressed Peppino. "What about the first week in July?"

That was agreed upon, and other business arrangements set into motion. They shook hands and said good-bye. Kay knew the Center actually sold itself, being what it claimed to be—"the finest retirement community in the country." But she played a part in it too, and she always felt fulfilled when a prospective resident left happy. Peppino Gallo left with a much better attitude then when he'd come in.

She did not immediately rise from her chair and get ready to leave, however, but sat a while longer, watching the red convertible grow smaller and smaller beneath a graying sky and a landscape brushed with shadows. Both men, she thought, were embarking on a new way of life. One had lost a wife—another was gaining one.

Daniel's got his life under control, he said. *Well, so do I*, Kay remembered. *"It's just that I constantly seem to be reminding myself of that.*

A short while later, Kay sat in Ella's kitchen, stirring ranch dressing into a crisp garden salad made from vegetables grown on the Center grounds. She gave Ella a run-down on what little she'd learned about Peppino Gallo. "I'm sure you'll be good for him, living right next door."

"He didn't look any too friendly and at my age, I'm not about to mollycoddle some old man in his second childhood," Ella staunchly affirmed and sipped from her cup of decaf.

Before Kay could swallow a bite of tomato and inform Ella that she hadn't meant to give an unfavorable account of Peppino Gallo, Ella had developed that mischievous gleam in her eyes. "It was the young one who impressed me," she said, nodding. "I guess he'll be coming around to visit if his grandfather moves next door."

181

"Aunt Ella!" Kay reprimanded, her fork poised in the air for emphasis. "You've got to stop trying to set me up. If the Lord has a man for me, He'll send him my way."

"The Lord helps those who help themselves," Ella replied pointedly.

"Thomas Jefferson said that—not God," Kay said.

Ella shrugged. "It's a good saying anyway. Now, you know that Daniel fellow is the most comely man that's come this way in a long time—maybe ever?"

Kay agreed, but from the moment Peppino mentioned the wedding, she'd told her emotions to take a hike up the mountain and stay there. "Peppino said Daniel's getting married," Kay said finally. "At the end of July."

Aunt Ella looked as if the bottom had fallen out of her fantasy world. Shaking her head, she took her empty coffee cup to the sink.

"Peppino said it's to be the biggest wedding of the season," Kay added, attempting to drive home the point that her aunt should stop the match-making she'd tried for years, often proving to be an embarrassment to her niece.

Aunt Ella sighed. "We're going to have to do something about you."

"Like I've told you, " Kay declared. "I've got my work, my church, friends, you." Kay didn't dare look at the skepticism she knew would abound in her aunt's eyes, as she added, "I'm perfectly happy!"

Chapter 3

"Perfectly happy," was how Kay felt after the long weekend retreat at the beginning of July. Her singles' group had hiked up to Mount Mitchell, the highest peak east of the Mississippi, had devotions around a campfire, and slept out under the stars. She had her life in proper perspective and was eager to see Aunt Ella and find out if her new neighbor moved in and if all was going well.

"The furniture was moved in yesterday but he didn't stay here overnight. By the way, he wants to be called 'Peppy.'" Her eyes lifted toward the ceiling and she muttered, "There's nothing peppy about him." She then cut her eyes toward Kay, saying pointedly, "He should be called Fuss-budget. I was on my patio, minding my own business but I could hear his booming voice, ordering everybody where to place each piece of furniture exactly right."

Sighing, she returned to her subject. "Anyway, I met the family. They're delightful. The grandchildren are precious—one girl and two boys, all teenagers. Peppy's son has a real estate business. The son's wife volunteers at the hospital and is active in church. Says she might volunteer here at the Health Care Unit."

"Oh, that would be nice," Kay replied, nodding.

"Think I'll dash over and see how things are going." She stepped out onto Ella's patio, around the brick-latticework partition, and onto Peppy's patio, then knocked on the side of the glass doors that formed the back wall.

"Well, hello there!" exclaimed Peppy with more enthusiasm than he had exhibited the last time she saw him. He pushed aside the screen panel. "Looks like you're out of uniform, Ms. English," he said and laughed at his own joke.

"Off duty, but dressed for the occasion," she said, with a broad smile. His approving look took in the red scarf around her neck, her white shirt, and her blue shorts.

"Come in," he offered. "See how you like my decor."

The decor's terrific, came her errant thought as the bright afternoon sunlight illuminated Daniel, in jeans and T-shirt, a perfect picture of health and happiness. He stood in front of the entertainment center, holding a video.

"You remember Daniel," Peppy said.

I tried not to, she was thinking, but she merely said a light, "Hello."

His eyes fell to the American flag name tag on her shirt, as if he hadn't remembered her. But, she did look different, with her naturally curly untamed hair hanging down around her shoulders and not dressed in her "costume," as Peppy had implied.

"Ms. English," Daniel acknowledged.

"Kay," she replied, and turned from his dazzling

smile to the furnishings.

"A bedroom's a bedroom," Peppy said, "but I sold my house furnished, so all this is new." His hand made a sweeping gesture around the living room.

On the beige carpet, deliberately neutral so that any decor would fit in, sat a modern couch, its weave a combination of brown and cream stripes, comfortably designed to accommodate a tall man like Peppy. Large cushions, various shades of brown, peach, and green were grouped invitingly in each corner. The end tables and coffee table were of light oak, like the entertainment center where Daniel was taking videos from a cardboard box and stacking them on shelves.

"You picked all this out yourself?" Kay asked, impressed.

Peppy grinned. "With a few suggestions from Daniel."

"Not many that he accepted, however," Daniel said meaningfully. Kay looked around and returned his smile, then focused on the tapestry over the couch. Its colors complimented those in the couch. "Impressive," Kay said. "Looks like ancient Rome."

"Indeed it is," Peppy said, walking over to her. "It's one of the few pieces I kept. Picked it up in Italy, but never really had a place for it before."

He turned away quickly. Kay exchanged a sympathetic glance with Daniel. Peppy and his wife must have taken that trip together. "Good-looking entertainment center," she said, walking over to the light brown recliner with an afghan tossed over the back of it.

185

Peppy nodded. "Things are shaping up. I do need to pick up some plants, maybe a tree or two. That silk flowers and tree shop downtown might be a good place."

"The best," Kay returned. "The owner is in my singles' group at church"

"You're single? Why, I would have thought a pretty girl like you'd be married."

An old girl my age, you mean, Kay was thinking. Daniel turned her way and she was sure a question lay in his eyes. If another person in this world implied, "If you ain't loving, you ain't living," she'd scream!

To prevent it, she glanced at her watch. "I'd better go. I'm sure you got a flyer about today's activities."

"Oh, yes," Peppy said, "but the family's already planned a barbecue for me. Invited relatives, friends and neighbors. The whole county, in fact, to celebrate my Independence Day. I'll be back tonight. My first night here, you know. Hey," he said suddenly, with those sparks in his eyes, "Why don't you come join us?"

"I was about to ask that," Daniel said, taking a step closer to them. "We'd love to have you join us, Kay. Bring your aunt along, if you like."

Kay stepped back, toward the doorway. "Thanks," she said. "But I always join in the activities here on the Fourth, then Aunt Ella and I drive down to the lake to see the fireworks."

Daniel thought Kay might return their invitation by asking if they'd be back before dark and consider seeing the fireworks with her and her aunt. But she didn't. He noticed that Kay looked affectionately at

Pops, but guardedly at him. Maybe he was mistaken, but he got the distinct impression Kay's cordiality extended no further than to his grandfather.

Such an attractive single woman probably turned down invitations all the time. Most likely, she was even committed to someone special.

Chapter 4

After breakfast the following morning, Peppy walked out onto his deck with a cassette player, looked over the four-foot high brick partition, and saw Ella looking at a magazine. If he'd known she was there, he wouldn't have come out. On his first visit here, she'd "inadvertently" peeked into Kay's office. When he moved in she'd come over to "welcome" him. He saw her in the dining room this morning "sneaking a peek" at him. Oh, he knew what these old women had on their minds. All of them— looking for a husband. Wanting to reel a man in like a fish. Well, he wasn't biting.

But. . .he could at least be cordial.

"Ma'am," he said.

Ella tightened her lip to match her determination. She wasn't going to allow that man to ruin her morning meditation. This was such a peaceful place and she liked to sit out on her deck after breakfast, have a cup of tea, plan her day, or read awhile. She liked to watch the hummingbirds glide down to her red salvia, drink from it's blossoms, and dart away.

"Miss Yella," he said.

She had planned to ignore him. But how could one ignore an obnoxious man who called you yella?

She turned, her lips taut. She looked up and her clear blue eyes, the color of the tranquil morning sky, lit upon him.

"Morning, ma'am."

"What did you call me?" she demanded

"Ma'am," he said.

"No. Before."

"Why, I said Miss Yella. That's your name isn't it. At least, that's what I understood. Sounds like the Yella Rose of Texas. You from Texas, ma'am?"

"No, I'm not from Texas. And my name is not Yella. It's Ella. Ella Hayes. Mrs. Hayes."

"Mrs? You're married?"

"I was."

"Well, Miss Ella. I'm a little hard of hearing sometimes. You'll have to forgive me." He lifted his hand and fingered the tip of his mustache. Just this morning at breakfast, June had remarked that when a man did that, he was up to no good.

Will I have to forgive him? Ella thought stiffly, then began flipping through the pages of the magazine. Up to no good, she remembered June saying. The last thing she wanted was for this man to think he could charm her.

Sassy ol' thing, Peppy was thinking as he laid the tape player on the brick lattice-work partition. He punched a button and Andy Williams began to croon about "blue skies." He stretched out on his lounge chair and joined in with "nothing but blue skies all day long."

My, he has an exceptional voice, Ella had to admit. Maybe she would suggest he join the chorus, then he wouldn't have to sing on the patio and disturb her reading. She got up, laid the magazine on her chair, and walked over to the partition to the wooden box of ivy whose trailing vines offered more privacy by covering the spaces between the bricks. His eyes were closed and his singing almost drowned out Andy Williams. She coughed.

His eyes opened. "Oh, is the music bothering you?"

Ella had a strong feeling he had selected hearing, and she could play the game too. Looking him straight in the eye, she said as sweet as you please, "No, nothing is smothering me."

His mouth fell open, wondering if she was putting him on. Then, behind that clear blue gaze he saw a hint of mischief just before she focused on the ivy and began to pick off withered leaves and let them drop in a pile at her feet. This woman was trying to get his goat.

"You trying to get my goat, woman?"

"No. But I'm going to get that tape player if you don't turn down that off-key singing."

He raised up. "Off key?"

She nodded, letting a withered leaf float down at her feet. "I'm sure Andy's voice warbled on that last high note."

"Would you mind?" he asked, gesturing toward the cassette player.

Ella turned down the volume and did tell him about the chorus. "It could use a voice like yours."

He scoffed. "I haven't sung in public since. . .in a long time."

Ella knew what that meant. He was still lamenting over the loss of his wife.

Peppy didn't know why he had even sung with the tape, unless it was to irritate his neighbor woman that, for some weird reason, he wanted to put in her place. Or maybe he didn't want anybody to think he belonged here—not even his own self.

He lay back on the chaise lounge and felt the morning sun lie softly on his arms, folded against his chest. Just as he was about to doze off, she said, "You missed it."

He squinted at her. "Missed what?"

"The parade yesterday."

"Well, I doubt that I would have missed much. I was told that you people walk or ride around the roads till you get to the dining room. The last parade I went to was downtown. The highlight was a little boy, dressed in red, white, and blue, marching down the street, beating on an aluminum pan with a big spoon." His eyes closed. "What kind of parade is that?"

Feeling riled, Ella's voice rose. "Oh, some of us old biddies hobble along with our walkers in front of us. My friend June was on her crutches. Some shuffle while others crawl. It takes about three hours just to get around to the dining hall."

She looked over and the pleased expression on his face indicated he believed that! If Kay thought she could be a Christian example to this man, she'd better think again. She couldn't remember when anybody riled her so! Her voice rose even higher. "Actually, not that you're interested, but you need to be educated—" She

191

paused, and smiled then, seeing how his mouth tightened as if he were insulted.

In glowing terms, Ella began to describe the parade. "The band led the way," she explained as she continued to pinch off little brown leaves. "Our chorus marched behind them, singing songs like 'The Battle Hymn of the Republic' and 'The Grand Ol' Flag.'"

He imagined everyone waving flags. Suddenly, it was like Peppy saw a warning flag go up in front of his eyes. This woman wanted him to join the chorus. She said "our chorus" just now which meant she belonged to it. Yep, as he suspected, she had more than singing on her mind.

"Some wear costumes like Uncle Sam and those big white top hats. Others wear jogging shorts and—"

His eyes opened and flew to hers. "You're making this up."

"I don't lie, Pepper!"

"Peppy!"

"Peppy?"

"My name," he said irritably."

"Oh yes, didn't I hear that somewhere?" she questioned, as if it were unbelievable.

He frowned and raised the back of the chaise to sitting position. Didn't this woman know that you get to a man through his stomach and not by aggravation? But he wasn't about to let her know she was getting to him. "They really had a parade like that?" he asked, trying to stick to the conversation.

"Sure. And that's not the half of it. The cyclers, in

their athletic shorts and shirts and helmets, rode together. There were a few mopeds too and we have two couples who have those double-seater motorcycles. They go off to those big motorcycle conventions a couple times a year."

Peppy stopped looking at her but his head was moving from side to side as if he had an uncontrollable tic in his neck. She knew he was having difficulty believing her. "The highlight though was Craig Preston and his wife, on that riding lawnmower. It's a big yellow thing and they had it all decorated with streamers. Craig and Vestal sat up there waving their flags and their hands like nobody's business."

Peppy shrugged and asked gruffly, "If everybody's in the parade, who sees them?"

"Some residents, our friends and relatives. Health Care Unit patients come out in wheel chairs or are propped up at their windows. And of course, the employees. It's a big event. They roast and smoke two pigs on the huge barbecue spits. Then there's a low country boil. They put everything in it: miniature corn on the cob, little red potatoes, sausage, shrimp, east coast spices. Some people from downtown call and throw their names in the pot for the barbecue simply because we have the best barbecue around. The owners of this center help with the cooking."

"No kidding?" Peppy said, wonderingly.

She nodded. "Oh, and I forgot to mention that some residents drive their cars in the parade."

Peppy chuckled. "My red convertible would have

been perfect for that. I could have decorated it with blue and white streamers and looked like a flag."

"Ummhmm," Ella mumbled.

"Pardon?"

Her eyes took on an innocent look and she repeated, "I said, 'Ummhmm.'"

Peppy lay back against the chaise again, trying to enjoy the sunshine. The joy was gone though. That "Ummhmm" of hers and the nonchalant way she kept picking off those dead leaves seemed to indicate she thought he was all talk and no action.

Ella could readily see his face had reddened. Was it the sun or his blood pressure? Turning away from him and the partition, she grinned. This little assignment of Kay's might not be so bad after all. She hadn't really had a challenge in quite a while. "Oh, my," she said suddenly, gathering her magazine and teacup, realizing how time was flying. "I'm about to miss my poetry class. Our group has a wide range of interests—Anything from Beowulf to Ogden Nash, and some even like to discuss nursery rhymes." She laughed lightly. "Are you interested in poetry?"

"Not at the moment," he said blandly.

That didn't surprise Ella. "Oh," she said, right before going inside. "You know there's a council meeting in the Assembly Room at 10:30. You're to be introduced."

"Yes, ma'am," he said dully. Ella raised up on her tippie toes to see him. His eyes were closed. She suspected he was going to lie there all day and atrophy.

Shortly before 10:30, Peppy strutted into the Assembly Room. He'd changed into dress pants, short-sleeved white shirt, and a wide, bright red bow tie. After the business session, he stood in line beside twin sisters, Ina and Una. They'd obviously shared quite a bit with Maxine, the interviewer, who told the residents that Ina, a retired schoolteacher, had lived in a nearby city until her husband died, then came to the Center. Una had lived in Minnesota and worked as a librarian until her retirement. Her husband died ten years ago. She decided the Minnesota winters were too cold for her, and too lonely.

Maxine had said the residents didn't have to say anything if they didn't want to, but the sisters took turns talking about their interests. Ina had already begun a novel she'd always wanted to write but never had time and she wondered, with all the wonderful activities available, if she'd have time now. Una was an accomplished organist, a bridge player, and a published poet.

Peppy hadn't planned to reveal anything other than what he'd told Maxine. He had an uneasy feeling that he might not fit in here after all. Everyone he'd met were professionals in their field and they all led interesting and busy lives. He too was educated, had run his own business, had special interests, but as far as activity, well, he just hadn't done much of anything in a while. But it was his turn. "I'm interested in gardening, music . . ." He cleared his throat. "And my red convertible."

That brought a few chuckles. He never used to be at a loss for words. Could even have been called the life of the party. That quality had kind of left him. What else should he say? Instinctively, he twirled the tip of his mustache, which always brought smiles. "By the way, call me Peppy, please," he said with a forced smile.

That did the trick. Congenial laughter followed and it was time for other residents to pass by and shake hands. He had to admit these people were warm and friendly. They might even believe he was peppy—if that neighbor of his, over there pouring juice and coffee, whose blue eyes cut around at him when he made that last remark, didn't tell them differently.

Chapter 5

That afternoon at four o'clock, Daniel called the Center and asked Kay if he could stop by. Kay knew he had no reason to call unless it was about Peppy. "Is there a problem with your grandfather?" she asked, concerned.

His tone was serious. "That's why I need to talk to you."

"Then, by all means, come on," she invited.

Less than thirty minutes later, he rushed through her office door, in dress pants, short-sleeved shirt, and tie. Her concern increased, realizing he must have taken off from work.

Daniel felt like telling her how lovely she looked. He'd seen her hair up, he'd seen it down, but he hadn't before seen it pulled to one side like that and fastened with a gold barrette. Her auburn hair and green eyes were such a striking combination. But after a polite welcome of, "Hello, Daniel," she gestured toward the chair opposite her, so he sat.

"Hi, Kay. Sorry if this is keeping you," he apologized.

"I normally leave at 5:00," she said.

"And I need to get back for a 5:30 appointment," he said. "So, I'll try to be brief."

Kay nodded. "What's your grandfather's problem?"

After all the rush, now he was hesitant. How was he going to handle this diplomatically? He didn't want to offend Kay, but he wanted to help Pops. "This is harder than I'd thought," he said, uncomfortably.

"We're equipped to evaluate any kind of problem, Daniel," she said, trying to put him at ease. "Small or great. He can go to the Health Care Unit, or if it's something difficult or embarrassing to talk about, I can send a nurse or a counselor."

Daniel knew he was giving the wrong impression, making things worse. "No, nothing that personal. I guess you'd say it's a preference."

"Preference?"

"Pops wants to move to another apartment. He thinks a male neighbor might be more suitable."

Kay was clearly surprised. "His living next door to Aunt Ella is a problem?"

"So much so, he's threatening to leave here if changes aren't made."

Kay was mystified. "I thought he was adjusting so well. Everyone likes him."

"Not everybody," Daniel corrected. "He says Miss Ella doesn't like him."

"Why does he think that?"

"He says she nags him—doesn't like him and lets him know it."

Kay shook her head. "I don't know how he got such an impression. Aunt Ella is the sweetest, most caring person in the world. She spent her life on the mission field in Korea. She's the most dedicated Christian I've ever known. After my parents died, she took me in, gave me a home, became a mother to me, sent me to college, gave me her car when she moved here. . . She—"

"Whoa!" he said, leaning forward in his seat to make his point. "I don't doubt all that. The first time I met her here, she was polite and gracious. She came over when we moved Pops into the apartment, eager to welcome us and help any way she could. I think she's a fine woman and I like her."

"But. . .your grandfather doesn't?" She could not imagine such a thing!

Daniel sighed. "I'm in a spot here. Pops is crazy about you. He said if I do anything to alienate you, he'll never forgive me. In fact," he said, his tone quite serious, "I'd never forgive myself."

Kay quickly glanced down, telling herself she was misinterpreting his meaning. He was talking about his grandfather. "In this short time I've known him," she could say honestly, "he's one of my favorite people. I know, that underneath all that growling, he's just a big lovable teddy bear."

"You've got him pegged," Daniel said, smiling warmly. "Kay, I wouldn't have brought this up, but he's the dearest person in the world to me. From what I've seen, I'm convinced the Center is the best place for him. I don't want to see him leave here."

Kay nodded. "Any kind of change can be hard at first, but I honestly think he belongs at the Center. Let me talk to Aunt Ella and see if I can get an insight into this."

He stood. "Thanks, Kay," he said sincerely, leaning over her desk slightly, his eyes searching hers warmly. "I'm sure we can work this out. I hope I'm not imposing."

Feeling slightly inhibited with his standing over her, Kay stood. "Not at all. This is not just my job, Daniel. It's my mission. I truly believe God has put me here for a purpose, and I consider every one of these people my family. Feel free to talk to me about your grandfather anytime."

"You're truly remarkable," he said, and he thought he saw a becoming blush on her cheeks. "Maybe we could talk about this further, over dinner."

"That's not necessary," she returned immediately.

"It's something I'd really like to do."

Kay stared. "I thought you had an appointment."

"I do," he said, "but I can call and someone else can handle it for me."

"I'm sorry," she said, "I have other plans." She opened a desk drawer and took out her purse.

He felt the rebuff was pretty clear! The impact of her attire registered then. Her bone-colored dress was a flowing silk, perfectly accented with gold jewelry. Of course, she'd have plans. He could imagine her at a fine restaurant, having a candlelight dinner, with someone special. *Lucky guy!* he was thinking. "Thanks again," he said. "Have a good evening."

"You too," she returned, without looking at him again.

Later, Kay stopped short just as she entered the bridal

shop, feeling the color drain from her face and the smile leave her lips. A man stood inside, and she recognized his profile. It was Daniel, now wearing a suit coat with the attire he had on in her office a short while earlier. Standing in front of him, looking up at him with a special glow in her eyes, was a pretty, petite girl with short black hair, talking excitedly about wedding plans. Daniel's handsome face lit up with that dazzling smile of his and the girl followed his lead in walking toward a beautiful gown.

Kay did an about-face, tugging at Peg's arm. "Let's leave," she said.

"We just got here," Peg protested.

"Come on." She grasped Peg's arm and they hurried out of the shop. "We can come back later. Let's eat first."

"You look faint." Peg said. "Didn't you eat today?"

Kay stopped, once they were past the glass windows. "Oh, Peg. This is foolish. We can go back."

"No, we're not," Peg said. "You need to talk."

Kay knew that was true. These feelings were weighing heavily on her heart. "But your upcoming wedding was supposed to be tonight's agenda," she said, apologetically.

Peg scoffed. "You listened to me moan and groan about Tim for years, and how my life was over. It was you who told me my life hadn't begun, and its worth didn't depend on Tim. It took a long time, but I learned that you were right. Now, if you have a problem, I'm listening."

Kay was grateful for the dimly lit restaurant, and the

corner booth Peg asked for. "It's nothing drastic," Kay admitted, after they ordered.

"Good. Get it out of your system before it gets drastic."

"Daniel was in the wedding shop and the whole situation disturbed me more than I had admitted to myself." Kay then unburdened her soul to Peg, starting with the first time she saw Daniel. She told how she discovered he was getting married and accepted that. Now, her concern was about Peppy and Ella.

The waitress brought the food and Kay moved her fork around in it.

"What else?" Peg prompted.

"When he came to the office, he said he had an appointment. Thirty minutes later, he asked me out to dinner. Now, he's in the wedding shop with his fiancée. The situation disturbs me, Peg."

"You don't think he really wanted to go out and discuss his grandfather?"

Kay shook her head. "He made that pretty clear."

After a moment Peg asked seriously, "Do you suppose he's having second thoughts about getting married?"

"It didn't look that way in the wedding shop, Peg. Did you see them?"

"That couple in the corner? Yeah. They seemed pretty engrossed in each other."

"Exactly," Kay said. "I don't know what to think. What kind of man treats his fiancée that way? How would she feel if she knew this?"

"Not too good," Peg said honestly, thinking of James, the man she would soon marry. After a long moment of looking at her friend, she asked softly. "Have you told me everything?"

"Not the worst part."

Peg waited. Finally Kay looked into her friend's eyes with a forlorn expression. "I was tempted to accept his invitation."

Chapter 6

B y the next morning, Kay had accepted the fact
that she couldn't know Daniel Gallo's intentions and decided it was best not to dwell upon
it. Maybe he'd just wanted them to be friends since the
welfare of Peppy and Ella was uppermost in both their
minds.

Regardless, she couldn't answer for him, but only
for herself. Talking honestly with Peg, then praying
about it, helped put things in perspective for her. Keeping herself on the straight and narrow was her goal and
finding out the situation between Aunt Ella and Peppy
was her responsibility.

The best judge of what was happening with Peppy
would be Aunt Ella, who was delighted when Kay
offered to stop by and have dinner with her in the
apartment.

"How's your neighbor?" Kay asked, after their supper was brought in and she took the foil off her plate.

Ordinarily, Ella might have said, "Which one?" but
it seemed nowadays everyone's mind was on the musta-
chioed one. She lifted her eyebrows, feeling they ought
to have a prayer before getting into that subject. "Let's
say grace," she said.

After grace, Ella cut a bite of meat, said simply, "I

reckon he's fine." She poked the food in her mouth.

"Several that I've talked to think he's adjusting quite well. And frankly, I think he's adorable."

Ella huffed. "You and two-thirds of the population."

Kay laughed at that. Females made up two-thirds of the population. She asked, "What about you?"

Ella wiped her mouth with her napkin, then answered, "You know I'm not taken in by any modern-day Valentino."

Is that how Ella pictures him? Or the other female residents? Regardless, Aunt Ella didn't sound like a woman who had a personal vendetta against Peppino Gallo.

Kay probed further. "Daniel is concerned about his grandfather's adjusting here. I told him if anybody knew Peppy's real state of mind, it would be you."

Ella scoffed. "There's nothing wrong with his state of mind that I can't handle. Isn't that why you put him next door to me?"

"Exactly," Kay replied and the two looked affectionately at each other. No way was Kay going to let Daniel Gallo's insinuations make her insult Aunt Ella, the kindest, sweetest woman in the whole world.

Downtown, Daniel and Peppy were sitting at a table in the Chinese restaurant, discussing the situation.

"Kay wasn't upset about my wanting to move, was she?" Peppy asked.

"Not upset. Just concerned. We both have your best

interests at heart. But I was careful saying anything against her aunt. It's a touchy subject."

"Kay's a wonderful girl," Peppy said immediately. "Beautiful too. Fortunate for her, she didn't get those mountain lion genes of her aunt's, always snarling at you."

Daniel leaned over his plate. "Let me give you a word of advice about women, Pops?"

A look of incredulity came onto his grandfather's face. "About women? You—" he pointed his fork at Daniel, "you are going to tell me all about women?"

Daniel leaned back and glanced around, wondering if his grandfather's burst of laughter had disturbed other diners. They didn't seem to notice. "Maybe I've learned a few things over the years," he insisted.

"Go for it," Peppy said and attacked his chow mein as if the conversation were a waste of time.

Daniel knew there wasn't much he could tell his grandfather, but he had to try. "With some people, Pops, arguing is like a drug. The more they get, the more addicted they become until it's an all-consuming passion. Don't argue back. She'll find someone else to argue with."

Peppy snorted and glanced over at Daniel. "You're saying, if that neighbor of mine says, 'Jump!' then I'm to ask, 'How high?' "

Daniel laughed. "Not exactly. What I'm saying is, practice what you've preached to me over the years. Remember? 'A soft answer turns away wrath. Turn the other cheek.' "

"Easier said than done," Peppy mused. "She sets me off."

"Try it, Pops," he said. "Try a little kindness."

But Daniel had his doubts when Peppy looked at him and declared, "Son, sometimes it takes a lot more sugar than a person's got, to sweeten up a sour ol' lemon."

Late in the afternoon the following day, Peppy walked out back, frowning as he stood at the edge of the patio, looking over the flower bed that had been neglected since the other occupants of the apartment had moved out.

Suddenly, he stiffened, hearing the sliding of a screen door. Maybe he could sneak back into his apartment real quick.

No such luck!

"You planning to jump?" he heard her say loudly.

Jump? Then he realized how he must look, standing there on the edge of the patio, staring down like he was on a bridge spanning a body of water far below. He felt inner laughter start to shake his insides as he thought, *Or throw somebody else in!* He would've chuckled out loud but he didn't want to encourage her. She was everywhere he looked already.

Forcing his lips down and drawing his eyebrows together, he glanced over. She looked placid as you please, with needlework in her hands. "What did you say a thing like that for?" he questioned gruffly.

"Well, I know you're having a hard time, being in that transition period."

"What?"

"Accepting the inevitable," she said. "We have to admit we're growing old and we're going to die. Maybe tomorrow, maybe today."

She was rankling his nerves. If he wanted that, he could have stayed with his teenage grandchildren. "You're wrong," he blurted out. "I do accept it. I just don't like it. I don't like feeling helpless. I don't like the aches and pains and failing eyesight and not being able to hear everything and pretending I heard the punch line to the joke when I didn't even hear the joke. I don't like getting tired when I didn't even do anything to get tired about. I don't like having worked all my life for a nice home and giving my wife beautiful things, then she ups and dies. No I don't like it."

"Ummhmm," Ella said smugly. "Like I said, you're in that transition period."

He tried with all his might not to insult her. "You know all about it, don't you?" and it took all his strength not to add, "Miss Yella!"

"I know a lot," she explained. "I've been in that self-pity state myself. Believe me, it's best to focus on others."

"You sure focus on me a lot," he blurted out. "Weren't you in there running around this morning, making sure my welcoming party was a success?"

"I'm on the committee," she said blandly.

He stared at her, but she didn't look up, just sat there not missing a stitch and with that Mona Lisa smile on her face. Other women smiled *at* him. She smiled *about* him. "Anyway," he said, wanting to end the conversation right now. "You don't know what kind of period I'm in. You don't even know me." He felt his blood pressure rising. "Woman, do you know you could drive a man to distraction."

"At least I can drive," she chided.

He walked back to the edge of the partition. "Are you implying something?"

"Oh, you talk about that little red convertible of yours like it's your white horse and you're the knight in shining armor. But I never see you in that car. I suspect you don't drive anymore. Did you fail to get your license?"

Peppy glared at her for a long time, trying to remember Daniel's advice. *"Don't argue,"* he'd said. Without another word, he turned and stormed into his apartment. Seconds later, he strode out on the deck again and around that brick partition and Ella feared he might fall flat on his face. He didn't, but hurried over, huffing and puffing, and held out a driver's license. "Look at that," he said. "Does that look like I couldn't pass my driver's test?"

Ella reached into her sewing bag and took out her reading glasses. "Almost eighty-one," she exclaimed, looking over the top of the glasses perched halfway down her nose. "Why, my goodness gracious. No wonder you're so cranky."

"Cranky!" he snorted and strode down the walk, adrenaline flowing through his veins like a ribbon in the breeze. As he crossed the bridge, she wondered if he

209

might go over to the pond and jump in. No, he was headed for that red convertible. He put the top down. Maybe he was going back to his family. She did feel a stab of conscience and wondered if she'd gone too far. Her eyes focused on her needlework, but her fingers didn't move to sew another stitch.

Suddenly, she jumped, hearing a car horn.

That didn't happen often. No one had a reason to toot a horn around here. The speed limit was walking speed—about 10 miles per hour and a stop sign at every intersection. Then she scoffed. What was that man doing, out there on the street, making motions with his hands like that?

"Come on, Ella," he called, now coming across the bridge. "Let's see who can drive this thing."

"Why no," she murmured, but that shiny red convertible suddenly looked like a white horse. However, the driver was no knight in shining armor. Rather, he was an agitator, just like the insides of an old washing machine she used to have.

"Just come take a look," he challenged. Now, how was he going to take Daniel's advice if she didn't cooperate?

That man was going to have the entire community out watching if he didn't be quiet. With a sigh, she got up, dropped her sewing into the chair, and walked, just as briskly as he, out to the car. "It is beautiful," she admitted.

"And did you see me drive it?"

"I didn't look," she said.

"Come on, let's go for a ride."

"It's almost suppertime."

"We won't go off the premises," he promised.

She shook her head.

"Chicken!" he accused.

"Chicken?" she mumbled and stared at him. Why, he was talking like a high school boy, daring a girl to get in the car with him. Well, maybe a little drive.

She got in and he carefully maneuvered the car down to the stop sign, then turned and she turned her head when she saw a couple of women walking on the sidewalk. She didn't want to cause a scandal. Oh, no. Gloria and Irene saw her. Why, she'd be the talk of the community. Then he drove out in front of the building on the long stretch of road, then picked up speed after turning onto the back road, bordered by the trees going up the mountain.

She felt the warmth of the sun on her face and the softness of the wind in her hair. For an instant she felt young again—even daring, sort of like a high school girl. He even turned on the radio and for an instant she went back in time. Then before she knew it, the car stopped and she was back where they'd started.

"You could have parked back there in your space and I could have walked down."

"No, ma'am. A gentleman always sees a girl to her doorstep." He got out of the car, came around and held the door she'd already opened, and made a gallant bow.

She half expected him to make a snide remark, but when he straightened and his eyes met hers, she didn't see any mischief in them, but a look of a boy wanting approval.

"You *can* drive," she said. "That was nice. Thank you."

"You are most welcome, fair lady," he said and she wondered if he thought he was some kind of knight in shining armor.

Peppy chuckled all the way to his parking place. Yep, Daniel had hit this nail right on the head. At last Peppy found the way to deal with that woman. He couldn't win an argument with her. He'd just kill her with kindness!

Chapter 7

At the end of July, for several days, El Niño had a field day with the landscape. The clouds rolled in, bringing with it all the fury of a summer storm's lightning and thunder boomers, remained as a gully washer all the next day, and calmed down to a steady rain by Saturday. Kay spent the day cleaning her apartment. She wasn't sure she should even go to the Singles' meeting that night at church, but she'd promised to take a cake and Peg called, insisting she was stopping by and they'd ride together.

"This weather's depressing," Kay commented.

Peg wouldn't let her get by with that. "Weddings are depressing," she said, "when they're not your own. I've been there, remember?"

"I settled my single status long ago, Peg," Kay insisted.

"I know. But some things have to be taken to the Lord more than once."

And that was the discussion of the program that night. After they ate, Peg suggested the group talk about their singleness.

"Easy for you to say," a single mom said. "You're getting married—when is it, November?"

"Yes, but I've been single for ten years after my

boyfriend jilted me, leaving me feeling unwanted and thinking I'd never love again. My life was ruined. Now I can see that Tim would have been wrong for me. God brought me and James together, after we've had time to learn that marriage isn't just butterflies and bells and racing heartbeats."

Betty, in her thirties, responded with understanding. "I've felt the same," she admitted. "Every time I come to one of these meetings, I have to push back the thought that we're losers. I look around and see that the youngest here is in her mid-twenties. The younger ones are married or out on dates. It's not easy."

"Depends on where you are in your life," said Marge, a divorcee with two young children. "I stayed with my abusive husband because I thought I couldn't make it without a man. But I'm making it, with God's help, and we're a happier family than when we were afraid every time he sat down with a bottle, knowing where it was going to lead. Now I can be grateful that my former husband left us."

Susan agreed. "So many times I've cried out to God to send me a man, as if that's the answer to all our problems. Frankly, I joined the Singles' group, hoping I'd find a good Christian man to marry."

John could relate to that. "That was my reason too," he said. "After my wife died, and I had the total responsibility of my three children, I almost gave up at times, knowing it was a hardship on my parents, taking care of them while I worked. And it was hard on the children, not having a mom. I thought the answer to my problems was a woman to take all that work off my hands. I've learned the hard way, and now I'm able to teach it to my children, that our ultimate self-worth doesn't depend upon our relationship with the opposite sex, but upon our reliance on God. We're not better off without my wife and their mother, but I can honestly say we're closer to God and we've experienced His workings in wonderful ways."

James spoke then. "I guess my experience is a little different. I've taken a lot of pride in my singleness, as the Apostle Paul seemed to do. I've enjoyed living alone, having the freedom of a bachelor's life, feeling I could serve God better as a single man. I've felt I had a better acceptance of my status than the rest of you. I believe that might be what the Bible calls 'the pride that goes before a fall.'" He gestured toward Peg. "I fell!"

Everyone laughed, including Peg, who punched him on the arm and gave him a pretend mean look. His arm went around her waist and he added sincerely, with the look of love in his eyes, "I didn't even know I needed a wife. But the Lord has given me this love for her and it's hard to imagine going on without her."

Kay realized this was just what she needed. "I make jokes about always being a bridesmaid, never a bride. But the awareness of my single status is very real. And frankly, despite my resolve, I find myself looking at every single man, wondering, could he be the one?"

"The world seems to think we're supposed to be looking for a man," said Marge. "My family and fellow-workers are always asking who I'm going with, or telling me Mr. Right will come along. It's hard not to feel like a total failure by not being married."

"We all have our weaknesses," said John. "I have a fellow worker, a Christian, who has a problem with his temper. We talk about it. He prays about it, but it's something he knows he has to give to the Lord daily, and continue to control. We all have our weaknesses, but as a group, I think dealing with our singleness is our biggest challenge. Not just because of what we might want within ourselves, but because of what the world as a whole expects."

They all agreed. Peg closed the meeting with a verse of Scripture: "Seek first the kingdom of God and his righteousness."

Thank You, God, Kay could sincerely pray after returning to her apartment, *for the blessing of my singleness.* She felt confident in the fact that her sense of fulfillment depended, not upon a man, but upon her relationship with God.

Kay had mentioned to Ella that she'd seen Daniel and his fiancée at the bridal shop when she went there with Peg. Nothing was in the Sunday paper about the wedding. Ella decided to ask Peppy about it, when she got the chance.

Her chance came on Monday evening after supper when Peppy went out and began working in his flower bed. She'd seen when the maintenance crew brought the gardening tools, and when Peppy had brought several boxes of plants and set them on his patio earlier in the day.

Ella walked out to her own flower bed, feeling it was her duty to clear the air, just like that summer storm had done, and hoped her efforts wouldn't end up as devastated as the flower beds. "I just hate to see my little impatiens beheaded and strewn all over the back lawn," she said.

She knew he was pretending not to hear because she saw his nostrils tighten when he took that deep breath. But he just kept ignoring her and digging out the dead and wounded plants.

She walked over to the partition. "Beautiful evening," she said.

Peppy looked around suddenly. "I don't believe what?"

"What?"

He looked exasperated. "What did you say?"

"I said," she said louder, "it's a beautiful evening."

"Oh. I thought you said 'you don't believe me.'" He looked around as if he hadn't noticed the evening before. "It quit raining," he said and returned to digging holes in a row closest to his patio.

She walked right over and stood not two feet from him and spoke loudly, so there'd be no misunderstanding.

"I guess congratulations are in order."

He stood and shook the dirt off a root and threw the damaged plant aside. "For what?"

"Your new granddaughter-in-law."

He reached for the shovel. "When did this happen?"

"The end of July. Remember?"

He wondered to what lengths that woman would go just to talk to him. "Nobody told me anything about it," he said brusquely, driving the shovel into the dirt.

Ella began to smile. "Kay told me that you said Daniel was getting married and it was to be the wedding of the season."

Peppy stared at the dirt in front of him, with his foot pressed against the edge of the shovel. Daniel had implied that Kay didn't like him very much. This might explain it. She thought he was getting married. He couldn't image anyone not liking Daniel. "Kay misunderstood. Daniel was involved in the wedding of the season. But he was the coordinator—not the groom. After I retired, Daniel took over Precious Memories, the bridal shop. That was my business, you know."

Ella dared not let him see how pleased she was with that bit of information. But Kay did say Daniel might be engaged. "I would expect a man his age to be married."

Peppy kept digging out weeds and grass. "After Daniel did his stint in the military, serving in that Middle-East conflict, he came home to discover his girl had found someone else. He was in a slump for awhile, but he's adjusted. He has friends, but no serious attachments that I can see." He straightened out his back like he might be getting a kink in it. "Kay's a mighty pretty girl. Is she spoken for? Boyfriend or anything?"

"No, and believe me, you're too old for her."

"Hah! Not if I was about ten years younger—" he began.

"Ten years!" Ella repeated. Now it was her turn to say "Hah!" Ordinarily, she wouldn't stand and listen to such talk, but this was tickling her imagination. Daniel wasn't married—or engaged! "I would have thought the wedding business would be a woman's kind of work."

He scoffed, taking plants out of a cardboard box. "A consultant does more than sell wedding dresses. In fact, one could use several degrees in this kind of business. Daniel had his business degree before he went into the service. He helped at the store while getting his Master's in Counseling. It's not whether you're male or female but what's up here that counts," he insisted, pointing at his head. "Anyway, the three of us loved working together. Then Marybelle. . ."

He paused, stuck a plant in a hole he'd dug. Ella wasn't about to finish the sentence for him.

"She. . .died," he said finally. "That changed everything."

"You mean Daniel came out of his slump and you got in, just like those black-eyed Susans you just shoved in that hole?"

Ella watched his face turn red and he pushed the dirt around those roots like the plant was going to escape. Finally he said gruffly, "We're talking about Daniel here."

"It just seems like a woman's kind of work to me," she said.

"You don't take anybody's word for anything, do you, ma'am?"

Ella lifted her eyebrows, looking at him in amazement. "Why, you say Daniel's not married. You say he's not engaged. You say Kay misunderstood. You say he runs that wedding shop as good as any woman. You say you ran it better than a woman. Is there some reason I shouldn't believe you? Are you trying to convince me of something?"

When he stood, brushed the dirt off his gloves, took them off and tossed them down on the ground, Ella scooted around the partition and returned to her apartment. *That man is not hard of hearing,* she told herself. *I know he heard every word I said out there.*

It took Peppy nearly twenty-four hours before he remembered that Daniel said kindness to an argumentative woman would render her speechless. The "red convertible venture" had worked. What could he try this time? Yes, he had it! All the way downtown and back, he chuckled. He felt a joy inside he hadn't felt in a long time, putting something over on that woman and she didn't even know it. And she thought she was so smart.

With a twinkle in his eye and a grin he couldn't keep from spreading beneath his mustache, he knocked on Ella's back door after supper. Disappointment washed over him when she didn't respond. Well, he would just go ahead and begin his little chore.

Over an hour later she came out and was visibly shocked to see that he was almost finished with replacing the battered impatiens with new ones. "I wouldn't expect you to do that," she said, amazed.

No, she wouldn't! he thought to himself triumphantly, trying to appear contrite. "I hope you don't mind, but you didn't answer your door, so I thought I'd just go ahead and replant your flower bed."

Now what was he up to? she wondered, looking askance at him, but he just kept working that bed. Then he said, "There're some Precious Memories albums I'd like you to see. They're right inside on the coffee table if you'd like to have a look."

Well, it was still daylight, and he was on his knees in the flower bed, and she didn't see anyone out at the moment who might spread gossip about her going into a single man's apartment. She didn't want him to think she was a prude or afraid of him, but neither did she care to be chased around a coffee table, especially not by a man with dirty hands—and who knew what this man had on his mind? She went inside, but kept her eyes on him, in case he made a wrong move.

However, he didn't get up to go wash his hands until after she came out and went over to her patio and sat down. The pictures showed Peppy with brides, some with him wearing a chef's hat. His wife, according to the names beneath the pictures, was all smiles and looking at Peppy like she could burst with pride. It took a good-hearted man to get a woman to look at him like that. Maybe he was different when he was younger.

It kind of brought back memories, some she'd put out of her mind, about her and her husband Mitch. She didn't even realize she was staring off into space, into a bygone era, until Peppy pulled up a chair and was sitting right next to her. "What are you thinking about, Miss Ella?"

"I'm thinking," she said distantly, slowly returning to the present, "about weddings."

"Well, I hope so," he replied. "That's what these pictures are all about."

"I mean. . .close weddings."

"Huh?" he snorted and drew back, his eyes wide, ready to jump up and run. Maybe he'd overdone this kindness thing.

Ella managed her most innocent smile. "I have this beautiful grandniece, as you know."

"Kay's getting married?"

"Of course. Someday the right man will come along and she'll fall head over heels in love."

"I'm surprised that hasn't happened already," Peppy said.

"Kay had to mature very early. You see, she had a lot family troubles during the years most young people are dating and having fun. She lost her parents, then came to live with me. She was so grateful that I sent her to college, she just took over most of the household chores and worked hard at her studies. By the time I sold the house and moved here, she got her own apartment, but all the men her age had married or were only friends."

Peppy cleared his throat, as if stepping in where angels fear to tread. "Would you, um, consider my Daniel for your Kay?"

To his surprise, she didn't fly off the handle. She

nodded slowly. "I'll need to know more about him, but from what I see, I'd say he's a likely prospect. But right now, they seem to have this tension between them."

Both sat silent for a moment. The summer sun sank low behind the mountains, painting the sky with a rosy glow. A bird took flight from the clump of trees out by the creek. The sky would soon turn gray. This was much more important than whether or not he and Miss Ella got along.

"This reminds me of ol' Jack," Peppy said quietly, still contemplative. "You know that two-foot-long catfish out back in that pond? You throw bread pieces his way and he swims around slowly, checking out the situation. Then suddenly, with mouth wide open, he lunges and gulps down those tasty morsels like they're a gourmet meal."

Ella pretended such had never entered her mind, but gloated inwardly as he began to give words to the thoughts coming on in his head like somebody had flipped a light switch.

"My Danny boy's just swimming around right now. A lot like ol' Jack. But Miss Ella," he added, with twinkling eyes and a broad smile, "that Miss Kay is gourmet loaf." Then he twirled his mustache and nodded vigorously. "You just go right ahead and cast your bread upon the waters."

Chapter 8

Dinner!

That was Peppy's ploy to get Kay and Daniel together. Carefully-laid plans were set into motion. He went to Kay's office. "You know your aunt and I haven't been getting along like two peas in a pod," he said.

"I've suspected it," Kay replied with a knowing smile.

"Well, I admit, I've complained a little—sort of down on the world. But I'm trying to make amends. I asked her over for a home-cooked real Italian dinner."

"How sweet," Kay said.

"Whoa! Not to hear Miss Ella tell it. She says she's not the kind of woman who goes alone to a man's apartment, and that just made matters worse. Well, I wonder, Miss Kay, since you've been so nice to me, if you'd come. Maybe that will prove to her I don't have ulterior motives. I really do want to make up for being such a grouch. And it might just give you and me a chance to talk about how I might fit in better at the Center."

"You really don't need to go to any trouble, Peppy—" she began.

"Compared with what I've done in the past, this little dinner is, so to speak, a piece of cake." He leaned forward, his hands propped on the edge of the desk.

"We start with stuffed mushrooms. Followed by my famous chicken cacciatore. Mmmm. Magnifico!" He lifted his fingers to his lips and kissed them. "Prosciutto and melon, crusty garlic bread of course, and for dessert, strawberry slush."

Kay fell back against her chair. "I gained ten pounds just listening to that."

"No, no. I know how to cut calories." He straightened and patted his stomach, not bad for a large man, even though he was obviously holding it in.

She thought too, now with Daniel married, Peppy might be trying to form relationships with others. That was good. "If you're sure. . ."

His smile lit up his face and his brown eyes sparkled. "I'm positive."

"What should I do?" Ella asked later, when he told her the bait was on the hook.

"You'll get your chance another time," he said. "We have to do a little casting and sometimes it takes a while before you get a bite and reel them in. It's best if we let them think we need them to help you and me get along."

"That shouldn't be difficult," she said and he gave her a quick look.

Remember kindness, he reminded himself. *I'm doing this for Daniel.*

The day of the dinner, Ella heard him singing, and the loudest was the repetition of "O, Solo Meo." The aroma of something delicious floated out Peppy's back door and invaded Ella's apartment; her stomach growled its eagerness.

Peppy said it wouldn't be dressy, but to show she was making an effort, Ella had her hair done that day and it looked right pretty with those soft white waves. She wore a little makeup, a light blue dress, and one-inch navy pumps. Not to overdo, she clipped on small pearl earrings.

She arrived a little early, just to make sure everything was going as scheduled and to help if needed. When she knocked, he called, "Come in."

Oh my, it looked as good as it smelled. Although the sun hadn't set, the room was lighted by the soft glow of candles. He'd moved his kitchen table into the living room and covered it with a peach-covered tablecloth, matching the cloth napkins. A fresh floral arrangement sat in the center, flanked by two long-stemmed peach candles in crystal holders. The light danced and reflected in each tiny prism of the crystal goblets. Tiny pastel flowers with pale green leaves rimmed the china plates.

Ella looked up as Peppy came to the kitchen doorway. Over his clothes, he wore a big red apron bearing the words "Super Chef." "Looks good and smells good," she said, a mite self-conscious, not having expected it to be so lovely and so formal.

"Think it'll be good, huh?" he challenged with a satisfied smile.

"Well," Ella scoffed, turning toward the entertainment center, "proof of the pudding is in the eating." She surveyed the videos behind the glass doors. "I've never seen a man who could cook like a woman. Most open a couple of cans, throw them on the table, and say they cooked."

"You wouldn't believe the compliments I've had," he growled.

"Nope," she said. "I wouldn't. Unless they were too scared to tell you the truth. You have an awful temper, you know. Reminds me of my Uncle Rudy. He used to storm around making everybody quiver and he even slapped his wife around a time or two."

"I'd never do that," Peppy was quick to say. "I believe in treating a woman kind and gentle. They're the weaker sex, you know."

Ella cut her eyes around at him then, and this time he was shaking, trying to hold back his laughter. Then he couldn't and he guffawed. "Gotcha that time!"

"Yeah," Ella acknowledged and turned away, not wanting him to see how pleased she was. This was the first time she'd seen him laugh since he moved to the Center. Matter of fact, she didn't remember hearing a man laugh like that since Mitch—so many years ago. It was good. Yes, good to laugh. Good to hear it. She reached for the tissue she'd slipped in the side pocket of her dress and wiped her eyes.

"What's the matter? You got allergies or something?"

"Onions," she said.

"Younguns?" he blared. "You talking about our Kay and Daniel?"

That dried her eyes! "Onions," she said louder. "You did put onions in the cacciatore, didn't you?"

"Sure. You don't like onions?"

"I love 'em," she said. "If they're cooked good."

"They will be," he promised. "Let's just hope they're not overcooked." He turned back into the kitchen just as his front doorbell rang. "Get that please?" he asked.

As expected, it was Kay, looking beautiful with her shiny curly hair down around her shoulders. She'd taken off the jacket of her sleeveless dress and was especially beautiful in the candlelight. She was as impressed with the room as Ella and lavished great praise upon Peppy. "Are you expecting a fourth person?"

"I'm sorry, I probably should have told you. But I've had Daniel drive out here several times bringing items that I forgot to order and that you don't have in the store here. So, out of courtesy, I asked him to join us, and by George, if he didn't say he would." Just then, Daniel walked up to the glass doors. Ella thought he looked mighty fine in loafers, dockers, and knit shirt.

Daniel greeted them all warmly. He and Peppy embraced. Kay spoke politely, but her thoughts were running rampant. *Where is his wife? Why aren't they on their honeymoon?* But that was not her business. She walked over to the glass doors and looked toward the road. Maybe the new wife was bringing a gift for Peppy and was coming in a different car. But there were four places at the table. She was not going to be a fifth wheel —nor was she going to spend the evening sitting across the table from a married man, who had recently asked her out, even if she offended Peppy and Aunt Ella and they both decided to move away from the Center!

Just then, Daniel came up beside her. "Could we step outside a moment, please?" he asked.

Kay was glad to do that. She needed a breath of fresh air. They walked across the patio and stood in front of the flower bed. "Look, I'm sorry about this," he apologized. "I could see you were shocked when I came in. Things like this can be embarrassing. I can make an excuse and get out of here."

Kay couldn't see that would solve anything. His leaving wouldn't erase the fact that four of them were here and expected to have dinner. This was his grandfather's home now, and if anyone were to leave, it should be her. "Your grandfather has obviously gone to a great deal of trouble. If either of us leave, it could cause worse tension between him and Ella." She would make her own excuse, as soon as possible after eating—if she could get through the meal.

"Soup's on," Peppy called, clanging a spoon against a pan.

They went inside. Peppy asked the women to be seated and Daniel to bring the plates. He dished the food onto the plates, and Daniel brought them to the table. When the men sat down, Peppy asked Daniel to say grace.

Kay felt it was a beautiful prayer, but she couldn't concentrate on it. She was silently asking God to help her—but was uncertain what He should help her with. After the "Amen" however, she could not bring herself to look across at Daniel.

They all began to eat. She could truly compliment

Peppy on the food. "It's wonderful," she exclaimed, looking at Aunt Ella for confirmation. Aunt Ella's expression gave it to her.

"He used to run a restaurant," Daniel said.

"Another of my specialties," Peppy said, and Ella had to cough to keep from choking, "is southern-fried catfish."

"Now, you're not going to try and catch Ol' Jack?" Ella feigned consternation.

"Never! This place would rather get rid of me than their mascot, Ol' Jack." He chuckled then and his large frame began to shake.

Daniel and Kay exchanged glances then, as if to say they didn't know what was so funny about that, but each laughed politely.

After they'd stuffed themselves with the fabulous meal and the mouth-watering dessert, Peppy offered after-dinner coffee and invited Kay to sit on the couch and look at his albums.

"I'll pour," Daniel offered.

"I couldn't hold another thing," Kay said and continued to stand. Aunt Ella moved over to the recliner and took the coffee Daniel brought. He set Peppy's on the coffee table, then brought his own to the table and pulled a straight chair around.

Kay moved toward Peppy, ready to thank him, make an excuse, and leave. He seemed to know that and looked up with a wounded puppy look. "You might enjoy looking at these," Peppy said. "They're all about Precious Memories, the store I used to own."

"You owned Precious Memories?"

"Until a couple of years ago. I sold it—"

"I was in there a few days ago," she decided suddenly to say. Nothing had been mentioned about Daniel and his wife. In fact, Daniel had hardly spoken during the entire dinner. Her own conversation hadn't been very stimulating. In the interest of the missing wife, someone should say something! She looked at Daniel then. "Your fiancée is very pretty."

He sputtered and held the cup out to balance it. "Fiancée?"

Did he think she didn't know? "Well, I suppose by now she's your bride."

"This is interesting," he said. "Could you tell me her name? I'd like to meet her."

"Didn't you. . .aren't you. . .I mean. . .did you break up?"

He shook his head and held his arms out, as if dumbfounded. "There's nothing to break."

By then, Peppy's chuckle had become a full-blown laugh. "You're going to break that cup and saucer if you don't quit flailing it around like that. They thought you were getting married," he said, then explained to Kay. "I sold the business to Daniel—for a whole dollar. Now, he owns the place. I told Miss Ella. She didn't tell you?"

"Must have slipped my mind," Ella said.

Kay glared at Ella but tried not to appear mortified.

"No wonder the tension in here was thick enough to cut with a knife," Peppy said. "I thought maybe my defroster was messing up." He laughed. "So, you thought he was getting married, and so you turned a cold shoulder to him, and he thought you weren't interested."

Then Ella took her turn. "So that's why you two have been acting like the other one had some kind of communicable disease?"

Kay was wondering how she might apologize to Daniel. She looked at him, but he set his cup on the table, looking thoughtful. Then he looked over at her. "You said you were in the shop?"

She nodded, hoping to gracefully get out of this mess.

"Then," he said stiffly. "You're getting married?"

"Me?" She pointed to herself. "No! My friend Peg is." Then she smiled. "Now *you're* assuming things."

He smiled back, that dazzling, million-dollar smile, and little flecks of gold glinted in his dark eyes. Kay felt warmth flooding to her face.

Aunt Ella rose to the occasion. "Well, Kay," she said. "Maybe you could find something there that you think Peg might like."

Still speechless, Kay dropped onto the sofa. Ella coughed lightly. Daniel looked at her. He noticed she was tapping her cup with a finger.

Realization dawned. He went into the kitchen, poured a cup of coffee for Kay, and set it in front of her on the coffee table. Her eyes didn't quite meet his, but she said, "Thank you."

Daniel sat down again. He and Ella exchanged warm smiles.

Chapter 9

Kay waited until after her first dinner date with Daniel to share the news with Peg. "We had a great time, Peg," Kay said and laughed. "It was really funny after we recovered from all the misunderstandings, wrong assumptions, and judgmental attitudes." She admitted, "Mine was the worst!"

"You and Daniel clicked, huh?" Peg said with a big smile.

Kay's face lit up. "We both admitted we liked each other right away, but that remark Peppy made about the wedding of the season at the end of July got us off to a wrong start."

"Isn't it great how God works," Peg said. "You were tempted to go out with him, even when you thought he was engaged. But you said no, and now look. Oh, Kay. He could really be the one for you."

Kay censured the idea. "It's too soon to be thinking like that, Peg."

Peg was not to be put off. "You know my brother Bill? He met Sarah and right away knew she was the mate God had chosen for him. They were married three months later. Now, six years and three children later, they're still in love."

"I know God can work that fast, but I don't know if

He has revealed anything like that to Daniel. I am not making any more assumptions," she asserted staunchly. "I'm taking this slow and easy. I'm not rushing into anything."

"Things aren't moving fast enough to suit me," Peppy said to Ella. "Daniel says they're seeing each other as good friends, going out with their singles' group and with friends."

"We got them together," Ella said. "Now they have to move at their own pace."

"Reminds me of a song," Peppy said and he began to sing, "On top of Ol' Smoky, all covered with snow. I lost my true lover, from courtin' too slow."

"You need to be in the chorus," she said.

"That's another subject," he snapped. "My concern is Daniel and Kay. So we just sit back and hope?" he asked bluntly.

"Oh, not at all," Ella contradicted. "We must have faith in them. And faith calls for action. Go get those albums. Our next move—in secret of course—is to plan their wedding."

Peppy was so dumbfounded, he obeyed. But he still couldn't believe it even after they were settled on her couch and the albums and brochures spread out on her coffee table. "You're really serious," he said.

"Of course."

Peppy sighed. "I've never seen a girl I thought would be more perfect for Daniel. But, I haven't planned a wedding since. . ." His voice trailed off, then he said it. "Since Marybelle died."

Ella lifted her chin and her level gaze assailed him. "At least you said her name without choking up."

"It's been hard accepting the way things turned out. In earlier days I worried about things like losing a job, my children, my hair, and even an argument." He laughed uncomfortably. He seemed to lose enough of those with Ella. Then the awful pain tightened his throat. "But I never suspected I'd lose my wife. Wives are not supposed to die before their husbands."

"A man's not supposed to cry either," Ella chided.

"I'm not crying."

"No, and God didn't make little green apples."

His blurry eyes began to get dry and hot. *Remember kindness,* he reminded himself. *That's the only way to deal with a woman like her.*

"How long ago you lost your husband?" he asked.

"Fifteen years," she said, folding her hands on the notes she'd been writing about the wedding. "I don't suppose there's a better man on earth than he was."

"Are you saying I'm not a good man? Is that what you're getting at?"

She looked at him then, with her sky blue eyes so clear it seemed that nothing disturbed them. That disturbed him!

"Why, I wasn't even thinking about you," she said quietly. "You shouldn't be so sensitive."

While he quietly fumed, Ella said gently, "I've lived a long, good life. A life of service to the Lord and to

235

others on the mission field in Korea. I had a wonderful husband, a good marriage. Oh, we had our ups and downs, our share of illnesses, and failures. But all in all, I've been blessed. And now, I shouldn't go around blaming the Lord because He doesn't give me heaven on earth. This is a wonderful place to live out my last years and I can't complain."

Peppy knew she was trying to teach him something about acceptance, but he wondered if she'd really had as good a life as he. Maybe she hadn't had as much to miss as he did. "Did you have children?" he asked.

Ella gazed off in the distance, wondering how much of her life to share with him. She didn't want to be the teary one.

Peppy thought she wasn't going to answer. Then she said softly, "I had several hundred children."

Peppy stared, questioningly.

"Mitch and I didn't rear any children of our own. But the good Lord knew what He was doing. When I've seen other parents, so busy with their little ones, and all the time and attention that demands, I feel that God blessed me with time to concentrate on their little hearts and minds. We started schools, planned lessons, planted seeds, and there's been a great harvest in Korea."

"Do you hear from them now?"

"Oh, yes. I get birthday cards, Christmas cards," she smiled. "And even Mother's Day cards."

"Then you don't really know, or can't understand how I can't manage to live with my own family, my own flesh and blood. I must seem like a heathen to you. You lived with hundreds of children. You could probably live with any of them now."

She smiled. "Yes, I believe I could go and live with any of those families and be well-cared for and respected. But I understand about families. I have been a child. I have been a teenager and I gave my parents the fits."

"Noooo," he said, but she saw his grin.

Ella nodded. "Why, in high school I wanted to run off and get married to this boy who was the cat's meow. Then, a little later, I was running from God, running from His call to the mission field. I wouldn't even go to church and I tried a few things I shouldn't have. I don't know how my parents put up with me. You see, it's easier to deal with those who are not our closest loves. Our emotions get in the way. Our fears get in the way. I wish my mother were alive so I could tell her all the things I love and admire about her. But if she were alive, I'd be just like others I see—exasperated with her quirks, aware of all the little faults and weaknesses, resentful if she mentioned mine. That just seems to be the nature of us human beings. So, no, being on the mission field is easier than being a Christian example to your own family. It's not a lack of love on your part or your son's part. It's just that roles switch and that's as much a transition as a teenager becoming independent. You were the authority figure, and now it's changed. They are the authority figures. It's not easy to go backwards, to being dependent— to have your child tell you what to do, instead of your telling them. And it's not easy for them either."

"How did you get so wise?" he asked.

"By being on the outside, looking in," she said. "When a child was hurt on the playground, I could be objective and do what I was supposed to do, while a mother would be hysterical, unable to do anything but cry and ask questions that couldn't be answered. Oh, I cared, but with a difference. It takes all kinds. In a way, it's harder being on the outside, but it's so needed to have an objective viewer, an objective teacher."

"I've never seen anybody so content as you," he said, wonderingly.

Ella stared down at her hands. "Oh, I have my moments," she admitted solemnly, as her own pain nudged at her and forced its way into the forefront. "You talked about statistics," she said, "and about wives living longer than their husbands. Well, according to statistics, children are supposed to outlive their parents. But our lives are not governed by whomever looks at charts and puts down figures."

Peppy had the feeling he'd rather deal with her chiding rather than this seriousness. But she wasn't looking at him now, just out at the mountains as if he weren't there. She said quietly, "My baby never even got to take one breath of air."

She looked as if she wasn't taking in any air just then, staring out distantly. Peppy wasn't sure he could speak. Finally, he said softly, "Your. . .baby?"

A deep breath trembled through her body. Moving the album over to him, she sat straight and elegant. "The happiest time of my life was when I had a child growing inside me. But that little baby—she was stillborn—never had a chance." Her lips trembled and her eyes clouded. "I never even got to hold her in my arms."

By the time Peppy could mumble, "I'm sorry," she had stood, indicating he should leave. He said a quick, "Good night," and left the apartment. At least he'd had his Marybelle for over four decades and raised three children and several grandchildren. Miss Ella didn't even get to hold her own live baby for one instant.

Now, he asked himself, *how am I supposed to grieve without feeling guilty?*

Chapter 10

The month of September proved to be a cooling time, not only of the weather but of Peppy and Ella's attempts at getting the young couple together. They were positive that would happen and planning the wedding zoomed to the top of their priority list. Two or three nights a week they met at Ella's and became engrossed in that wonderful dream. But for the time being they had given up trying to put their dreams into action.

The first three weeks of October were spectacularly beautiful, as the leaves were changing and the mountains were arrayed in glorious color. The flower beds boasted gold, red, orange, yellow, and burgundy fall asters, daisies, mums, and marigolds, while the mountainsides changed daily from a lush green to varying shades of gold, yellow, brown, red, and orange.

"Daniel just called," Peppy said excitely one glorious afternoon. "He wants the four of us to drive up on the Parkway to look at the leaves."

A short while later, Ella and Kay climbed into the back seat of the little red convertible. Daniel drove, with Peppy beside him and with the top down they began the ascent up the Parkway, letting their hair fly free in the wind, stopping at lookouts to view the changing leaves for miles and miles.

The four of us together like this seems so right, Ella was thinking. *I just know it is.*

In mid-October, the weather forecast was for chilly days and overnight temperatures were to drop below zero. Bulbs were dug up and potted plants taken to the greenhouse. Peppy volunteered to oversee the fall and winter care of the plants. Baskets hung from the ceiling, others were placed on tables, and exotic plants were put in special places.

The weather played trick-or-treat during the last week of October.

Peppy got his flu shot.

Then he got the flu.

That hung on for several days and was followed by a cold and sore throat. He wondered if God were punishing him since he hadn't joined the chorus. Now, he couldn't if he wanted to. The weather was cold, messy, rainy and all he felt like doing was staying in his own bed, although he could have gone to the Health Care Unit.

Daniel stayed with him and slept on the couch during the second week of his illness. Peppy felt a little better when a doctor made a "house-call." He checked him out several times. A nurse came twice a day when he had a fever, and once a day after it receded.

After his temperature returned to normal, it seemed half the Center came to see him, male and female, residents and employees. He'd never known so many people to show concern, not even at church.

"Am I dying?" he asked Daniel.

"No, they just care about you."

"Care? If I don't die of natural causes, that woman next door is going to drown me with homemade chicken noodle soup she brings everyday."

"I notice you eat it," Daniel accused.

Peppy had to admit it was right good. He really did appreciate the concern even though he suspected his doorway might begin to sway from all the people standing against it, talking to him, encouraging him. Kay came every day after she got off work. Ella and Kay insisted he had to be well for the Duck Dinner at the end of November.

"I don't like duck the way most people cook it. Too greasy," he growled.

"They don't serve duck," Ella replied, but aggravated him by not telling why it was called a Duck Dinner. Obviously, a conspiracy was going on, because Kay said he had to get well and find out for himself.

Finally, he threw back the covers, proclaiming, "The only way I'm going to get any peace is to get out of bed. These people won't let me be."

Then he discovered what the Duck Dinner was all about!

"It's the event of the year," he was told. "Every-body attends. Although some of the residents go to Florida for the winter, they stay or come back for the Duck Dinner."

Several stories were bandied about on how it got it's name. It seemed the Center wanted a formal dinner to celebrate and honor all who had turned ninety the previous year. Some wanted to call the occasion "Order of the Garter." Another who had been in World War II wanted to give it a military term, "Ruptured Duck." His friend agreed, saying it could have a double meaning since so many mallards spent their summers on the pond and lake. They finally decided on "Order of the Duck" and it was eventually shortened to "Duck Dinner." Those who reached one-hundred-years-old became a member of the Supreme Order of the Duck.

"It's a little . . ." He paused and decided not to say "funny" to Ella. He said, "Bizarre," instead.

"You won't think so when you get there," Ella assured him. "Now, wear the finest outfit you have. Oh, by the way, I'd like to ask a favor."

Seeing that she really was reluctant to ask, he encouraged, "I won't do worse than say no."

She explained that, although there was no real contest with prizes, there was competition with table decorations. Usually, groups were formed, by halls or friends and they tried to outdo each other. "I thought maybe," she said reluctantly, "with your creativity and expertise in wedding planning, you might give me a few suggestions."

"Who's going to be at your table?"

"So far, June and Pansy."

He wasn't giving an inch and reveled in her discomfort. "Then what would that do to my table?

Those ladies would never forgive me if my table looked better."

"Well, I suppose, if you insist, you could join us at our table. After all, you do live on our hall. And you could ask a couple of men to join us if that would make you feel better."

"Are you asking me for a date, Miss Ella?"

"Oh, my goodness gracious no. Some do, though."

He looked at the floor so long, Ella wished for a hole, so she could sink into it. "It was just a thought," she said. "I'm just trying to be neighborly."

He glanced up at her, his lips turned down in a scowl. "I'm really not up to decorating two tables that are going to compete with each other, so okay."

He turned away as her face lit up. Glancing over his shoulder just before walking away, he said gruffly, "I knew I'd have to pay, one way or another, for all that chicken soup."

The gala event began with a reception at which residents viewed the tables decorated with ducks, flowers, autumn leaves, and fruit. A pyramid made with birthday cards from foreign countries served as a centerpiece for one table. Another used a newborn baby doll and another displayed an elaborate wooden carving of father time with a clock as his chest.

Peppy's table made a bold statement, expressing the personality and creativity of Peppino Gallo. The tablecloth was deep blue lame that shimmered like moving water in the flickering candlelight. He had centered a small battery-operated fountain, with water falling down the rocks and forming a pool at the bottom. Peppy placed one miniature mother duck, followed by nine baby ducks that appeared to swim around in the pool of water. On the table, he placed a miniature couple with the man holding over their heads a bright, multi-colored paper umbrella. Alternating at each place was a male, then female figure, holding its own umbrella representing the fall colors: red, yellow, orange, green, brown, and gold.

"So bold, yet elegant," Ella complimented. She thought it reflected Peppy's personality and creativity, as had the residents' flower beds. And tonight, with the aura of glamour and excitement all around, she allowed no adverse thoughts but admitted that he sure looked spiffy in that white long-tailed tux, frilled white shirt with the ruffles trimmed in black, and a white bow tie. My goodness, that night, Colonel Sanders and his chicken dinners couldn't hold a candle to Peppy Gallo and his duck delights.

Peppy didn't mind sitting beside Ella. She was a lovely lady with her wavy white hair, those clear blue eyes, smooth skin, makeup that enhanced her beautiful face. Simple, but exceptional, was her soft mauve gown with it's high neck, long sleeves, straight cut. It flattered her elegant frame and the split at the side of the dress, reaching to above one knee, could give the impression she was a model instead of a missionary. Her mauve high heels glittered, as did the diamond and ruby rhinestone necklace and earrings. Her personality sparkled just as bright as she laughed delightedly with her friends, receiving as many compliments on her looks as Peppy did on the table.

Closed-circuit TV was set up in the Assembly Room for the spillover from the dining room so residents could see the ceremonies and entertainment of a string quartet. The evening was perfect, from the before-dinner music played by a resident, a former concert pianist, to the awarding of certificates and ceramic duck pendants to nonagenarians. The meal was excellent, from the entree of lamb to the grand finale of raspberry mango cheesecake and classical music recordings after the festivities ended. Reluctant to leave, everyone socialized, commented, and complimented.

There was all the glitter and glamour of a night at the Oscars' for actors. Those nominated for this award, however, were ninety-year-olds and they sat at a special table. For the one-hundred-year-olds, it was like being inducted into the hall of fame. For those few hours, once a year, rather than thinking back to younger years, each resident looked forward to reaching that magic number of ninety, and being revered at the century mark.

"I have only one regret," Ella voiced as the six of them later headed for their apartments. "I wish Daniel had been here to see Kay."

They all nodded and agreed how lovely she had looked, and how professional her welcome was to all the guests. She had worn a short black dress with thin spaghetti straps. Her glorious mane of hair was pulled back on one side, fastened with a pearl clip, and framed her face on the other side. Her pearl tear-drop earrings set her face off perfectly.

"I'm more determined than ever," Peppy exclaimed, "that my grandson fall in love with that beautiful girl."

Daniel had felt all along that he could fall in love with Kay. But the more he got to know her, the more convinced he became. He attended Peg's wedding, not only as coordinator, but as a guest, having become friends with Kay's friends and an active participant in their singles' activities.

Peg was a beautiful bride, but Daniel couldn't take his eyes off Kay. As she walked down the aisle, looking so lovely in the short black dress, then stood at the front of the church, he knew he wanted her to be his wife. When the minister asked James, "Do you take this woman. . .to have and to hold. . .to love and to cherish," Daniel whispered within himself, *I do.*

Chapter 11

Conversation about the Duck Dinner had barely wound down when December parties began to roll and it was hard to find time for anything else.

During the first week of December a tremendous tree was set up in the middle of the dining room. Decorations included ornaments that residents had given or made over the years. Then new ones were brought each year. They strung cranberries and popcorn, drank eggnog, and enjoyed the Christmas spirit. After they decorated they got in a circle around the wall of the dining room and sang "Silent Night."

The entire month was one big celebration. Various outside groups came to perform or sing. The employees and administrators gave parties and a festive brunch for the residents. Various halls, lodges, and condos had their own group parties in their lounge areas. There were parties every few days. Residents trimmed their own trees, some of them donated by businesses. At tree trimmings there were hot cocoa, cookies, and singing.

The Men's Club presented a special Christmas program and invited everyone. Churches came with their musicals and programs. Caroling groups came, and to Ella's and Peppy's delight, Daniel brought a caroling group.

Instead of employees and residents exchanging presents, they pooled their money and donated it to a local charity.

The Christmas Eve program was traditional, beginning with oyster stew and salad, then a Christian service with a special speaker and music.

On the twenty-first, Peppy went to be with his family over the week of Christmas and into the New Year. The whole family would be there over a part of the holidays.

When Peppy returned on a cold, icy January day, he felt like he was back home and he realized he was adjusting. He'd enjoyed his family and they all had made him the center of attention; he bounced the smallest grandchildren on his knees and even joined in singing with the family. But as he stepped into his apartment, he had a feeling of having come home. It was good. His own place. And he'd made friends here. There was so much to do, he'd never be able to do it all. And there was one bit of news he was eager to share with Ella.

On the day of his return, everyone greeted him like he was a long, lost friend. He didn't see Ella. The next day she wasn't in the dining room. After lunch, he knocked on her door but didn't get an answer. He tried the knob and the door was locked. He called more loudly and pressed his ear against the door to determine if she had the TV on and maybe couldn't hear him.

He went to his own apartment and banged on the bedroom wall and called her name, but still no answer. He could have used the phone but by now he needed to see Miss Kay in person.

"Aunt Ella has bronchitis," Kay told him. "It's pretty bad and she's in the Health Care Unit."

It was the worst case she'd ever had. After several days of rest and medication having no positive effect, she'd been taken to the Health Care Unit.

The winter sun came out and poured out its golden sunshine on the hills and mountains. Peppy bundled up and went out to feed Ol' Jack and wondered how his Daniel and Ella's Kay would ever fall in love without them to help prod them and keep them together. He threw bread on the surface of the water, where it reflected the sun like gold, and he was reminded that all that glitters is not truly gold. Even Ol' Jack was sluggish and didn't seem to care whether or not he ate. Peppy knew how he felt, but whether fish or human, one had to keep up his strength.

He went to see her and didn't like the way she lay there, so helpless, so pale, with her eyes shut. He saw others, some confined to beds, some to padded recliners, some who had lost all their memory, and he wondered if they wouldn't like to have their memories, even painful ones. Some walked the halls with crutches, others with walkers.

He'd been told it was best he didn't go in while she was still feverish. He looked at their wedding plans for the young couple but it wasn't the same without her to challenge him. It was then he realized all her chiding hadn't been that at all—it had been challenging. And she was probably smart enough to have done it all intentionally. Okay, so she'd forced him out of his doldrums, made him face facts, made him count his blessings, gave him a reason to get up in the morning and that was to plan a wedding for his grandson. Then, she up and got sick! *Why?* His eyes lifted toward heaven. *Seems I've been down this road before, Lord.*

Daniel had considered proposing to Kay after the holidays, but that was put on the back burner while Ella was so ill. He called daily and spent many evenings with Kay at Ella's beside.

They were all concerned and many prayers were being said. Ella's condition was grave. She'd seem to improve, then she'd get sick again. Nothing would stay in her stomach and she had to be fed intravenously. Her fever went up and down like it was riding on a roller coaster.

Peppy stopped by Kay's office at least once a day, sometimes more. When Kay said Ella had lost about ten pounds, Peppy got really scared. She hadn't had any to spare in the first place.

He stayed busy in the greenhouse, ate all his meals in the dining room, joined the Men's Club, went to all the Bible studies and requested prayer for Ella, and decided to donate an hour a day in the Health Care Unit.

He began to appreciate his own health, seeing the sick and helpless. He couldn't go into Ella's room, but he could see her from the doorway, looking as pale as the sheets, and he couldn't even tell she was breathing.

It wasn't until after Valentine's Day—the loneliest day of the year for all the residents who had lost their sweethearts—that Kay called and said he could see Ella for a few minutes.

He hurried down to the Health Care Unit. Kay was with her and somebody had fixed her hair and put on some makeup but she still looked peaked. Her eyes didn't sparkle and they didn't even seen to focus well. She was propped up on pillows and wore a beautiful white silk bed jacket, but she looked frail. She tried to talk but no sound came, so Peppy did the talking, while she lay her head back with her eyes closed. He told her about his family over the holidays, emphasizing that Daniel had brought Kay to a family dinner and a party. He thought a faint smile hovered about Ella's lips.

When Kay said he'd have to leave, Ella opened her eyes and her mouth, but no sound came out, so she just nodded as she closed her eyes.

That night her fever returned and it took another day before it normalized. She was able to whisper a few words this time when he went to see her. "Maybe, after all these years, I'm going to see my little girl. I don't know if she will look like a baby, or be all grown up, but I think God will play reruns for me and let me see every second of her life."

Peppy reached for her hand. It felt thin and cold. "Don't give up," he said. "Isn't that what you tell people like me?"

"Yes, but," she began and had to turn her head and cough. "This keeps coming back. But I want you to go ahead with our plans."

"As soon as you're up and around," he replied, but the next day she'd had a relapse.

Peppy didn't know what else to do. He went to the chapel.

"Lord," he prayed. *"I don't know if this means any-thing, but if You let her live, I'll use this rough ol' voice for Your glory instead of growling at Miss Ella all the time. I promise. I'll even join the chorus. I know we can't make bar-gains with You—but God, I'd just be so grateful if You'd heal Miss Ella."*

Spring came. Ella's health returned and Peppy joined the chorus.

Yellow sunshine warmed the earth, tender shoots made their appearance, tiny buds appeared on trees, tender green leaves sprouted, grass became a velvet car-pet, birds sang, squirrels darted about, and the hearts of the residents turned to their most tender project—the spring Thrift Sale. Every year, they made thousands of dollars that they donated to the nearby community children's projects.

The first unseasonably warm day arrived. Ella decided to take a walk outside for the first time in months. Peppy went with her. When they stopped at the pond and threw bread to Ol' Jack, he asked if she felt up to getting back to their wedding plans.

"Oh, yes. That's my top priority now," she said. "I would like to hold a little great-great niece or nephew in my arms—one that is somehow a part of me. Been a long time since I held a baby."

"Are you sorry the Lord didn't go ahead and take you?" Peppy asked.

"I wouldn't mind going, but I guess He still has a reason for me to be here."

"You don't seem to be bitter about your baby," he observed.

"I was when it happened. I was giving my life to God on the mission field and I blamed Him for taking my little girl. I didn't want to serve Him anymore."

"But you did."

"Oh my, yes. God just let me rant and rave and cry till my tears went dry. Then He took me in His arms and held me till the grief went away. I missed her every day of my life. Not a day goes by I don't think of her. But I think God saw something that would happen to her and blessed us by not letting it happen. He took my baby when she was perfect and she's never known evil, or hurt, or hatred, or fear. She only knows the love of God."

They walked away from the pond and he pointed out the crocuses blooming near a clump of trees. She looked contented and appeared so calm. "I guess if you can forgive God for all that," he dared to say, "then it wouldn't be too hard for you to forgive an insensitive old codger like me."

She shrugged and kept walking toward the bridge. "If you asked, I might."

"What do you think I just did?"

"Hinted," she said as they crossed the bridge and headed down the walk toward their patios.

He felt she was getting back to normal, raising his blood pressure just like the old days. "Why don't we just stick to the business of planning a wedding for those two young people of ours?"

"Fine," she said as she stopped onto her patio. "My plan is, now that you're practicing in the chorus, for you to sing at the wedding!"

He waited for the punch line. It didn't come. She just smiled at him before going into her apartment. He stood for a moment, thinking. She hadn't exactly said so, but he reckoned that her cordiality meant she forgave him.

Maybe she even liked him!

Peppy was having a change of heart. The closer he and Ella got to finalizing those wedding plans, the more guilt-stricken he felt. It was probably all Ella's fault, but regardless of who was to blame, he had to talk to his grandson.

The last thing he'd want to do was alienate Daniel, but he wanted to get this off his chest. He confessed that he and Ella had planned a wedding for him and

Kay. Then he waited for the tongue-lashing.

It didn't come. Daniel began to chuckle. "I could think of worse things."

Peppy could only grin sheepishly. "There's more," he said. Then he unburdened his whole heart to Daniel, all the hurts of the past years, all his regrets, all the changes taking place inside himself, and all his hopes that he might make his remaining days more productive.

"Remember the lectures you gave me when I came back from service? And when my girl had found someone else? You told me God could turn things around, heal my breaking heart, and bring someone into my life that would make all that seem like a bad dream."

Peppy lifted his eyes in surprise as Daniel said, "You were right, Pops. Now, I want to make a suggestion."

Peppy spread his hands and shrugged. "That *kindness* suggestion worked. Throw another one on me."

Daniel walked over and put his hand on his grandfather's shoulder. Little flecks of gold began to dance in Peppy's eyes when Daniel said, "Let's you and I go look at engagement rings."

Chapter 12

On the Fourteenth of June, exactly a year since the Gallos first came to the Center, guests packed the Garden Room, beautifully decorated the way Ella and Peppy had planned. Garlands of ivory and peach silk roses draped the railing above and along the bridge beside the fountain.

June, an accomplished organist, and Frances, a concert violinist, provided music while the minister, Bible in hand, took his place in front of the lush green garden. Daniel was subdued, but Peppy strutted like a peacock with his tail-feathers spread, and looked just as awesome, drawing all eyes to him. The dapper old man, dressed in an ivory-colored tux with light blue lapels and cummerbund, looked as if he'd pulled off the caper of the century.

Kay and Ella appeared at a doorway, far across the room, on the other side of the garden. Both wore ivory-colored silk dresses. Kay's hemline was at her knees and her lovely auburn hair fell about her shoulders like a coppery halo; fastened in it was a headband made of blue ribbon and peach flowers. Ella's dress was long and flowing, a perfect compliment to her elegant stature.

When the two women reached the bridge, the setting became a fairyland. Audience lights were turned off. The recessed lights around the skylight high above the second floor were switched on, spilling down upon silver stars, hanging by invisible threads, and formed a soft circle around the minister, Daniel, and Peppy.

The scene was an outdoor wedding—inside. While the silver stars gleamed in a night sky, trees shimmered with blue and white lights like fireflies around a beautiful fountain. It became a night filled with romance and drama like none of them had seen before. Small lights along the bridge provided a pathway for the bride and her attendant.

As the two approached the minister, looking like angels from another realm, Peppy began to sing "Serenade," one of Ella's favorites, the song she had suggested. The lyrics and music transported her into another world. As he sang, "God speed your love to me," she was thinking, *Well, we're coming, but the plans were to move slowly so everyone could experience the drama and beauty we planned.*

Stay back, tears, she warned. *Don't dare ruin this makeup and drip on the most beautiful dress I've ever seen in my life.* She looked at Kay, then followed her lead and gazed at the two most handsome men in the world as they gazed at them like they were beautiful nymphs floating over the lighted pathway from the fairy tale forest.

"Dearly beloved," the preacher began when they stood before him. "We are gathered here to join this man and this woman in holy matrimony. Ella Eugenia Hayes, do you take this man, Peppino Alonzo Gallo to be your lawfully wedded husband?"

Peppy stiffened, as Ella turned those clear blue eyes upward and held his gaze. That woman knew how to make him suffer. Finally, her eyes glowed like those little blue lights on the trees, and her smile lit up his life and her lips said, confidently, as if this was exactly what she wanted, "I do."

Much later, after the elaborate reception in the Assembly Room, Daniel and Kay dropped Ella and Peppy off at the airport, then waited until they boarded the plane to Miami, where they'd begin their honeymoon cruise. Afterward, Daniel sped along the Interstate, headed for the Center where Kay had left her car.

"Now, we have plans to make," Kay said, "if we're going to get their things moved into the condo."

Daniel smiled. "I'm glad that came available. It's hard to imagine their deciding which apartment to live in."

Kay agreed, and laughed with him. "I suppose they'll concentrate on their own lives now and not ours?"

"Not a chance," he said. "I saw the delighted way Ella applauded when you caught that bridal bouquet."

"And Peppy was pleased as punch when you caught the blue garter."

"Yep," Daniel said with a shake of his head as he passed a car, then returned to the right lane. "They'll never give us a moment's peace. I expect they're going to be badgering us from now on."

From now on? Then. . .Daniel has no plans for making

our relationship permanent any time in the near future?

His turning on the radio indicated he didn't intend to pursue the subject further. Kay leaned back, listening to the soothing music and counted her blessings. The evening had been so romantic. The sky was star-spangled. She was riding along with a wonderful man. She would dwell on the fact there was hope—even seventy- and eighty-year-olds got married.

When they arrived at the Center, he didn't even offer to kiss her goodnight. "I'm beat," he said.

Kay knew the feeling. After she walked over to her car, he got out. "I almost forgot," he said. "Ella and Pops made me promise to tell you there's something for you on her kitchen table."

"I'll come out tomorrow," she said.

"They said tonight." He shrugged. "Maybe it'll spoil or something."

Spoil? "Okay," she said. "But you go on. I know you're tired."

"No, I'll go with you."

She unlocked the door, switched on the light, and went into the kitchen. There, on the table, was a big box, wrapped in white wedding paper and a huge blue bow. Printed on a small card was, "Open now."

Kay took the box to the living room and sat on the couch. Daniel stood at the door, looking as curious as she felt. She carefully removed the ribbon and the paper, then opened the box. Inside was another box, beautifully wrapped in bright colorful paper.

She glanced at Daniel. "This looks like the handi-work of Peppy Gallo!" He grinned, agreeing.

Inside that box was another. Then another!

It was sweet of them to leave her a present, but enough was enough! Tonight she didn't feel like fun and games, telling herself, *Weddings always make me cry.*

Finally, with boxes and papers strewn all around, she was holding a small black velvet jewelry box. She lifted the lid and there, glittering like a star, was a diamond ring. She lifted her eyes to Daniel. "Aunt Ella and Peppy wouldn't do this, would they?"

"They might," he said. "But they didn't." He got down on one knee and took the ring from the box. Lovelight was shining from his eyes and Kay felt her heart would burst with joy. "I love you, Kay. Will you marry me?"

"Oh, yes, Daniel. I love you too."

He took the ring and slipped it on her finger.

Soaring through the diamond-studded sky, with the overhead lights turned off, Peppy and Ella looked out the first-class windows. Ella hadn't flown since she'd come back from Korea. "I'd forgotten how the lights on earth look like stars from here," she mused. "And they're above us too. Reminds me of God's telling Abraham that His descendants would be as numerous as the stars in the sky."

Peppy reached for her hand and held it. "I know how Abraham must have felt when he started out on his journey. God is setting my feet on a new path that's exciting, challenging." He grinned and his free hand reached up to twirl his mustache.

Her blue gaze, enhanced by the silvery moonlight, met his eyes skeptically. "Well, you can feel like Abraham all you want. But don't expect me to be another Sarah and have a child in my old age!"

The two began to chuckle, as Peppy put his arm around her and drew her close. She snuggled against his shoulder. He bent his head and their lips touched in a sweet, promising kiss. Then he smiled and they settled back against the seat, two older people with young honeymooners inside themselves, feeling the warmth of the other.

Ella kept gazing out the window, thinking over the past year and how her fondest dreams had come true. Kay had found her man, and Ella had gotten her own—the handsomest man around. She glanced at Peppy's face then. He was dozing, his jaw had slackened, and his lower lip drooped. In another minute, that man would be snoring.

She nudged him in the ribs. He jumped, his eyes flew open, looking glazed. "I was just saying," Ella said sweetly. "I can't remember when I've seen so many stars."

He cleared his throat. "What? Where?"

"The stars," she said. "Above you."

He patted her hand and grinned. "My stars! I love you too."

Yvonne Lehman
Yvonne's an award-winning author from Black Mountain, North Carolina, in the heart of the Smoky Mountains. Her novels for Barbour's **Heartsong Presents** line include *Drums of Shelomoh, Southern Gentleman, Mountain Man, A Whole New World,* and *Hawaiian Heartbeat*. Married and the mother of four grown children, Yvonne teaches at a local university, and is the founder of the Blue Ridge Christian Writers' Conference.

Wrong Church, Wrong Wedding

Loree Lough

Chapter 1

Breena winced as her heels click-clacked against the polished marble. If she had arrived on time, her footsteps would have blended with the rest of the pre-wedding din. Grabbing the first available seat —on the aisle, second pew from the back—she heaved a relieved sigh and sat. *This is the lumpiest cushion I've ever. . .*

" 'Scuse me, miss," drawled the tall stranger beside her, "but you're sittin' on my Stetson."

As the flush of embarrassment heated her cheeks, Breena handed the flattened black felt hat to him.

"Well," he said, turning it this way and that, "it used to be my Stetson. . . ."

"I-I'm so sorry. I never even saw it. I. . ."

He shot her a playful half grin. "It's all right." As if to prove it, the cowboy winked. "I was thinkin' of gettin' me a new one, anyway."

A white-gloved hand reached up from behind and tapped his shoulder. "You're a guest in the house of the Lord, for goodness sake," an elderly woman warned. "Show some respect and *be quiet!*"

Like a little boy caught with his hand in the cookie

jar, he shot Breena an "uh-oh, we're in trouble now!" expression and dutifully faced forward. She did the same as her seat mate tried unsuccessfully to reshape his mangled headpiece.

This has definitely not *been your day, Breena Pavan!*

First, her hair dryer's motor blew up, forcing her to let her short, dark curls air dry. Then the power went out altogether, and she had to apply her makeup by the light of the tiny bathroom window.

She was halfway to the church when she realized she'd left the wedding gift on the hall table, and on the way home to get it, her right front tire decided to go flat.

She had managed to get the spare on without incident, but as she tucked the jack back into the trunk, her knee brushed the license plate, snagging her panty hose. She might have made it to the church on time . . .if that *first* drug store had carried anything other than leotards.

Unfortunately, things had started going wrong long before she got out of bed this morning. Take yesterday, for example, when she realized she'd misplaced the invitation to Todd and Sandra's wedding. It had taken several phone calls to find someone who knew when and where her old school chums would be getting married. "One o'clock, St. John's," Todd's harried sister had said.

Breena glanced at her watch. Unless it had suddenly gone the way of her hair dryer, she was only ten minutes late. No one seemed to have noticed her tardiness, and once she had a chance to replace the cowboy's hat, all would be right with the world again.

At least, as right as *her* world could be. . . .

She settled back and listened to the preacher's clear voice, reverberating from every rafter in the cavernous wood and marbled space as he read from Genesis: " '. . .and she shall be called Woman, because she is taken out of Man. Therefore shall a man leave his father and his mother, and shall cleave unto his wife: and they shall be one flesh. . . .' "

The bride and groom exchanged vows, shared their first kiss as man and wife, and turned to face the congregation. She hadn't realized Todd was so tall. *And when did Sandra put on all that weight around her middle?* The church had been decorated with white roses and daisies, and gigantic pink satin bows hung from the end of each pew. *If I ever have a wedding,* Breena thought dreamily, *I hope it's as pretty as this one.*

As the congregation stood, the newlyweds linked arms and proceeded up the aisle toward the back of the church. It wasn't until they drew near that Breena realized. . .

. . .they weren't Todd and Sandra!

It had never occurred to her to ask Todd's sister *which* St. John's. . . .

She hung her head and closed her eyes. *Only you could end up at the wrong wedding.*

But why should she be surprised? Ever since she'd attended that faith rally with her college roommate, it seemed that nothing concerning religion had gone right for Breena. She slumped onto the seat and hid her face in her hands.

The cowboy sat down beside her. "Are you all right?"

Breena shook her head. *No,* she answered silently, *I most certainly am not all right. In fact, there's so much wrong with me, it'd take a ream of paper to list everything that...*

"Can I get you anything? Tissue? Water, maybe?"

Again, she shook her head.

"Please," she heard him tell the folks on his other side, "feel free to step around us; seems the lady's feelin' a mite dizzy. . . ."

She felt humiliated, embarrassed. . .but dizzy? *Well, going to the wrong church* was *a dizzy thing to do. . . .*

"I noticed you came in alone," the cowboy said. "Same here. Something came up, and my date had to cancel at the last minute."

If she didn't know better, Breena would have said he was gearing up to ask *her* to replace his date! But why would he do that, when she'd mashed his hat and gotten him scolded?

"We could go in my car, pick yours up afterward. Or I could follow you, if you'd rather. . . ."

She'd never seen bigger, greener, longer-lashed eyes on a man in her life. A thin streak of bright white gleamed in his coal-black hair. And that mischievous, slanting smile made him *GQ* material, for sure.

"So what do you say?"

Still focused on the dark mustache arching over his

lips, Breena licked her own lips. "Um, say? To what?"

Chuckling, he repeated, "To joining me at the reception."

Again the warmth of a blush colored her cheeks. "I, uh, I'm afraid I can't."

Tucking in one corner of his mouth, he shook his head. "Figures."

Blinking, she raised her eyebrows.

"Ain't it just my luck to have a li'l gal who's prettier than the bride sit down next to me. . .and she's already spoken for."

"It isn't that, it's just. . ." *Be quiet, Breena; you sound like a little ninny!* She'd ended up at the wrong place at the wrong time *again*, and now she was gearing up to ramble like a raving lunatic.

She had no business even considering his invitation. He was obviously a devout Christian. She could tell by the way he'd closed his eyes during the ceremony, nodding and whispering "Amen" and "Praise Jesus" when the minister's words touched his heart. With her history, Breena knew better than to involve herself with a man like that.

"I shouldn't be here," she blurted. And for the next five minutes, Breena held his attention as she told him about her erratic, unlucky, unbelievable morning.

"Sounds like my afternoon. . .I suffered a hat-mashing and a tongue-lashing in a five minute stretch." He grinned. "You look smashing, by the way. . . ."

Breena returned the smile. "So you see," she concluded as if he'd never interrupted, "I'm supposed to be

271

at a different wedding, at a different St. John's."

"Which one?"

It was a simple question that ought to be followed by a simple answer. Breena sighed, knowing full well she had no idea which St. John's Todd and Sandra had been married in. She cast a forlorn glance at her watch. *And they're definitely married by now!* She shrugged one shoulder. "If I knew, I'd. . ."

He tucked in one corner of his mouth and frowned, thoughtfully stroking his thick mustache with thumb and forefinger.

He's probably thinking up a good excuse to make a quick getaway, Breena told herself.

His laughter began gradually, quietly, then bubbled up and boiled over like stew in an unwatched kettle. The delicious sound echoed through the now-empty church, bouncing back to wrap around her like a warm, friendly hug.

"That's some sense of humor you've got there. Ever consider becoming a stand-up comic?"

What would you think if you knew I wasn't joking, Mr. Perfect? she wondered, smiling wryly.

"Sorry," he said, extending a hand. "Forgive my bad manners. The name's Keegan. Keegan Neil."

The way he was pumping her arm up and down, she wouldn't have been at all surprised if water started trickling from her fingertips.

"And you are. . . ?"

"Oh. Um. Breena." She wriggled free of his grasp. "It's nice to. . ."

"Breena," he repeated. "Interesting name. Sounds Irish."

Smiling slightly, she nodded. "My mother was born on the Burren."

"And my ancestors hail from Edinburgh. Breena," he said again.

He had the deep, rich voice of a Galveston radio disc jockey. She'd always been partial to baritones. . .and Southern accents. . . .

"Is it a nickname for Sabrina?"

She shook her head. "Nope. It says 'Breena' on my birth certificate."

"Short and sweet and to the point. Just like its owner." He gave an approving nod. "I like that."

Breena either had a fever or she was blushing.

"This other wedding," he said, interrupting her thoughts, "did the invitation say you could bring a guest?"

"Well, yes, as a matter of fact, it did."

"So the *other* bride and groom are expecting you to show up with an escort?"

Another nod. "I invited a friend, but he woke up with an ingrown toenail."

Keegan's eyes and smile widened. "He. . .*what?*"

She shrugged the other shoulder. "An ingrown toenai—" The merriment on his face told Breena he'd heard her just fine the first time. He couldn't believe such a thing could waylay a man.

"No, really. His toe is all swollen up—twice its normal size," she explained, "and every step is torture. He

273

didn't think he'd be much fun if. . ."

By now, Keegan was wiping tears of mirth from his eyes. Without warning, he placed both hands on her shoulders. "Breena, go with me to the reception. Doesn't matter one whit which one. You choose." Another chuckle popped from his lips. " 'Cause you're the most fascinatin' woman I've met since I left Texas." He paused. "That ain't entirely true, and I can't tell a lie, 'specially not in church." His left eyebrow rose. "You're the most fascinatin' woman I've ever met, *period.*"

Before she knew what was happening, Keegan had sandwiched her hands between his.

"Say you'll spend the rest of the day with me. I'll promise not to bite."

If you knew the truth about me, Mr. Good Christian, you wouldn't be so interested in spending one more minute with. . .

Grinning, he jammed the now lopsided Stetson onto his head and poked out his elbow, inviting her to take his arm. "Shall we?"

Breena hesitated, because in truth, she *wanted* to spend more time with him. She tucked her hand into her pocket. He appeared to be a good man, a kind man. She guessed him to be twenty-nine or thirty; his eagerness to get to know her better told her he was probably looking to settle down, raise a family. He needed a good and kind woman, a *Christian* woman to help him accomplish that. And after what happened to her all those years ago in college, well, Breena knew for certain *she* wasn't that woman.

He was still standing there, arm extended, waiting patiently for her response. *He deserves an answer. Deserves far more than that.* "I can't," she said, regretfully.

His tantalizing smile disappeared and both brows dipped low in the center of his forehead. "Why?"

She lifted her chin. "Are you 'born again,' Keegan?"

"Yeah, of course. . . ."

"A steadfast believer?"

He frowned. "I reckon you could put it that way, but I still don't understa—"

"Then you don't belong with the likes of me."

His eyes narrowed. So did his lips. "I hate to repeat myself, but *why?*"

"Because. . ." *Oh, just spit it out, Breena!* "Because a man like you has no business hanging around with someone who's been rejected by God, that's why!" Snatching her purse from where she'd laid it on the pew, Breena left the way she'd entered. . .heels click-clacking across the shining marble floor.

"Breena. Breena, wait. . . ."

Keegan watched helplessly as the door closed behind her.

Rejected, he repeated, scratching his chin, *by God?*

It was a concept he simply couldn't comprehend. He'd been involved in the church for as long as he could remember, and never had anyone said such a thing.

During his elementary school years, Keegan had organized the collection of food to feed needy families at Thanksgiving and Christmas. In high school, he'd helped build a homeless shelter. As a college student, he'd worked with inmates at the state penitentiary. If those men—some of whom had committed murder, rape, armed robbery—could be forgiven their sins, *what in tarnation gives* her *the idea she had been rejected by God?*

Keegan headed for the door, the heels of his boots resounding in the unoccupied chapel. The noise reminded him of the sound her skinny-heeled shoes had made as she'd run away. She had such pretty little feet, such curvy calves. *And the biggest, brownest eyes I ever did see. . . .*

He'd looked evil in the eye enough times in that Texas prison to know a sinner—repentant or otherwise —when he saw one, and—Keegan snorted to himself— *It's not like she killed somebody or somethin'.* Her eyes reflected the bright, sweet soul of a child. Yet there was more. . .something faraway, something sad. . . *Wonder what that's all about?*

Why not ask her? He could look her up in the phone book, give her a call, convince her that no one with eyes like hers could have done anything to cause God to reject her. He could ask her. . .if he'd thought to get her last name.

Still, there was one way he knew he could help her: Prayer. Again he pictured her lovely face, her friendly smile, her sparkling eyes, and knew he'd be praying for more than her well being and peace of mind. . .he'd be praying for God to help him find her.

Breena. . . Even her name was lovely. . . .

Something in her had called to Keegan, and something in him had answered. Breena had been in his life for thirty minutes, at best; she'd been gone for perhaps thirty *seconds*. . .

. . .and already he missed her.

Chapter 2

God must have wanted Breena to attend Todd and Sandra's reception. She took a left turn out of the parking lot of the *wrong* St. John's when she should have taken a right, but she didn't realize her mistake until she'd gone about a mile. By now thoroughly frustrated, she tried to take the expressway as a shortcut home, only to get caught in a huge traffic snarl behind an accident. Exasperated, she pulled off at the next exit, and while she was trying to establish her bearings she looked down the street. . .and spied the Chapel of St. John just a few blocks away.

She arrived at the banquet hall a few minutes before the newlyweds, found a seat at a big round table, and did her best to join in the conversation with Todd's neighbors and co-workers. As she pushed a piece of wedding cake—the awful kind, with an unidentified fruit filling and that frosting that leaves a coating of lard on the roof of your mouth—around her plate, her thoughts persistently drifted to Keegan Neil.

Keegan Neil was on her mind again as she climbed the

spiral staircase leading from her workshop to the apartment above. Sighing, she hung her purse on a peg in the hall closet and flipped the switch beside the front door. Soft light flooded the room, puddling on pale oak table tops and washing over the cushiony brown sofas that flanked her floor-to-ceiling fireplace. Breena loved everything about her home, from the panoramic view visible through a row of arched windows to the rough adobe walls where she'd hung her collection of antique lutes and mandolins.

Before she'd rented the property, the upstairs space had been an artist's studio, complete with kaleidoscopic paint spatters dotting the warm hardwood floors. She hadn't scraped them up because she liked the way the multi-hued splashes brightened the otherwise dull boards. Using those drips and drops as her color palette, Breena had matched scatter rugs and throw pillows to the bright shades, giving the open area a lively, eclectic look.

She'd carried the cheery look downstairs and into her workshop, too, coating the trim boards, doors, and windowsills with brilliant enamels.

Breena enjoyed her home, but she relished her work even more. Music—and anything to do with it—had always been her heart's desire. Her love of music had, at the age of ten, inspired her to take apart the battered old piano in her grandmother's back room. Hours after closing the door to that oversized closet, she emerged, eyes shining with victory at having turned an out-of-tune beast into a beautifully singing instrument. Fingers swollen and bruised from struggling with stiff wire and rough wood, she'd placed both hands on her hips and announced her plans for the future to her family: "I'm going to be a piano tuner when I grow up!"

Her parents had exchanged patronizing glances. "Only Breena could say a thing like that," her mother had said. And because of it, Breena had made up her mind right then and there to prove she could do it. She studied hard to reach her goal. The job, her research taught her, involved more than a talent for the keyboard. It required a good ear, physical strength, dexterity. . .and a slightly reclusive nature, since the best tuning work is done in solitude. Not that Breena didn't like chatting with her customers, but in her opinion, the real fun began when the interview ended. She likened being alone with the instruments—and the music they made —to visiting heaven several times a day.

She'd always liked her lifestyle, free to come and go as she pleased, unencumbered by the tethers of a nine-to-five office job, or family, or beaus. Her only responsibilities were to her customers. . .and Hershey.

As usual, the cat leapt from his cozy bed—a threadbare afghan piled on the seat of a bentwood rocker—and padded toward her. The brown-striped Tabby wove a figure eight around her ankles, alternately chirping and purring his affectionate greeting. "It's good to see you, too," Breena said, scooping him into her arms.

Digging a fish-shaped treat from a foil-lined pouch, she let him nibble it from her open palm, then stooped to put him back on the floor. "Don't look at me like that," she said, wagging a finger in his direction. "You know the rule: More than one a day and you'll get fat and lazy. And we don't want that, now do we?"

Hershey's hollow-sounding meow told her that was *exactly* what he wanted. He looked up at her with big green eyes. . .which reminded her of Keegan.

Keegan Neil. It was a fine, strong name that fit the man well, she thought.

But why does the name sound so familiar?

Breena headed for her bedroom, slipped off her heels, and put them on the shoe shelf in her closet. *No point straining your brain trying to remember, because even if he is everything you've ever wanted in a man, you can't have him. Not with your past.*

Breena hung her dress on a padded hanger, shrugged into jeans shorts and a T-shirt, and climbed down the spiral staircase that led to her workshop.

A mahogany baby grand, Breena's pride and joy, dominated the center space. Someday, she hoped to own a home of her own. She could see it in her mind's eye— a two-story Victorian with a covered, wrap-around porch. Through the tall, narrow windows to the right of the red-painted door, folks would be able to view her grandmother's oak dining room table and matching claw-footed chairs.

And the baby grand, placed at an angle, would be visible through the living room windows to the left of the door.

Mind on your work! Breena scolded herself. She turned on the overhead lights with one hand and grabbed her tool bucket with the other. She'd promised to have the little spinet repaired and ready by mid-week. *No way you'll make that deadline if you don't get cracking!* The piano needed new wires and hammers before it could be returned to the customer's home for its final tuning.

Pulling on a pair of well-worn leather gloves, she hunkered down and began the arduous task of removing the old strings. The last one hit the floor as the grandfather clock struck twelve. Glancing around her as she got to her feet, Breena chuckled. *You look like some kind of weird bird sitting in a wire nest.*

Yawning and working the kinks from her neck, she put away her tools and headed back upstairs. *First thing tomorrow,* she told herself, *you'll finish that job.*

She wanted to get on to rebuilding the old player piano she'd bought for a hundred dollars at an estate sale a month ago. It would take time to get it up to playing speed. Time, and a myriad of new innards. Patience, she knew, and hard work would turn the miserable old clunker into a sweet-singing instrument that would easily fetch ten times what she'd paid for it. . . .

She stuffed her shorts and shirt in the hamper and, after a quick shower, stepped into her favorite sleepshirt—white-cotton and covered with thousands of little black Zs.

Hershey made himself comfortable at the foot of the bed as Breena pulled back the covers. He knew the routine, and curled into a comfy ball, blinking as she got onto her knees and folded her hands.

"Dear Lord, I know it must be hard, listening to my

petty wishes and concerns. . .feeling as You do about me. . . ." Breena paused, for this had always been the hardest part of her nighttime prayers: Should she continue in the hopes the Lord would accept her as He'd accepted her roommate, as He'd accepted all those other kids that night at the rally, or say a final "Amen" and let God have some peace? Tears filled her eyes as she fluffed her pillow and cuddled into it. *Why am I so inept when it comes to praying!*

Her parents had taken good care of her. Thanks to their tutelage, she knew which fork to use at dinner, how to introduce adults to adolescents, when to speak . . .and when not to. . . . The Pavans had been upstanding members of the community, and taught her to be a responsible citizen as well.

But though they'd done themselves proud, feeding and clothing and educating their daughter, they had not seen to her spiritual needs.

Until Breena went away to college, she hadn't been aware she *had* spiritual needs. By contrast, her roommate Melissa seemed filled to overflowing with unbridled Christian joy. When Breena asked her *why* she was always so happy, Melissa had said in what Breena would soon recognize as her matter-of-fact way, "Because God loves me, of course."

Hope had simmered in young Breena's heart: Could God love her the same way He loved Melissa? But always on the heels of that hope came despair: Why *would* God love her that much? After all, Melissa hadn't been responsible for her own mother's death. . . .

Everyone (except her father) had said it wasn't Breena's fault. But she knew better. It didn't matter that immediately after the funeral, she'd turned her life around. Her mother was still just as dead as if she had continued pulling the adolescent pranks that had distressed her so.

Besides, what had she done lately to earn God's love? She hadn't worked to help feed the poor, or baby-sat toddlers so their parents could attend Sunday services, or visited people confined to nursing homes, as Melissa had. Why, until her roommate dragged her to Good Faith, Breena had never even set foot in a church!

"Better late than never," had been her new friend's advice.

Cliché or not, it made sense, and Breena began helping as Melissa went about her Christian duties. But even after months of volunteering, Breena sensed something was missing, and she shared her concerns with Melissa.

"Do you pray?" Melissa had asked. "Because the more you pray, the closer you'll feel to God. . . ."

For Breena, talking to the Almighty—even alone in a room—had seemed painfully awkward. He knew better than anyone what she was. . . .

"There's a faith rally this weekend," Melissa had said. "*Dozens* of people are saved every week. I can't believe I didn't think of this before!"

With that memory still bright in her mind's eye, Breena punched her pillow. "Saved, indeed," she muttered. "The only thing 'born again' in me that day was the knowledge that God doesn't want me."

Hershey, confused by Breena's tossing and turning, walked to the head of the bed and touched his nose to hers.

"Good heavens, Hersh, your schnoz is as cold as ice!" she said, grinning despite herself. "Here it is only June, and already I know what to get you for Christmas: A nose warmer!"

He butted his forehead against hers.

Scratching under his chin, she chuckled. "You sound like a chain saw when you purr like that."

Hershey peered into her eyes, his big green orbs reminding her again of Keegan Neil.

Taking a deep breath, Breena kissed the top of the cat's head. Why Keegan had chosen that moment to pop into her mind, she didn't know. He hadn't even tried to hide his interest in her, a fact that both thrilled and depressed her. "I should have let him come with me to the reception," she told the cat. "One afternoon, watching me in action, and he'd know how wrong we are for each other."

She rolled onto her side and scrunched the pillow under her neck. "Keegan Neil. . .Keegan Neil," she chanted. "Why *does* that name sound so familiar?"

Turning to her other side, Breena began reciting the twenty-third Psalm, hoping it would calm her enough to induce sleep, as it had so often in the past.

But something told her that even after she'd whispered, " 'and I will live in the house of the Lord forever,' " the name Keegan Neil—and the man—

285

would still be very much on her mind.

A shard of bright sunlight seeped under the window shade, angled across the burgundy peonies decorating the rug beneath her bed, and slanted across Breena's face. Throwing an arm over her eyes, she slapped the alarm's snooze button for the second time. "It can't be seven o'clock already," she groaned. Monday mornings were always the worst. She had spent Sunday in her normal routine of reading the paper and drinking coffee, followed by the usual awkward phone call to her father, and then laundry and trying to straighten up to get ready for the week ahead. Occasionally she would think about going to church but the thought of all those happy faces only made her sad.

Rear end high in the air, Hershey walked his front paws forward and indulged himself in a long, luxurious stretch. After an equally expansive yawn, he sat up straight and stared until Breena said, "Quit lookin' at me like that." Ruffling his fur, she tossed the top sheet aside. "It isn't like you're gonna starve if I don't feed you at the stroke of seven. . . ."

But the stubborn look on his furry face clearly said, "that's what you think!"

Rolling her eyes, Breena gathered him close. "You're good training, Hersh," she added, kissing the top of his head. "If I ever have kids, I'll have the patience of a saint!"

Gently depositing him on the black and white tiled kitchen floor, she started a pot of coffee, and as it brewed, opened a can of cat food for the Tabby. "Now, I have lots to do this morning, so I don't want you pestering me for treats 'til at least noon. Got it?"

Noisy chomping was his reply. Smiling crookedly, Breena headed back to her room. "If I ever have those kids," she tossed teasingly over her shoulder, "I hope they're more grateful for their meals than you are!"

Half an hour later, showered and wearing capri-length stretch pants and a baggy T-shirt that said "Everyone Wants to Save the Dolphins. . .Who's Gonna Save the *Tuner?*" Breena grabbed her purse and headed for the garden center across town. Ordinarily, she shopped at Papa's Nursery and Crafts just up the road, but the ad in Sunday's paper claimed that the Grand Re-Opening of the newly refurbished That's the Way It Grows was going on from seven AM to seven PM. Any establishment that offered those hours *and* a sale deserved her business.

Leaving her mini-pickup in the gravel lot, Breena headed straight for the hothouse, determined to find something that would thrive in the raised gardens she'd built on her deck. *No petunias!* she cautioned herself; *the ones you planted two weeks ago have already wilted.* Walking up and down the aisles of colorful blooms, Breena stooped now and then to read the care-and-feeding directions of each variety.

It was as she studied the instructions for growing impatiens that a deep Texas drawl said, "I'd invite you to set a spell, but there's not a Stetson in sight. . . ."

287

Chapter 3

Breena quickly straightened from the impatiens table, wide-eyed and clutching a small pot of pink flowers to her chest.

"Sorry," Keegan drawled, "didn't mean to scare you."

Brushing potting soil from her T-shirt, she put the plastic container back where she'd found it. "It's okay; I'm wearing my sneakers."

His brow furrowed with confusion as his mustache slanted above a half-grin. "Um. . ."

She matched his smile, dimple for dimple. "Well," she explained, "if my shoes hadn't been laced up good and tight, you'd have scared me right out of them."

He chuckled softly. "Sorry," he said again. And then, "You're up and about bright and early. Guess you didn't go to that reception yesterday. . . ."

I could say the same for you, she thought, taking note of his faded jeans, scuffed cowboy boots, and red T-shirt. "Oh, I went. I just didn't stay 'til the bitter end is all." Sighing, she added, "I have a million deadlines. Seems 'bright and early' is the only time I have to run errands.'"

His intense scrutiny unnerved her. Tapping a fingertip to her lips, she added, "I wonder where they keep the marigolds?"

He quirked an eyebrow. "*They* keep 'em in the next greenhouse. . ." He pointed to the airplane-hangar shaped building beside them. ". . .with the rest of the sun lovers."

One brow rose on her forehead. "Sun lovers?"

He nodded. "You know. . .plants that need a minimum of six hours of unfiltered sunlight a day?" Gesturing toward the vine-covered ceiling above them, Keegan told her, "These guys in here need plenty of natural light, but no direct sun."

Breena wondered how he knew so much about the subject. *Seems more the cattle branding type to me,* she thought, her gaze traveling from his pointy-toed boots to his callused hands.

Nonchalantly, Keegan plucked a wilting bud from a nearby stem, tossed it onto the bark chip-covered floor, then pressed two fingertips into the pot. Frowning, he called to the teenage girl, stacking wood pallets near the door. "Billie, let that go for now. These guys need water."

"Have hose, will spray," the chubby redhead replied as Keegan returned his attention to Breena.

"You. . .you *work* here? Isn't it a little—"

"Sissified for a cowpoke to trifle with flowers?" The grin above his mustache slanted slightly as his eyebrows twitched once again.

Breena blushed. "I didn't mean—"

"Yes," he said, rescuing her, "I guess you could say I work here."

The redhead stood beside him, with a dripping hose

nozzle in one hand and the hose itself in the other. "You want I should water the sun lovers when I'm through in here, Mr. Neil?"

Keegan nodded. "And tell Marcellus to unload that shipment of azaleas the tree farm delivered yesterday. That 'half price' ad ran in this morning's paper, and I have a feeling we're gonna be swamped in a couple hours."

That's where Breena had seen his name. . .in the newspaper advertisement. . . .

Grinning, Billie saluted smartly. "Yessir, Mr. Neil, sir. I'll get right on it, sir."

"You forgot to click your heels," he teased, winking. "Don't let it happen again, or I'll have to dock your pay." Then, "Did Agnes get the checks written?"

"Yessir," the teen said around a giggle, "put the stamps on the envelopes myself, first thing this morning."

"Good." He nodded approvingly. "What about the new schedule?"

"Me an' Agnes worked—"

"Agnes and I. . ."

Breena noted that the girl accepted his correction good-naturedly.

"Agnes and I worked on that after we stuffed the pay envelopes. Agnes thinks you'll probably need to hire two more kids to round out the summer staff."

He raised an eyebrow. "But I thought Marcellus had signed up for a whole slew of summer school courses."

"He did. But he's mostly goin' nights and weekends, remember?" Adjusting the water spray, she turned and began showering the plants behind them. Giggling again, she called over her shoulder, "He loves this place so much, he can't stay away."

From the easygoing atmosphere, it appeared Marcellus wasn't the only one who loved this place.

With a hand on Breena's elbow, Keegan led her farther down the aisle. He tucked in one corner of his mouth. "Kids," he said, shaking his head, "you've just gotta love 'em."

Breena could tell by his easy rapport with Billie that he meant what he said, and she added another item to her quickly growing "Reasons to Like Keegan" register. She noticed the shards of a broken clay pot, lying beneath the flower table. *If you have a lick of sense,* she warned herself, *you'll toss that list before your heart ends up like that. . . .*

"They'll behave responsibly," he continued, "if you give them a chance to prove what they can do, that is. My whole staff is made up of folks under the age of eighteen. . .kids who have had minor altercations with the law, mostly, or whose folks don't do their jobs. . ." Smiling, he nodded toward the office, where Agnes's white-haired head was visible through the opened window. ". . .and kids over sixty-five, of course."

His staff? Breena pictured him the way she'd seen him yesterday in the church, crisp white shirt tucked into sharply-creased trousers that exactly matched the dark flecks in his camel-colored sports coat, highly-polished brown boots, a gold-banded watch on his left wrist. Dressed as he was now, he could easily have been a customer buying petunias for his wife on his way to the hardware store. Though he'd changed his wedding attire for a more casual look, he still stood tall, his broad shoulders and wide stance telling anyone who took the time to look that this was a man who had every reason to feel confident.

Breena took the time to look. . .

. . .at his long, muscular legs and thick upper arms.

. . .at his square jaw and piercing green eyes.

. . .at the streak of snow-white that flashed through his shiny dark hair. *He's too young to be going gray; it's almost like he got hit with a shot of bleach. . . .*

As though he could read her mind, Keegan ran a self-conscious hand through his hair. Feeling a twinge of guilt, Breena bit her lower lip. She hadn't meant to stare.

She turned her attention to the basket of ivy hanging above them. "So tell me," she began, trying to sound nonchalant, "how long have you owned this place?"

He plucked a brown leaf from the plant. Breena frowned inwardly, wondering how he'd spotted it amid the mass of glossy leaves.

"Nearly a year." He glanced around, pocketed both hands, loosed a satisfied sigh. "Inherited it when my granddaddy died. He practically ran it single-handedly, and didn't pay much attention to the details those last couple of years. I've been dotting i's and crossing t's and doing *a lot* of clean-up ever since he passed on."

"Your grandfather wasn't from Texas?"

"He was born there. Lived in Lubbock 'til World

War II." Keegan's eyes brightened with a memory. "My grandma was an Army nurse and he was a fighter pilot. He got himself shot down, and, well, as they say, 'the rest is history.'" Keegan shrugged as a smile of remembrance tugged at the corners of his mouth. "Nonna's people owned a restaurant in Baltimore, and after the war, the whole Citerony clan settled in Little Italy. Grampa worked hard, saved his money, bought himself a couple dozen acres here in Howard County."

With a jerk of his thumb he indicated a farmhouse in the distance. "Built it himself while he readied the land for planting. Grew Christmas trees, mostly, but he farmed all the usual stuff, too."

Everything about Keegan fascinated her, from his family tree to that streak of white in his dark hair. "The usual stuff?" she asked, pretending to be engrossed in the velvety ruffled leaves of a red-flowering geranium.

"Corn, wheat, soy. . . Had himself a vegetable stand during the summer months, and sold salad fixin's to the neighbors."

Breena was beginning to feel like a parrot. "Salad fixin's?"

Trapping its stem between thumb and forefinger, Keegan nipped off a purple and yellow pansy. "Tomatoes, bell peppers, zucchini. . ."

"Oh," she said, fingering the waxy green stalks of a pink begonia, "salad fixin's."

He took a step nearer and tucked the flower behind her ear. "So tell me, Breena, what kind of plants are you in the market for today?"

Was it the perfume of the thousands of blossoms surrounding her, or his nearness that made her head spin? Breena looked into the face so near her own. *It isn't the flowers,* she admitted. *It definitely isn't the. . .*

"Earth to Breena. . .earth to Breena. . . ."

She mirrored his grin. "I need to replace the petunias I bought two weeks ago."

His inquisitive stare prompted her to quickly add, "They died."

"In just two weeks? What'd you do to the poor things?"

Shrugging, she sighed. Not once had she kept a houseplant or a goldfish for more than a few weeks. When she was still living at home her father had often teased her about it, saying "Some folks have green thumbs; yours must be black, 'cause everything you touch dies!" His nervous chuckle hadn't hidden the fact that his joke wasn't a joke at all. . . .

"I honestly don't know," Breena defended. She didn't like it, but her father's opinion of her was one she'd more or less learned to live with. And why not? After what she'd done, Breena believed she deserved every cutting barb that came out of his mouth! "I watered them every day. Fed them. Made sure. . ."

He crossed both arms over his chest. "Did you stick 'em in the ground, or in a planter?"

"I built a raised bed for them. On my deck. So they'd get plenty of sunshine, and. . ."

He adjusted the pansy he'd stuck behind her ear, reminding her of a doctor, investigating his patient's symptoms during an examination. "Did the blossoms wilt before they fell off?"

"Yes. . ."

"And the greenery turned kinda yellow?" he asked, wrapping his finger with a lock of her hair.

Nodding, Breena wondered if he could hear her heart hammering. *He's certainly standing close enough. . . .*

The same finger gently brushed a wayward curl from her forehead. "Sounds to me like you pampered the poor things to death."

You must look like one of those dashboard doggies, the way you keep nodding.

"I know they don't look it, but petunias are hardy li'l things. A small dose of fertilizer when you put 'em in the ground, water when the soil is almost dry. . .that's all they really need."

She watched as he ran that very busy fingertip across his mustache. There had been just one romantic relationship in her past, and he had been clean-shaven. *I wonder what it would feel like to be kissed by a man with—*

Keegan licked his lips, a prankish grin playing on his face. *Had* it been a thought? Or had she spoken the words aloud? If she *hadn't* said what she'd been thinking, how was she to explain the fact that he seemed to be considering the same idea?

His face loomed nearer and, one hand on her shoulder, whispered in her ear: "Shhh. . .don't move."

Breena's joints locked involuntarily at his soft command.

"Don't be scared. . . ."

Her muscles tightened in response to his warning. Why would she be afraid of a little old kiss?

". . .but there's a spider in your hair. . . ."

Long, thick fingers combed through her locks, and then he said, "Gotcha!"

He stepped back, holding a daddy longlegs between thumb and forefinger. Both brows rose on his forehead as he studied her reaction. "You're not scared of bugs." It was more a statement than a question, and Keegan's admiration was apparent in his voice, his eyes, his smile.

"You act like you expected me to leap onto that bench over there, wringing my hands and squealing like a piglet." Breena laughed at the picture her comment conjured. "Bugs are okay. . .in their own environment." She narrowed one eye and held a fist in the air. "But let one drag its woolly li'l tail into my house, and. . ." With an affirmative nod, she shook the fist, warning any would-be eight-legged intruder what might happen if it dared venture into her world. She pocketed the threatening hand and added in a tiny voice, "I've never been stung, so I'm leery of bees and wasps and things. . . ."

Keegan chuckled quietly. "And mice?"

She furrowed her brow. "What about them?"

"Are you scared of 'em?"

Breena shrugged. "Nah." One brow arched in suspicion. "Why," she asked, grinning, "is there a mouse in my hair?"

"No, but there's one on the floor, right behind you. . . ."

Peering over her shoulder, Breena saw it, wee and white, pink tail flicking, whiskered nose wriggling, front feet pawing at the bark mulch. She got onto her hands and knees for a better look, held out her hand. "What a cutie you are," she cooed. "Whatcha diggin' for?"

From the corner of her eye, Breena spied a calico cat, golden eyes glowing, hunched to pounce.

"Gus," Keegan admonished, "don't even think about it."

The cat sat, flat-eyed and ears back, watching as the minuscule rodent disappeared behind a stack of bagged pea gravel.

Breena scrambled to her feet, dusted the knees of her stretch pants. "Why'd you name her Gus?"

"Because she was a gift from an old girlfriend whose name was Augusta."

There was no explaining the hot flash of jealousy that coursed through Breena's veins. She'd only met this man the other day. And there could never be anything between them, what with him being such a devout Christian and her being. . .

"How'd you know Gus was a girl?" he asked, interrupting her thought.

"Because, male calicos are very rare."

Eyes narrowed, Keegan regarded her carefully.

"I learned it on a cable station dedicated to teaching kids about animals; this veterinarian in Australia did a whole segment on calicos."

The thick mustache tilted above a rakish grin. "Is that right?"

He hadn't tried to hide his interest yesterday, and there was no mistaking the admiration glowing in his green eyes now. Breena took a deep breath—to stave off another blush and keep her curiosity under control—because cats and mice and spiders and plants were the last things on her mind. *Whatever happened to dear, sweet* Augusta? was her sarcastic, silent question. Breena waved a hand in the direction of the flower-laden table. "So what do you recommend?" she asked instead.

Keegan leaned his backside against the table, where hundreds of impatiens bloomed, and crossed both arms over his chest. "Dinner. Tonight. My place."

Chapter 4

The moment Keegan opened the door, his massive bulk was illumined by the glow of candles. They were everywhere. . .on the mantle and hearth, on the coffee table, lining the windowsills. The scent of freshly-struck matches wafted on an air current, tickling her nostrils.

"Bless you," he said when she sneezed. Stepping aside, he gave a grand, welcoming gesture with a sweep of his muscular arm. "C'mon in and set a spell. Help yourself to the cheese and crackers. How 'bout some iced tea?"

"Sounds nice," she said.

As he rummaged in the kitchen, Breena surveyed his living room. She'd more or less expected to find his tastes leaning toward Western decor—big buttery leather sofas and chairs, dark wood, brass lanterns rather than lamps, statues of cowboys on rearing stallions, framed prints of dusty cattle drives. . . Instead, well-worn books lined the ceiling-to-floor shelves flanking a flagstone fireplace, and vases of fresh flowers decorated the tables. Potted plants with shiny green leaves, illuminated by strategically placed spotlights, stood in each corner of the room.

There were gauzy white curtains at the windows, topped off with valances that matched the upholstery of the two wingbacks facing the woodstove insert. And beneath it all, thick-piled cream carpeting.

From where she stood, Breena could see into the dining room, bathed in its own shimmering candlelight. He'd set the claw-footed oak table for two, complete with a five-piece service of china, crystal water goblets, and enough flatware to serve a small army.

The scents drifting in from the kitchen inspired her to lift her chin and close her eyes. She took a deep, lingering breath. Just as Keegan entered the room, a tall tumbler of iced tea in each hand, her stomach rumbled loudly.

"I think I can hold out a little while longer," she said in response to his teasing grin.

Their fingers touched when she accepted the offered glass, and Breena shivered involuntarily in response to the warmth of his skin as it grazed hers.

Gently, Keegan grasped her elbow and guided her through the dining room. "I thought it'd be nice to sit outside 'til the grub's ready." Throwing open the French doors, he stepped onto the sun porch.

Here, as in the living room, Breena was stunned by the cleanliness. Apparently, he'd been married, and "the little woman" hadn't vacated the premises very long ago. The evidence was everywhere—in the artistic placement of every knickknack, in the positioning of each article of furniture, from the perfect blend of color and texture and style to the use of lights and shadows to enhance every item's shape. She shrugged one shoulder and sighed, feeling a pang of pity for the woman who had let a man like Keegan Neil go!

"Pull up a chair," he instructed, opening several tall, sliding windows, "and take a load off."

She sat in the wicker rocker nearest the door and nodded at the hat rack in the corner. "You have quite a collection. . . ."

"Yeah," he teased, "and I plan to keep 'em right there when you're around."

Breena laughed as the ceiling fan overhead whirred softly, and the breeze it roused caused the candle flames to dance, reminding her of the tiny ballerina that twirled and turned in the little pink jewelry box her father had given her for her tenth birthday. She still had that box, still kept trinkets and baubles inside it.

"Say, why the long face?" Keegan asked, sitting in the chair beside hers.

Sighing, she shook her head, then stared into her glass, as if the answers to all her problems swam among the sparkling ice cubes. "No reason," she said, resuming her former smiling demeanor. "Just remembering. . ."

"An old beau?"

Had she been mistaken? Did she hear a tinge of envy in his deep voice?

"No. . .nothing like that." She should be more careful with her responses, pretend there was a long line of old beaus in her past. Isn't that what the women's magazines would advise?

But Breena saw no point in playing hard to get with

Keegan Neil. He wasn't going to "get" her, period, because once he found out about her wretched past, he wouldn't want her. He deserved better, far better than the likes of her, and she knew it.

It had been fourteen years since her mother's death, and Breena had taken over the role of doting on her grouchy, emotionally distant father. Even though he never appreciated anything she did, looking after him was the least she could do. After all, it was her rotten behavior that had caused the stress that induced her mother's heart attack. If she'd been a good girl, her father would still have the love of his life to look out for him. . .instead of a penitent, guilt-ridden daughter. . .and Breena would still have her beautiful, loving mother. . . .

It happened this way sometimes. . .shame and regret building up and building up until it had nowhere to go but down her cheeks. Before she even realized she was crying, Keegan was down on one knee, enclosing all of her fingertips in one, big hand. "Hey," he whispered, wiping a tear from her lashes, "don't do that. . . you'll smear your mascara."

Scolding herself for exposing him to her weak-willed display, Breena stiffened her back. Sniffing, she blotted her eyes with the tissue he'd handed her and pulled herself together. "I-I'm not wearing any mascara."

One hand on each of the rocker's arms, he squinted in the dim light, then ran a fingertip across her lashes. "Well, I'll be a donkey's uncle. They're soft as my old granny's rabbit fur coat."

She opened her mouth to apologize, to thank him

for the compliment, to tell him she'd never seen bigger, greener eyes in her life. . .

. . .and a loud groan issued up from her stomach instead.

Breena covered her face with both hands. "I'm so embarrassed," she admitted, voice muffled by her palms. "Blubbering like a baby, then growling like an old lion." Peeking between two fingers, she added, "What must you think of me?"

"I think," he began, his voice thick and unsteady, his gaze unwavering, "you're the most gorgeous thing on two feet." He stood, pulled her to him, and wrapped her in a warm embrace. "And I think," he tacked on, "we'd better get some food in that belly of yours before you drop over in a dead faint."

Despite the warm June night, Breena was cold when he let her go. Hugging herself to fend off the unexpected chill, she watched him head back inside.

"I hope you like spaghetti," he said over his shoulder, " 'cause that's the main course." Stopping dead in his tracks, he faced her. "Hey. . .you're not one of those vegetarian types, are you?"

Breena's eyes widened and she blinked. "Who? Me? Give me steak over tofu any day!"

He gave an approving nod and started for the kitchen. "Good. 'Cause there're meatballs, too. Now, c'mon in here, and help me put the vittles on the table."

They chatted amiably over Caesar salad, spaghetti and

meatballs, and the spumoni he'd made for dessert. It took some convincing, but Keegan finally agreed to let Breena help him do the dishes. She washed, he dried. "Makes more sense," she explained, "since you know where everything goes. . . ."

Keegan chuckled. "That's what I like. . .a sensible woman."

Afterward, they returned to his sun porch. The night breeze had intensified, blowing out all the candles. "Are you cold?"

"A little," she admitted, settling onto the rattan sofa, "but it's so pretty out here, what with these big windows giving us a view of the sky and all, that I hate to go back inside, even though it's warmer."

Keegan tore the long-fringed afghan from the back of the matching easy chair, and gently draped it around her shoulders. Sitting beside her, he slid an arm around her waist and pulled her closer. "Warmer now?"

Nodding, Breena stared straight ahead, into the star-studded inky sky. The heat from his side seeped into her, warming not only her body, but her spirit, too. Self-recrimination for her mother's death had haunted her for so long, she hadn't felt worthy to let good and decent people close, for fear of contaminating them with her tainted past. Consequently, Breena had been cold and lonely for so long that being near him made her yearn for more.

Unconsciously, she rested her head on his shoulder and sighed. Eyes closed, she relaxed, and smiled from her heart for the first time in a long time.

It began gradually. . .his fingers playing in her short, dark curls, then softly stroking the back of her neck. Next, his lips found her temple, her cheek. Clasping her waist, Keegan drew her nearer. She knew he was going to kiss her; *wanted* him to kiss her. Logic reminded her they'd met only the day before yesterday. Still, there was no explaining it, but Breena felt as though she'd known him most of her adult life. *He deserves better than you,* she thought. *When he finds out what you did. . .*

She pictured the look of disappointment, of revulsion that had so often been painted on her father's face. Would Keegan's kindly smile turn down at the corners, his merrily twinkling eyes dim with indignation when he learned the truth about her? She'd known him barely more than forty-eight hours. . .more than long enough to know for certain that she'd rather die than see that. . . .

Far smarter—and safer—to leave now. Breena made a move to sit up, but Keegan's embrace tightened. "No," he murmured, "don't leave me. . .at least, not yet."

Did he realize what he was doing? Could he have known that she'd been thirsting for attention, for affection, such a long, lonely time? The answer eluded her and the question faded as his lips found hers. Breena drank hungrily, needily. Something inside her seemed to erupt; was she lost. . .or found?

Keegan inhaled a ragged breath and said, "I never meant for that to happen. . . ."

"Well," she interrupted, "it did." Breena ran a trembling hand through her hair, breaking the intense eye contact.

"Aw, don't look so sad, darlin'," he said, giving the tip of her nose an affectionate touch. "You didn't let me finish. I may not have meant for it to happen, but I'm glad it did."

Her heartbeat quickened in response to the sweet smile that slanted his burnished mustache. She had no right to feel utter relief at his words. *You're making mountains out of molehills,* she scolded herself, *dreaming like some silly school girl lost in the throes of her first crush.* Something told her that if she hadn't lived such a deliberately solitary life, this evening wouldn't seem like such a big deal.

But she had lived alone, and this evening *was* a big deal. The biggest in her life. If she were smart, she'd get to her feet right now, leave and not look back. If she stayed, she'd be hurt. Maybe not right away, but sooner or later. *Better never to have loved and lost,* she rearranged the age-old cliché, *than to love. . .and lose.*

When she pressed her palms against his hard, broad chest for leverage to stand, he wrapped each slender wrist with his thick, callused fingers. His coarse whisper sliced the silence. "You're lovely."

She looked deep into eyes that gleamed with a blend of affection and passion. *You'd sing a different tune if you knew the truth about me.* The thought reverberated in her head a time or two. What better way to test his intentions, than by putting it all out there?

"I killed my mother."

Chapter 5

Keegan's brows dipped low in the center of his forehead as his gentle smile settled somewhere between bemused disbelief and cautious concern. "You. . .*what?*"

"She had a heart condition, and I wasn't exactly the best daughter." Shaking her head, Breena said, "But I'm putting the cart before the horse."

Breena stood and began pacing in the space between the glass-topped coffee table and the sofa, repeatedly squeezing first one hand, then the other. "It all started," she went on, feigning a light, nonchalant tone, "when my parents separated. I was fourteen at the time, and it scared me half to death. As an only child, I'd always been number one in their lives. I couldn't believe they were actually considering putting their needs and wants ahead of mine. I mean," she rolled her eyes, emulating her fourteen-year-old self, " 'how dare they mess up my perfect, happy life with talk of divorce.' "

Keegan got to his feet, slid an arm around her waist. "Breena. . .please, sit down." He chucked her under the chin. "They say this indoor-outdoor stuff wears like iron, but I hate to put it to the test with your pacin'. . . ."

She read the gentle smile in his eyes and allowed him to walk her to the sofa. Hands tightly clasped on her knees, Breena continued. "They'd always been so proud of my achievements—academic, athletic, volunteer—and constantly boasted about their sweet, smart little girl." Her lips thinned as her gaze found his. "When they split up, I wanted to hurt them, the way they'd hurt me. I didn't think I had any ammunition except—" She took a deep breath. "Something told me the best way to accomplish that was to take their bragging rights away from them."

Keegan nodded understandingly. "Got yourself involved with a rough crowd, did you?" he asked.

She answered in a voice heavy with sarcasm. "That's putting it mildly; I rode home from school in a squad car almost as often as I took the bus." She shook her head. "Eventually, my folks worked out their problems and got back together, but by that time, I was in so deep with my low-life friends, I didn't have the courage to get out. I became—"

"The kids who work for me used to get into trouble regularly, too," Keegan interrupted, patting her hand. "That doesn't mean they are—or ever were—bad." Tenderly, he tucked a lock of hair behind her ear.

"—I became incorrigible," she rattled on. "My behavior worried my mother to distraction. She was under constant stress, a lot of it, because of me." Tears filled Breena's eyes, and she bit her lip to stifle a sob.

Seeming not to notice, Keegan quirked an eyebrow as his mustache tilted above a mischievous grin. "So what sort of weapon did you use to do her in?"

Breena scowled at him in disbelief. "That isn't funny, Keegan."

"Sorry. . .I was only trying to—"

"I know what you were trying to do. You were trying to make a joke because you don't think I killed my mom." She tucked in one corner of her mouth. "Well, thanks for the attempt, but it won't work." She went on as if there hadn't been an interruption. "The only weapon I needed was my—"

He held up a hand to silence her. "Don't tell me. . . your _behavior?_"

Breena, appearing not to hear the gentle sarcasm in his voice, focused instead on something beyond his left shoulder. "One question has always plagued me, though," she said, more to herself than to Keegan.

Balancing both elbows on his knees now, he peered into her face. "And what would that be, darlin'?"

She met his eyes, and in a small fluttery voice said, "My parents never told me Mom had a heart condition. If—" Breena lowered her eyes, then her head.

With a wave of his hand, Keegan prompted her to continue.

"But if they had, would it have made any difference? If I'd known how sick she was, would _that_ have given me the courage to break away from those kids, to walk the straight and narrow again, _for her?_"

For a long while, neither Keegan nor Breena spoke. Finally, she broke the silence. "Well," she said, rising, "there you have it. My horrible history in a nutshell."

Hurriedly, she walked toward the front door and grabbed her sweater from the hall tree.

"What are you *really* hiding from?" His voice was stern, his face impassive as she opened the oak door.

She stood in the open entry. "Hiding?" she repeated. "I'm not—"

Keegan emitted a dry, cynical chuckle that silenced her. "You didn't kill your mama, darlin'." He jabbed the air with a forefinger. "Her heart condition did."

Standing taller, she lifted her chin. "Technically, that's true, but it was my behavior that—"

Keegan groaned under his breath, one hand in the air like a traffic cop, and said, "If you were still sixteen, I'd understand such an immature mindset. But we both know that you're not sixteen." He narrowed his eyes to add, "Let me get this straight: You want to be guilty of causing your mother's death?"

Blanching, Breena stammered, "Well, well, no. No, of course I don't. I don't *want* to—"

"Then don't be," he said emphatically. Then in a calmer voice, Keegan added, "God hasn't judged you as harshly as you've judged yourself."

Breena remembered that day in college, when she'd gone to the front of the big tent and accepted Jesus as her Lord and Savior. *If God hasn't judged me, then why did He—*

"I'll tell you what I think," Keegan said, breaking into her thoughts, "I think you're using this 'guilt trip' to keep people from getting too close. What's the matter. . .afraid you'll fall in love with somebody. . .

and let them down?"

Breena began to tell him about the day when she had tried to give her life to God, but as she stumbled through the story, Keegan lay a silencing finger against her lips. "Hush, darlin'." His voice and demeanor softened even more, "You've already said too much."

He wrapped her in his arms and held her tight. "I said it before, I'll say it again: You're a fine woman, Breena. Your so-called shocking confession didn't change my opinion of you one iota." He winked mischievously and grinned. "You seem to have all the answers; what's your answer to *that?*"

"I-I never pretended to have all the answers." Rolling her eyes in vexation, Breena snapped, "For your information, I didn't make my 'so-called shocking confession' to change your opinion of me. I told you because—" Breena stopped short of completing her sentence, because she knew he was exactly right.

He lifted her chin with a bent forefinger, then pressed both warm palms against her cheeks. Whether she deserved it or not, he seemed to like her, and his acceptance was like a healing salve on her lonely, aching heart.

Her heart turned over as his gaze slid across her face, a tingling sensation began in the pit of her stomach as his thumbs drew lazy circles on her jaw. The draft of air that sighed through the open front door swirled around them in cool, electrifying currents. Trapped in the invisible warmth of his welcoming arms, she silently urged, *Do it! Kiss me, already, so I can*

311

gather what's left of my dignity and leave!

As if he'd read her mind, Keegan's face moved nearer, until she could feel his faint breaths upon her face.

Breena closed her eyes to savor the moment, and like a giddy girl caught up in her own emotions, she waited. . . .

The soft touch of his mustache against her mouth put her on her toes, and what had begun as a feathery caress became an almost-timid kiss that sang through her. Breena ran her fingers through his soft, dark waves, hoping to imprint the feel of the satiny strands upon her brain. She wanted to remember the sound of his voice, his tender touch, the compassion that had glittered in his green eyes. This innocently provocative kiss in particular would be something Breena would treasure when she returned to her stark and solitary world.

Slowly, Keegan stepped back and, hands on her shoulders, turned her around and gently shoved her onto the front porch. He reached onto the hall table and picked up a huge bouquet of roses and baby's breath, wrapped in green tissue paper.

"What. . .what's this?" she stammered.

"Forty-eight flowers for forty-eight hours. . .but none as beautiful as you." He smiled broadly. "Of course, that's not exact. I wrapped these this afternoon. It's more like fifty-six and a half hours by now."

She cradled the roses as if they were a newborn child. Had it really been so few hours? Though Breena was in no emotional condition to calculate it, she had a strong suspicion that Keegan knew precisely how long it had been.

"Call me when you grow up," he said as the door swung shut, "and we'll pick up where we left off."

For a moment, Breena stood squinting into the bright glow of the porch light. There would be a pin-prick of light shining through the peep hole unless it had been blocked by something. . .or someone. . . .

Smiling ever so slightly, Breena lifted the flowers a bit. "Thank you, Mr. Maturity," she said, and turned to leave.

He'd been pretty hard on her, but Keegan believed he had no choice. Working with troubled kids had taught him that pity was never good medicine.

The truth of the matter was, he did feel sorry for Breena, mighty sorry. But he'd seen the same sad, self-punishing expression on the face of every adolescent he'd ever hired at the greenhouse. Each had responded to his version of "tough love" because, as Marcellus had put it, "You ain't no phony, man; you say what you mean and you mean what you say."

Marcellus had been Keegan's first "case," and there had been dozens since. Several, like Marcellus, had come to work at That's the Way It Grows, when Keegan took over and began to clean the place up. He didn't have any formal counseling training, which he liked to think set him yards apart from specialists in

313

child psychology. He believed God had called him to this task, because he surely had not asked for the assignment! Keegan had always relied upon the Almighty to provide whatever he might need, whenever he might need it, to help kids in crisis. The Lord had seen fit to bless him with an ability to get the kids to open up, to reveal pertinent facts about themselves that would help Keegan get to the root of their problems.

Other than what she had said at dinner, Keegan knew virtually nothing about Breena.

Well, that wasn't entirely true. When Breena paid for the flat of marigolds, she'd filled out one of the "May We Send You A Catalog?" forms that sat beside the greenhouse cash register, so he knew her name and address. He knew by the condition of her hands that she wasn't afraid of hard work. He knew she had an amazing sense of humor, and that she was beautiful, and sweet as cotton candy.

And her kisses were warm and genuine. *Mmmm-mmmm-mmmm,* Keegan said to himself, smiling at the memory. Something told him it meant every bit as much to her as it had to him.

The most striking thing he knew was that Breena actually thought she'd killed her mother. Why, he didn't know; certainly not for the far-fetched reason she'd given him. And for some off-the-wall reason she thought that God had rejected her. *Probably the two things are connected in her beautiful, mixed-up head. . . .*

Keegan pictured her, more beautiful than any woman he'd ever known, especially with tears shimmering in her big brown eyes, and heard the incredible sadness that dulled her otherwise musical voice. He had no earthly idea what could have put a cockeyed notion like that into her pretty head and kept it there all these years, but if it was the last thing he did, he sure as shootin' aimed to find out!

Breena was up all night, thinking about Keegan. He'd been a doting host; dinner was delicious, dessert spectacular! From the time she'd arrived to the time they'd returned to the sun porch, she and Keegan had talked and laughed, and genuinely enjoyed one another's company.

But all that changed the moment she began telling him about her past. Keegan's lighthearted mood had contrasted with her own dark disposition as he tried to convince her she hadn't been responsible for her mother's death.

Of *course* it had been her fault!

For the first time in fourteen years, Breena wasn't so certain of the answer.

She *hadn't* known about the heart condition, after all, a condition that had plagued her mother since shortly after Breena was born. Because of the ailment, her parents hadn't added to their family.

But there was still the matter of the unanswered question: If she had known about her mother's illness,

315

would she have become the good, obedient daughter again her mother had boasted about?

Until Breena could be sure, she'd continue to believe that her mother had died, long before her time, because of her,

What if the answer to the question is "no"? Breena asked herself. What if, after all this time, she discovered that something else had caused her mother to overreact, and hyperventilate, and. . .

Breena slumped onto the chair nearest the telephone and glanced around her apartment. She'd been punishing herself for so long that if the answer was no, her entire life would change. She'd have a chance at a real, loving relationship with her father, at a complete life of her own, maybe even with a devoted husband and children who would think she'd hung the moon.

She shook her head and got to her feet. Much as she wanted to be set free from the shackles of guilt and shame, it was simply too much to hope for.

It hadn't been pleasant, taking the blame for what had happened, but Breena had lived with it for so long that she had grown to accept, if not be comfortable, with it.

Too bad, she thought, because she liked Keegan. Right up to and including the way he got all gruff and tough with her at the end of their dinner. Breena understood that he'd been trying to give her another viewpoint to think about. Oh, she hadn't understood it at first, that much was certain! At first, she'd been furious with Keegan for his paternal demeanor.

But he'd been so sweet, so funny, so forgiving earlier that, once back on familiar turf, she couldn't help but wonder *why* he'd so suddenly changed.

She walked over to the snack bar that separated the kitchen from the living room. It had taken two vases and a jelly jar to hold the roses Keegan had given her. The entire apartment was alive with their honeyed scent. Breena withdrew one of the long-stemmed beauties from the water and, eyes closed, reveled in the feel of its velvety petals against her cheek. "Forty-eight flowers for forty-eight hours," she said in a singsong voice.

Suddenly she remembered how Keegan had taken her to task about her mother and she jammed the rose back into the vase.

Like an actress in a 1940s B-movie, Breena paced the width and breadth of her loft apartment, asking the seemingly unanswerable question, "Who does he think he is, expelling me like an unruly schoolgirl!"

Chapter 6

The frantic elderly woman paced back and forth like a nervous delivery room daddy-to-be as Breena tightened strings and adjusted the hammers of the ancient player piano. The instrument had been a tenth anniversary gift from the lady's dear departed husband.

Breena had always been glad for extra tuning or repair jobs. Mrs. Barber was a talker, and that was good, because the chatter would take Breena's mind off Keegan.

"It got out of tune once, back in '79 I believe it was," Mrs. Barber said, squinting one eye as she strained to remember, "but I never much minded the sour notes; they kind of reminded me of my Henry." She clasped thin-skinned, wrinkled hands beneath her double chins and smiled wistfully. The smile diminished, and she added, "Then this morning, I sat down to peck out a tune, and nothing!" The girlish pout erased ten years off her face. "You can fix it, can't you?"

Certain people and their pianos, Breena had discovered, forged relationships that would put some marriages to shame. *If folks gave this kind of care and attention to their spouses,* she'd often thought, *the divorce rate would plummet!*

"I'll do what I can," she promised. It was a bit like being in front of the tiger cage at the zoo, watching Mrs. Barber walk to and fro, back and forth. She seemed fit. . . for an older woman, but what if, like Breena's mother, she had a weak heart? Surely all this fussing and pacing around wouldn't be good for her. . . .

"So tell me, what's your favorite piano solo?"

Mrs. Barber's face lit up like she was standing in the spotlights on stage. She perched on the edge of the piano bench and crossed both arms over her ample bosom. "Hmmm. . ." She tapped an arthritic finger against her chin. "Guess I'd have to say 'Amazing Grace.' Umm-hmm. Definitely 'Amazing Grace.' Why, just a couple bars of that one can lift my spirits for hours, especially when I'm at work!"

This adorable senior citizen still has a job? "What kind of work do you do, Mrs. Barber?"

"Well, I retired last year, y'see. Hit the old seven-oh and decided it was time to slow down. Those first few weeks were fun, but then I started to *hate* havin' nothin' to do." Raising her chin and grinning with pride, she continued, "I'd been working for the same man nearly quarter of a century. When his grandson took over, I wasn't so sure I'd like the job, don'cha know. Turned out he's a better boss than his grandpa, and that's sayin' a mouthful, let me tell you!"

Crossing one knee over the other, Mrs. Barber smiled. "I asked the boss if he'd let me come back. . .

cut my hours, and—"

As long as Breena kept her talking, Mrs. Barber seemed content to sit still, which took some pressure off of Breena,

"What sort of work do you do?"

"I'm an accountant. I may have lost my figure, but I'm mighty good at mindin' other folks' figures," she laughed. "Best thing about this job," she whispered conspiratorially, one hand beside her mouth, "I found out I'm pretty good with things that grow. And long as I don't get greedy, the boss says I'm welcome to a freebie now and then."

Atta girl, Mrs. Barber, keep talking. . .and sitting. . . .
"What sort of freebies?"

"House plants, vegetable plants, border plants for the outside gardens. . ."

There had been a white-haired woman in the window of Keegan's office, and if Breena's memory served correctly, he'd called her Agnes. *Didn't Mrs. Barber say, "I'm Agnes Barber, and my player piano isn't playing."? Oh, come on, Breena. What are the chances Mrs. Barber is Keegan's Agnes?*

"Mr. Neil is the most generous boss I've ever worked for."

"Mr. Neil?" Breena swallowed hard.

"He lets me set my own hours. Long as the bills and the payroll checks get cut on time, I'm free to come and go as I please." Another gravelly giggle. "He's got me covered, let me tell you! Health care, pension, profit sharing. . .why, the man's generous to a fault."

Pension? Profit sharing? Full health care benefits. . . for a part-time, semi-retired employee? Breena had never heard of such a thing. Mrs. Barber was a fortunate woman to have such a concerned, caring boss.

Could Keegan have set up this piano house call? She'd never told him where she lived or what she did for a living. Breena couldn't remember ever telling him her last name!

Suddenly, her cheeks burned with a blush. *How ridiculous to think that a busy man like Keegan would be plotting to send me business.* Still, he did seem interested. They had shared a peaceful, pleasant dinner; four dozen aromatic, red roses filling vases in her apartment proved his thoughtful, romantic nature. He had kissed her—on the first date—and she had kissed him back. All this and they'd only known each other for three days! She was falling feet over forehead for a virtual stranger.

". . .and what a handsome young fella," Mrs. Barber was saying. "It's a wonder some slick female hasn't snapped him up by now."

"He's never been married?"

Mrs. Barber shook his head. "Nope."

"Ouch!" Breena pinched her finger in the teeth of her needle-nosed pliers. *Get your mind on your work, before you permanently maim yourself!* One sharp whack with the rubber mallet, and the piano's rollers snapped back into place. "Have a seat at the keyboard, Mrs. Barber, and rev 'er up; let's see if we've got this baby up and running."

321

"Here's to happy endings!" Mrs. Barber said as she depressed the foot pedal.

Immediately, a lively tune jangled from the big mahogany box. "Oh, honey, you've done it! You fixed my piano!" Mrs. Barber clapped her hands in time to the music. "Can't you just hear Al Jolson, puttin' words to this melody?" And with neither prompting nor invitation, she belted out the first bars of the ancient song. " 'Swanee, how I love ya, how I love ya, my dear old—' "

Smiling, Breena packed up her tools. Repairing and tuning pianos demanded ingenuity, dexterity, and physical strength. She'd never minded the hard-work aspects of the job, because they guaranteed the end result: seeing and hearing her customers' joy when they'd been reunited with their instruments.

Mrs. Barber stopped singing as suddenly as she'd started. "How much do I owe you?"

Breena filled out a work order, detailing the charges for parts and labor. "You can send a check to that address," she said, handing it to the elderly woman. Customers of Mrs. Barber's age came from a generation with a "do your best" work ethic and pride that demanded all debts be paid, on time and in full. But some lived on fixed incomes, and didn't always have the financial wherewithal to pay on the spot for service calls. Asking them to send a check to her workshop, she'd learned, gave them plenty of time to come up with the money, sparing them a boatload of embarrassment. Besides, Breena earned a good living, tending the pianos owned by area churches and schools.

Seventy years old or not, Mrs. Barber was quick. Too quick to let that one slide. "Oh, you're a sly one, honey." In no time, she'd dashed off a check in the full amount of the invoice. "There y'go," she said, tucking it into Breena's shirt pocket. "Now, I'm gonna give you a piece of advice. . .free of charge." And with a snort and a chuckle and an elbow to Breena's ribs, Mrs. Barber instructed, "Don't give anybody a free ride. You do good work; make folks pay for it!"

Nodding and smiling, Breena allowed the feisty lady to usher her to the door.

"You married, honey?"

"No."

"Engaged?"

"No."

"Got yourself a steady beau?"

Breena thought of Keegan. . .and that parting kiss . . . Sighing regretfully, she said, "No."

"What! Pretty and sweet as you are?"

Shrugging, she said, "Guess I just haven't found my Mr. Right yet." But even as she said it, Breena knew she'd found him.

The scent of roses floated everywhere.

Hiding under the blankets, then the pillow, did nothing but make her short of breath. Even getting up and closing the door didn't block out the sweet, soft fragrance.

Breena tossed and turned for an hour before surrendering. "That's the trouble with a loft apartment," she muttered, firing up the teapot.

Hershey's "since you're up anyway, why not feed me?" expression told her she'd get no sympathy there. Breena fed the cat, then rummaged in the cupboard for a tea bag. *Chamomile is supposed to have natural relaxing properties,* she thought. Breena brewed it extra strong.

Lounging in the overstuffed easy chair near the windows, Breena stared into the vast, velvety sky that blanketed the city below. It was a bright, clear night, complete with a silvery crescent moon and thousands of winking, blinking stars.

Was her mother up there among it all, enjoying an equally beautiful view of earth? Breena's gaze slid toward the bookshelves that flanked the fireplace. On a high shelf, illuminated by the beam of a carefully aimed track light, stood Breena's most treasured possessions: A five-by-seven black and white photograph, and a white leather journal.

In the sterling-framed picture, her mother stood alone, one shoulder leaning against the trunk of an ancient weeping willow, smiling serenely, her dark curls cascading down her back like a fur cape. They say the camera doesn't lie. The snapshot, taken on her parents' honeymoon to Niagara Falls, had captured her mother's physical frailty.

And the diary had likely captured Annie Pavan's emotional fragility. As a girl, Breena had watched as her mother, pen in hand, filled in the faint blue lines that striped each page. Her sweet smile, whether she'd been recording chickadee behavior or reacting to a rainbow, told Breena more than the written words could have. . .

But Breena didn't know what Annie had penned in the log, because she'd never been able to bring herself to open it. What if she scanned the precise script and confirmed a link between her wayward behavior and the physical symptoms of Annie's emotional condition?

Better to let sleeping dogs lie, she'd told herself each time she was tempted to pore over her mother's secret thoughts. By now, it had become a habit. . .this business of avoiding unpleasantness. . .so much so that Breena barely realized when she was doing it.

She realized this: She missed her mother!

When had she last said "I love you" to Annie? Sometime before her parents' separation, that much was certain. It had become one of the most agonizing facts of her past. . .that her mother had died, never knowing how much Breena had always loved and appreciated her.

And there was no going back now. No re-doing things done wrong. No repairing the damage her own self-centered, immature mindset had caused.

Keegan had been right about that, Breena admitted. Thirty years old or not, she had a long way to go before she could say she'd truly grown up!

Breena forced herself to look away from the keepsakes and focused again on the heavens beyond her window. Surely her mother was up there—*somewhere,*

She'd been a good and decent woman—and Breena suspected she'd been close to God, though shy of talking about Him.

"At least she's not in pain any more," a neighbor had said at the funeral. "She's in a better place now," someone else had responded.

Happy, and living eternally, without pain. Sixteen-year-old Breena had hoped it was true. She still hoped it was true.

Her eyes filled with tears. "I miss you, Mama," she whispered.

Chapter 7

"You can't get a good night's sleep if you've left dishes in the sink."

It was a proverb coined by his mother, one he'd heard hundreds of times growing up. Raised single-handedly by this loving but no-nonsense, by-the-book woman, Keegan learned to make hospital corners on a bed that would put a Marine Corps drill sergeant to shame. She'd taught him how to cook dozens of mouth-watering gourmet recipes, and how to keep house. Anymore, his fastidiously clean house was second nature.

Trying his best to stifle a yawn, he put away the dishes he'd just washed. Living alone all these years, he'd never seen a need for an automatic dishwasher. But the concept—and the contraption itself—was looking better and better.

The clock in the front hall gonged nine times. He rarely hit the hay before ten, but after staring at a computer screen all afternoon he was completely exhausted. *Give me some perennials and a pile of dirt any day of the week.*

One of the more interesting and exciting jobs he'd

held to pay his way through college had been a summer at the "Smith and Wesson" detective agency. His boss, Ernie Sisneros, looked about as much like the stereotypical private eye as the queen of England looks like Mr. Rogers. There had never been a Smith in Ernie's family, and the closest he'd ever got to Wesson was when he fried up a panful of hash browns. But the name gave folks the confidence to call, and Ernie gave them the belief he'd solve their cases.

Keegan had learned a lot that summer. Though the mainstay of his job had been delivering subpoenas and summonses, he'd been assigned to "searches" now and then. He knew how to find things and people and information.

Determined to discover the truth about Breena and her mother, Keegan had parked himself in front of the InfoSeek computer at the library immediately after lunch, and hadn't looked up until a quarter to five. By the time he had completed his other errand and was jamming the key into his front door, it was nearly seven.

Just as he'd suspected, Breena had *not* killed her mother. A rare, genetic heart defect had been the cause of death—the kind of disease that would have done her in even if she'd spent her life in a convent.

When he was finished at the library, it hadn't been easy to ring the doorbell of the house where Annie Pavan had died. But Keegan knew he'd get no rest unless he found out why Breena felt responsible for what had happened.

Who better to ask than the only witness to the tragedy?

Breena's father was a nondescript little man with dark hair gone mostly gray, blue eyes that peered suspiciously from a face that was a roadmap of lines and wrinkles, and a mouth that seemed set in a permanent scowl.

He'd been reluctant to let Keegan inside, grumping and groaning about how thoughtless young folks were these days, dropping by unannounced and the like. But by the time he showed Keegan out, anyone watching might have thought Robert Pavan was saying good-bye to a lifelong friend.

Both men learned a lot in the hour they were together. Keegan learned (or rather, re-learned) the age-old lesson, "Never judge a book by its cover." And Breena's father figured out that, because of his own behavior, his only child had spent the past fourteen years blaming herself for her mother's death.

Keegan didn't have a clue what to do next, but as he slid between the sheets, he had every confidence the idea would be there in the morning. God had put him and Breena together; there wasn't a doubt in Keegan's mind about that. There also wasn't a doubt that God would show Keegan the way to help free Breena from years of misplaced self-recrimination.

Keegan hoped the path to that end wouldn't be a long and winding one, because Breena deserved to know how much God loved her, as soon as possible. And Keegan was ready to end his search for the right woman, which before had always come up empty-handed.

He knew that a good relationship—a good *marriage*—must be built on a firm foundation. And though he was convinced that Breena had accepted the Lord at that youth rally years ago, she didn't seem to understand how to trust God for her life here and now. Breena might the woman God intended him to spend the rest of his life with, but she was on mighty shaky ground right now.

But once this mess from Breena's past is cleaned up. . .

Keegan was asleep before he could finish the thought.

Her apartment was beginning to look like a South American jungle. Four times in the six days since she had met Keegan Neil a delivery truck from That's the Way It Grows had pulled up outside her workshop. Now, in her apartment, there were green and flowering plants on every table, every shelf, every windowsill, and indoor trees in every corner. She had to admit they warmed the place up considerably. "But really," she said to Hershey, "where does he expect me to find the time to water these babies?" Not that it mattered, because in a month, every one of them would be dry and brown and dead.

The cat's bored yawn was interrupted by the doorbell. "That's what you get for being so insensitive," she teased as Hershey disappeared into Breena's bedroom.

She always entered the apartment by way of the workshop downstairs, because the driveway was right beside the entrance. Guests and the occasional Girl Scout cookie pusher used the front entrance, which required a climb up a flight of wide, metal steps. *That's weird,* she thought, positioning herself in front of the peep hole, *I usually hear people long before the bell rings. . . .*

Through the peephole, all Breena could see was a bouquet of mixed cut flowers. *Keegan, are you ever going to quit?* She flung the door open and her heart hammered when she saw her father on the landing, one hand in his pocket, the other holding the flowers.

"Hi," he said in a small, timid voice. "I brought you these."

In a voice that sounded like it came from outside of herself, Breena thanked him for the flowers and waved him inside. "If I'd known you were coming, I would have—"

"Baked a cake?"

Breena couldn't remember the last time she'd seen that playful light in his blue eyes, and she had to fight the impulse to throw her arms around his neck. *Why is he here?* "I was just about to run to the grocery store. There's a sale on chicken; I could get a roaster and fix you a nice—"

"Breena," he said, wending his way into the kitchen, "aren't you going to show your old man around?"

"Well, well, sure," she stammered, "of course. Just. . . just let me put these in water first."

331

While Breena arranged the bouquet in an empty mayonnaise jar, her father meandered into the living room. "Nice place you've got here. I like it." He stood with his back to her and his hands in his pocket, nodding approvingly. "You have your mother's eye for detail."

She'd lived in this apartment for nearly five years, but despite repeated invitations, he'd never visited before now. Breena set the flowers in the jar on the table and muttered a mousy "Thanks, Dad."

Robert Pavan touched a rose petal. "These from that greenhouse guy?"

Breena nodded and frowned. *That greenhouse guy? How does he know about Keegan? I've never said a word.*

"Must be mighty sweet on you; there are enough roses here to choke a horse!" With a sweep of his arm, he gestured toward the rest of the plants. "Rest of this green stuff from him, too?"

Another nod.

"Looks like he's taken quite a fancy to my little girl."

Had she heard correctly? Was there a tinge of pride . . .and *love*. . .in his voice?

"Got any coffee?"

"I-I brewed a pot just before you—"

"How about pourin' us both a cup, then, while I prowl around the rest of the place?"

She watched as he headed for the bedroom, where her unmade bed and a pile of dirty laundry would prove she was still a master at messing things up. "Have you eaten breakfast?" she called after him.

"Well, I dunked a couple Oreos in milk. . . .You know. . . ."

"Why don't I scramble you an egg, make some toast and—"

He met her eyes for the first time since she'd closed the door behind him. . .for the first time in too long. "Maybe later. Right now, I just want to talk."

Talk? About what? Breena's mouth went dry and her palms grew damp. Had he decided to come right out with it, say what he'd been feeling all these years about her part in her mother's death?

Mechanically, she placed cloth napkins, the sugar bowl, a tiny pitcher of milk, and one spoon on the table. Of the two chairs in her kitchen, she liked the one facing the window best. Many a morning, she'd daydream over the morning paper and black coffee as Main Street came to life. She perched on the edge of the other chair, leaving her favorite seat for her father.

"Still taking yours straight, I see," he said, pointing at her mug of black coffee.

A feeble smile was all the answer she could muster. *Funny,* she thought as he stirred milk and sugar into his mug, *I don't feel any relief at all, even though I've been praying for this moment most of my life, it seems.*

"Dad? Why are you here?" She sounded remarkably calm despite the turmoil that now raged inside of her. *Go ahead and get it over with,* she silently fumed. *Tell me you can never forgive me for killing Mom, so at least we can have an honest relationship, if not a loving one!* Now that the moment of truth had arrived, Breena wasn't at all

333

sure it was what she wanted. *At least the other way, I could pretend he loved me, a little. . . .*

"Keegan Neil stopped by to see me the other day."

Keegan? He'd gone to see Dad? Whatever for?

"Said he'd spent the day at the library, researching your past."

What? Breena picked at a nub on the placemat, and waited. . . .

"Before you came along, your mother used to tease me, saying living with me was like living alone. . . because I hardly said a word. . . ." He downed a gulp of coffee. "I've never been one for a lot of unnecessary talk."

Especially since the funeral. . .

"I don't know how else to handle this, except to get straight to the point."

Robert took her hands in his and forced her, by sheer will, to meet his eyes. "Can you ever forgive me, Breena?"

For a long moment, Breena could only stare in silent disbelief. "Forgive *you?* For what?"

"For letting you think you'd killed your mother." He looked away, but held tight to her hands. "All these years. . .I had no idea. . . ." He swallowed, hard, then met her eyes again. "I've been off in a world of my own. Going to work and coming home, watching TV, reading—" A dry chuckle punctuated his words. "Why, I believe I've read every book your mother collected, twice!"

"That would take two lifetimes, Dad," she said, smiling at the memory of her mother's library. The joke was. . .the whole house was the library, and oh, how she loved those books! Every one—even the paperbacks—wore a dust jacket, whether store-bought or fashioned from left-over gift wrap or shelf paper. Alphabetized, and organized by subject matter in the various rooms of the house, Annie could put her finger on a requested title in the blink of an eye.

Robert continued as though Breena hadn't spoken at all. "If I hadn't been such a self-centered—" He shook his head. Then, boring deep into his daughter's eyes, said, "It wasn't your fault, honey. We knew right from the start that she wasn't long for this world."

"Then. . .then why did you two separate? Why all the talk of divorce?"

A deep sigh escaped his lungs. "Because she'd been badgering me for another baby, *for years,* and frankly, I couldn't take a minute more of it. 'You want to leave me, you do it some other way,' I told her."

"And so she went back to Grandma's," Breena whispered, nodding.

"I'd never been able to refuse her anything; guess she figured if I saw how much she wanted more kids, I'd give her that, too. But I wouldn't. *Couldn't.*

"Don't get me wrong, I would have loved a house full of kids like you. But she was dying when we met, and we knew that every morning was its own little miracle. She—"

"You did the right thing, Dad," Breena interrupted. "Another child would surely have—"

"No!" His fist hit the table with such force that

the lid to the sugar jar rattled. "Now, you listen to me!" He paused, shook his head again, and in a softer voice continued, "She was lucky to have lived *that* long. Every specialist I took her to after the wedding said she'd have two, three years at best. Having you is what gave her the extra time. Don't you *see,* Breena? You didn't kill your mother. Being your mother is what kept her alive when nothing in the realm of modern medicine could."

"But. . .but all the trouble I caused. All the—"

Chuckling, Robert squeezed her hands. "You're so much like her in so many ways, right down to that stubborn streak of yours. Breena, honey, haven't you heard a word I said? *Wanting* you kept her alive a full year longer than the doctors predicted; *having* you gave her *fifteen years more!*" His lower lip twitched as he struggled not to cry. "You didn't take her from me, honey, you gave me a lifetime with her, when all I'd ever expected was a few years, at best. If you're so all-fired determined to take responsibility for something, take it for *that!*"

He pointed in the direction of the living room. "I saw your mother's journal on the shelf in there. How can you not know how she felt about you? It's all there, in her own handwriting."

Breena could only sit there, shaking her head at the irony of it all. The solution to all her problems had been right at her fingertips for fourteen years.

"I said it before, I'll say it again," he began, "I'm a self-centered, selfish old man. I missed your mother so much, I never took the time to see that you were hurting, too. Plus—" Robert took a deep breath and let it out slowly. "Plus, looking at you, being with you, was a constant reminder of her." He squeezed her hands again. "I know I don't deserve it. . .putting you through all these years of misery. . .but please say you'll forgive me."

"There's nothing to forgive, Dad." It hadn't taken soul-searching, or deep thought, or time; there truly was nothing to forgive. Breena had her father back!

And she had Keegan Neil to thank for it.

Chapter 8

Breena Neil. Mrs. Keegan Neil. Mrs. Neil.

The moment she became aware what her pen had been scribbling, Breena dropped it on the table. Dreaming of becoming his wife was one thing. Putting it in writing was another.

Get hold of yourself, she scolded, gathering up billing statements, stamps, return address labels, *before you—*

The doorbell rang, startling her so badly she nearly dropped the whole stack. *What's wrong with you? That's the second time in a row you didn't hear someone on the steps!* After tucking the materials into a box marked "Bills," Breena hurried to the front door.

I should have gone to bed earlier, instead of staying up all night, reading Mom's diary.... Breena rubbed her eyes and looked through the peep hole again.

Keegan stood with one hand in his pocket and the other holding a bouquet of mixed cut flowers. *What is this? Are he and Dad in some sort of cahoots?*

"Hi," he said when she opened the door, "I brought these for you."

Tucking in one corner of her mouth, she accepted the gift. "Thank you. They're beautiful." Then, a nod of her head indicating the rest of the blooming gifts, she added, "You didn't happen to bring something to put them in, did you?"

Laughing, Keegan shook his head. "Sorry. Sometimes I get carried away. . .something you ought to know."

She put the flowers into a tall tumbler and filled it with water. "Something I ought to know?" she repeated. "Why?"

Keegan shrugged. "Well, I just thought that since we'd be seeing more and more of one another, you ought to be aware of my flaws."

"There's a small fortune in greenery in here, and you call that a flaw?" Breena giggled. "You've sure got a lot to learn about making a woman miserable. . . ."

He glanced around the apartment. "Say, I like your place. It's very. . .spacey, I mean *spacious*."

"You were right the first time. Spacey, that's me. Hey, I just made a pitcher of lemonade. Care for a glass?"

"Sure." He grinned mischievously. "A glass would be nice. You gonna put some lemonade in it?"

"Yes, and ice cubes, too." She propped a fist on her hip, pointed a maternal finger at him with the other hand. "Now park it, mister; you and I have some serious talkin' to do."

Both eyebrows rose high on his forehead as his smile dimmed. "Okay. . .but do you mind if I open the door. . .just in case I need to make a quick getaway?"

"I mind very much, as a matter of fact." And in response to his confused frown, Breena added, "I don't want you to get away. Ever."

Beaming, Keegan sat where her father had, just the day before. Laying one hand atop the other, he hooked his pointy-toed boots around the legs of the ladder-back, and waited.

"Thanks, Keegan," she said, sitting opposite him.

"Wow, you're pretty in the morning light."

"No one has ever done anything so nice for me before."

"Actually, you're pretty in *any* light, but you're especially pretty in—"

"I was up all night, reading my mother's journal. I learned a lot about her, learned a lot about myself, too."

He leaned forward, covered her hands with one of his own, and ran a fingertip over her lashes with the other. "Hard to believe those are real. What are you, part giraffe or something?"

"Giraffe!" she giggled. "What has a gira—"

"I thought for sure you were the type who'd notice details, like the color of a mouse's tail and the fact that calicos are mostly female." He narrowed one eye. "You tellin' me you never noticed before what long eyelashes giraffes have?"

"Well, I've noticed *yours,* Keegan. Are you sure *you're* not part giraffe?" She could feel herself blushing and she took a sip of lemonade in the hopes it would cool her. "Now, back to the subject at hand. . . . You were right, Keegan, about everything. I've—"

"That's the kind of stuff I like to hear. If *that's* the direction this conversation is taking us. . .then I'm sorry for all the interruptions." He rested his chin on a fist. "Go on, continue. What was I so right about?"

Breena rolled her eyes and said, "That I've wasted a lot of time wallowing in self-pity."

"I never said you were wallowing. I said—"

"Keegan, please," she said, laughing despite herself, "this is hard enough!"

"Sorry. . ."

"I understand you did a pretty thorough bit of research on me."

A warm stare was Keegan's only response.

"Well, for your information, I've done a bit of investigating into *your* background."

One brow rose slowly. "Is that a fact?"

"It is. Talking to Agnes is like—"

Keegan groaned, covered his face with one hand. "If you've been talking to Agnes, you probably know more about me than I do."

"I know that your favorite color is red, and that your favorite author is Jack London, and that you hate vanilla ice cream, and. . ."

"What're you smirking about, Breena? C'mon, 'fess up. . . ."

Breena had to be careful here. She didn't know much about men, but she knew this: A man's pride is easily shattered. Even so much as a hint that he might harbor an irrational fear could cause permanent injury to his tender male ego. "Um. . .and you're not terribly fond of thunderstorms."

"I should say not," he spouted. He sat back, crossed

both arms over his broad chest. "Let's see how *you'd* react if you got struck by lightning!"

"Oh," she began, chin up and shoulders back, "I know exactly how I'd react."

His chin rose a notch, too. "Well. . . ?"

"I'd shiver under the covers—day or night—until the storm blew over."

Keegan's laughter bounced off every wall in the apartment. "It's not something I'm particularly proud of," he said, suddenly serious, "being afraid of a little rain. I mean, what if you were caught outside in a storm? I don't know if I could trust myself to save—"

"First of all," Breena interrupted, pressing a palm to his whiskered cheek, "Agnes says you're lucky to be alive after that bolt knocked you down. You wouldn't be normal if you didn't get the heebie-jeebies when thunder strikes." Her fingers combed through his hair. "I'm genuinely sorry you've had to live with that for nearly a decade. . .although I must say, it was almost worth it. . . ."

"Worth it? What are you, a sadist?"

She returned his gentle smile. "No," she sighed, "but it did leave you with this sexy streak. . . ."

"Hey," he said, feigning a smoldering, Hollywood-type stare, "I was *born* with a sexy streak. That lightning bolt had nothing to do with it."

Giggling, Breena said, "No, silly. . .I'm talking about the streak in your *hair*."

With no warning whatsoever, Keegan got to his feet, pulling her up with him. "Did you see that Tom

Cruise movie. . .the one where he was a secret agent?"

Breena nodded as he wrapped her in a warm embrace.

"Your mission, Breena Pavan," he said, imitating the voice from *Mission Impossible*, "should you choose to accept it, is to meet me at St. John's. Today. One o'clock."

He didn't wait for an answer. Instead, Keegan kissed her as never before. And as she stood, reeling from its dizzying effects, he headed for the door.

"Which St. John's?"

Keegan shrugged. "That's for me to know, and for you to find out," he said, slamming the door behind him.

She found him sitting exactly where he'd been on the day they'd met. . .precisely one week ago. Breena stepped into the pew and sat down beside him. "No Stetson to soften the bench?" she asked, her voice echoing in the empty church.

He looked straight ahead. "Haven't you heard? Stetsons are on the endangered hat list."

"I suppose you're right. Please don't turn me in. I've seen the inside of enough squad cars."

He pretended to take it all very seriously. "I've heard of homicide and suicide, but *haticide?*

Breena bit her lower lip to suppress a giggle. "I need to get you a new one so you don't look like you fell off your horse and landed on your head."

"Hah!" Keegan snorted, then fell silent. For a long

moment, neither of them spoke.

"Why did you ask me to meet you here?" Breena finally asked, breaking the silence.

"To ask you to think about the future." He turned on the seat to face her. "And since I never do anything without the Big Guy's approval," he added, a thumb pointing heavenward, "what better place to do it?"

Their silly conversation forgotten, Breena's smile faded. "The future?"

"Well, sure." He said it as though surprised she hadn't been thinking the same thing. "What else?"

Breena licked her lips, which had gone suddenly dry.

"Don't ask me to explain it, 'cause I can't." He held up a hand to stave off any comment she might make. "I've never done anything spur-of-the-moment in my life." He grinned, and wiggled his eyebrows. "But then, you already knew that, since you talked to my biographer-slash-accountant.

"I need some spontaneity in my life. I make lists, and plans, and—" He grew quiet and still for a moment, then grabbed her hands. "I can't explain it," he repeated, "but I think. . .no, I know *that* when you walked in here a week ago and mashed my hat flat, you stole my heart. And darlin', I don't want to live another day without you."

He's. . .he's proposing?

"Keegan," she began slowly, "before you say another word, I think it only fair to warn you. . .I'm not really a Christian. You deserve someone who's as devout as you."

344

"What do you mean you're not a Christian? Didn't you tell me that you accepted the Lord at that youth rally that your college girlfriend took you to?"

"Well. . .yeah, but I don't go to church."

"So? We can set that right, startin' tomorrow." Keegan put his arm around her shoulder and gave her a reassuring hug.

Breena's mind was swimming with confusion. She had gone forward at the youth rally, with Melissa's encouragement, and she had prayed the prayer. But after all these years of feeling like God had rejected her for what happened to her mother, it was hard to know what she believed. She knew that Jesus was the Lord and Savior. But was He *her* Lord and Savior?

"Breena, listen. If you accepted Jesus back when you were in college, you don't need to do it again. If you've wandered away and made some mistakes, the Bible tells us to repent, or confess our sins, how ever you want to say it, and then get back in the saddle. I'd say God's been waitin' a mighty long time for you to come back."

"Keegan, I understand what you're saying, but that's not the whole story."

"Of course it is."

"No, there's something else. I don't think I'm born again."

"What are you talking about?"

"Well. . .after that revival meeting, Melissa told me I needed to get baptized."

"And. . . ?"

"And, it didn't take."

345

"Didn't take?" Frustrated now, Keegan frowned. "What didn't take."

"My salvation, my. . .my. . .whatever you call it, it didn't take. That same night, after the revival service, I got into the water with the pastor, and repeated all the right words, and when he went to dunk me. . ."

"What?" Keegan pressed. "When the pastor dunked you, *what?*"

"He dropped me."

The silence was so complete that Breena believed she could have heard one of Hershey's whiskers hit the marble floor, but she could tell by his lurching shoulders that Keegan was laughing at her. "What's so funny?" she demanded, crossing both arms over her chest.

"You think because the pastor slipped up, you're not saved?" Shaking his head, Keegan took a deep breath. "Breena, Breena, Breena. What am I gonna do with you?"

"Well, you can't marry me, that's for sure."

"I can, and I will. . . .if you'll have me, of course."

Breena looked up and was startled by the earnest gleam in Keegan's eyes. She quickly glanced away and began a serious study of the far wall.

"I know it's crazy, Breena, admitting that I feel this way after such a short time. But I love you! There's nothing I can do about it, so you'll just have to deal with that." He faced forward again and rested both palms on his knees. "But first things first. What you need is to get into a church where you can begin to grow and learn more about God's love for you. Then you'll have confidence about being saved."

"Well, maybe you're right," she agreed half-heartedly.

"Why are you so hard on yourself, Breena? Why not cut yourself a little slack? Give yourself a break once in awhile. The world is a tough enough place without beating up on yourself all the time."

She shrugged. "It *is* silly, I suppose, since you're so good at pointing out my character flaws—"

He faced her again. "Character flaws? Why, there isn't a single solitary thing wrong with you, and I'll whomp anyone who says otherwise."

When he saw the teasing glint in her eyes, he stopped talking and wrapped her in his arms. "Tell me something," Keegan whispered into her hair. "Do you love me?"

"I do."

"And do you want to marry me?"

"I do."

"When?"

She leaned back to get a better look at his wonderful, handsome, loving face. Breena had a pretty good idea what life with Keegan would be like, for he'd already shown his true colors. Without knowing how things might turn out, he'd risked rejection to repair the rift between her and her earthly father; and now he was helping her see that she'd never been abandoned by her Heavenly Father.

She could only hope and pray that, as his wife, she could give him all the things he deserved: She'd cook for him and clean and. . . *Wait a minute! He's the one with the immaculate house and the gourmet kitchen. Maybe he can teach me that stuff too.* Anyway, whatever Keegan wanted, that's what Breena wanted—no, that's what Breena *needed*—too.

"When?" he asked again.

She leaned over and kissed the tip of his nose. "I don't know what day, but St. John's. One o'clock."

"Um. . .*which* St.John's?"

"That's for me to know and for—"

Her reply was smothered by a hailstorm of kisses.

348

Loree Lough

A full-time writer for over twelve years, Loree has produced more than 2,000 published articles, dozens of short stories that have appeared in various magazines, and two books for *The American Adventure* series for 8- to 12-year-olds (Barbour Publishing). Loree is the author of eighteen inspirational romances, including the award-winning *Pocketful of Love* (**Heartsong Presents**), and "Reluctant Valentine," part of the bestselling romantic collection, *Only You* (Barbour Publishing). A prolific and talented writer, gifted teacher, and comedic conference speaker, Loree lives in Maryland with her husband, two daughters, and two constantly warring cats.